Nicholas Salaman is in his mid-forties. He was born in Somerset, educated at Radley and Oxford and spent nearly twenty years as an advertising copywriter. He now spends his time variously among advertising in Paris and London, running a herb and spice company of which he is co-owner, and writing. He plays the harpsichord.

He has written plays for the theatre and television, and has written one other novel, *The Frights*, which received ecstatic reviews:

'A galaxy of odd balls . . . excellent . . . majestically funny . . . bears comparison with P. G. Wodehouse, yet Salaman somehow stretches this comic manner to cover the deeper springs of human motivation.'
Times Literary Supplement

By the same author

The Frights

NICHOLAS SALAMAN

Dangerous Pursuits

GRAFTON BOOKS
A Division of the Collins Publishing Group

LONDON GLASGOW
TORONTO SYDNEY AUCKLAND

Grafton Books
A Division of the Collins Publishing Group
8 Grafton Street, London W1X 3LA

Published by Grafton Books 1984
Reprinted 1985 (twice), 1986, 1987 (twice), 1988

First published in Great Britain by
The Alison Press/Martin Secker & Warburg Limited 1983

ISBN 0-586-06030-8

Printed and bound in Great Britain by
Collins, Glasgow

Set in Times

'What men or gods are these? What maidens loth?
What mad pursuit? What struggle to escape?
What pipes and timbrels? What wild ecstasy?'

Keats
Ode on a Grecian Urn

PART ONE

1

When I saw him across the bar in the Bird in Hand, I knew that I would have to pursue the matter

There was something about his air that irritated me.

It was a sultry day, admittedly (the spring had previously been disappointing, but suddenly it was one of those late-March heatwaves which get you hot and bothered in your winter clothes), and I am not the most tolerant of men in any event. But even for me, there was something about his 'Do you do uh Pimms here?' that I found particularly offensive.

Not that Arthur, the barman at the Bird in Hand, does not like people asking for Pimms. Quite the reverse. He has got all the trimmings right down to a little glass jug with blue borage flowers in it which he has delivered every day from New Covent Garden, in hot weather, and charges through the nose for the privilege. But what it does is take up time with a great deal of fiddling about with the cucumber and such while other people, like me on this occasion, are waiting for their orders, especially this early in the season.

That was the first thing that got on my nerves, and the second wasn't far behind.

'Just exactly what I feel like. And, Tony, look at those sweet little blue flowers.'

Tony, my least favourite name. Arthur must have doubled across to New Covent Garden to collect them that very afternoon, fresh flown in no doubt from California, crafty.

What I wanted to know, though, was what a person like that was doing with an English girl – especially with one who measured up so exactly to my own mind's eye. She was blonde, with hair of that particularly gold-filament variety which seems to promise something better than our human clay. Her eyes were as blue as the borage flowers; her ankles as trimly turned as you could imagine. In my youth, I would have given my eye-teeth to have taken her to the tennis club ball.

It was not to be endured. When I finally obtained my glass of amontillado, it tasted bitter. I sat in the next but one booth to where they'd settled themselves, and watched them discreetly.

He was, it seemed (perhaps you've guessed?), a marketing executive. Everyone is, these days. Don't you hate that? Marketing Executive? What does it mean? We never had marketing executives before the Americans came over here in bulk. We never even had marketing, up till the late Fifties you never even heard the term, and I daresay we were none the worse off for it.

She was talking:

'How did the teach-in go? Thirty video executives in one room . . . sounds as if it'd make a pretty dense occasion . . .'

'Thanks very much.' He laughed in a manner which suggested to me he thought himself far from dense.

'No, what I mean is,' she said, squeezing his arm with what I considered to be lamentable over-familiarity, 'dense like the surface of one of those planets. Heavy. All that heavy talent and talk. Solemn things of mystic meaning . . .'

She had learnt a thing or two, it seemed, someone had taken trouble with her; at least, she knew her Hymns Ancient and Modern. 'Bethlehem of Noblest Cities' is one of my favourites (to the tune of course of 'Stuttgart'). But it simply made her fall from grace seem to me all the more distressing, because here she was going out with (one) a foreigner who was (two) a marketing executive, and (three) a Tony.

She was talking again. In my interest, and craning

a little to hear, I slopped a rivulet of amontillado over my trouser top, which was, as you can imagine, an embarrassment, and a thing I would never have done in normal circumstances, being economical in my movements.

'Did anything come of it?' she asked.

'The teach-in? No, not really. The usual run around the ball-park. Market Growth . . . New Product Development. But there is one thing . . . I just cabled back to the States . . . If I don't put too many feet wrong in the next couple of months, I could be head of the whole UK operation by the summer.'

'But Tony, that's wonderful.'

And she leaned over and kissed him full on the lips.

This, apart from being seen with him in the Bird in Hand by myself, was her first serious mistake.

I do not like to see public demonstrations of affection; there is all too much of it about; it encourages the young and spreads disease; besides, it is not the English way. But to see such a respectable-seeming and well-brought-up girl embracing a foreigner, one of a nation that had contributed so signally to our present abasement, brings me out in a cold rage which frightens even myself.

I sensed my body trembling, and gripped the table in front of me to steady my hands.

'Excuse me.'

I had become so engrossed and upset with my thoughts that I had not heard the request the first time round, and I looked up hurriedly. I am normally polite on the surface, polite if reserved. A quiet modest appearance seems to me the perfect cloak for a nature that is both deep and at times turbulent. Isobel, my wife, described me once in those very words. (My spectacles also lend a useful element of harmlessness.)

'Excuse me.'

Yes, the American, having drawn a blank with the booth next door, was definitely trying to engage me in conversation. Hastily subduing the uncomfortable feeling that I might perhaps have let my thoughts speak in my expression, I turned an absent-minded and supremely recessive gaze upon him.

I do not, as perhaps you will have divined, altogether approve of the human race these days: even my fellow-countrymen I find sadly lacking – look at the way they've allowed foreign influences to walk all over them. (Drake, where are you now?) But I have always believed in the importance of fieldwork. If one is a spy, in enemy territory as it were, as I more and more feel myself to be an alien in this slipshod, disposable, take-away society we have now become, it is all the more important that I blend with the background, biding my time.

The mien – I like that word, don't you?, not the sort you normally find in daily parlance; I am a lover of our native tongue, though largely self-taught, and often read a page or two of the Shorter Oxford Dictionary before retiring – the mien, as I say, that I turned upon him was mild and almost painfully innocuous.

'Oh, I'm so sorry,' I said. 'I must have been dreaming. Sorry.'

'I just asked if you had a light.'

The girl, rummaging in her handbag, held a cigarette in her hand. I disapprove of smoking, but most especially do I dislike the habit in young women. She was letting herself down with every minute that passed.

'Sorry,' I said to the man with well-concealed satisfaction and total anonymity, 'I don't indulge.'

He looked at me curiously, half (it seemed) about to say something, but thinking better of it. The girl was still rummaging. She had not even noticed me.

'I'll get a match from the bar,' he told her, turning his back on me with a nod, thinking no doubt to dismiss me for ever from his life, and made for the Löwenbräu font where Arthur was pulling a pint for a party in a tweed jacket.

Extraordinary, isn't it, with a noble tradition of brewing like ours, that we should need to import all this foreign slop. You can hardly find a tin of good English ale in an off-licence these days. A measure of our national decline. But I digress.

The American, departing at this point for the matches, allowed me a few moments' pause for speculation as to why a successful marketing executive did not sport that typical hallmark of success without which one would have thought all executive triumph would seem but as ashes, or so the adverts would have us believe. The same idea had apparently occurred to the girl, for when he returned with his Swan Vestas, she smiled and puffed on her King Size, filling her lungs with tar, and said:

'I thought every executive had a Dunhill lighter. It's supposed to go with the credit-cards and the Lamy pens.'

'I've been through about ten in the last couple of years. But I always lose them,' he said. 'Like umbrellas. They just walk. It's almost like I had a poltergeist in attendance.'

He shouldn't have said that, he really shouldn't. Because that's what gave me the idea.

When they finally left the pub, it was nearly eight o'clock, and I had been obliged to drink two further sherries, which is in excess of my normal preference, as a consequence of their ordering more Pimms. It induced a certain recklessness in me. Indeed, for the first time since my wife Isobel passed on, I felt the stirrings of some purpose in my life. I still at that stage had no idea where it would lead, but it was purpose nonetheless.

I followed them outside. I feared for a moment that the American would have one of those hulking great American cars parked down the street, and would drive away with the girl to some gilded haunt, but I was in luck. It was she who stopped beside a small black sports model. I dodged behind a chestnut tree, already beginning to curl and burst on every bough. (As I shall make clear later, I am a tree lover.)

'Goodnight, darling,' she said. 'See you tomorrow night. Supper at my place?'

'Sure,' he said. 'Fine. Terrific. Joanie's down at the cottage again, so we can . . .'

I wish I could report a better standard of dialogue, I really do, but I relay it as it happened. So the Yank was married and was playing fast and loose with this girl. (Her name I had established, was Chloe.) So much the better; it made me all the more confirmed in my antipathy towards him.

When Isobel was taken from me, it was as if all the colour had been bleached out of life, and I was left in a world of black and white again, the same as it had been before I met her. The idea that a man could fool around with a girl while having the inestimable comfort of a wife to return to, filled me with incomprehension and, yes, wrath. The American did not know how lucky he was.

I decided I should have to teach him a lesson, if not for myself, for Isobel and for all wives sitting in darkened houses waiting for their husbands to come home.

A dog came padding up the street, fidgeted among the rubbish at the foot of the tree, and sniffed vigorously at my trousers where I had spilt the sherry. I feared he might give me away, and shooed him off with silent authority which he took to be some sort of game. I would inevitably have been disclosed, since he had taken a firm grip of my cuff, but at this moment I heard the car door open and the girl Chloe repeating, or as you might say encapsulating, her farewells.

'Tomorrow, then. About eight-thirty. OK? See you. 'Night, darling.'

People do repeat themselves, don't they? Most of what they say means nothing, just noises, verbal grooming. Sometimes I think there ought to be a tax on speech. How many necessary words do we use in a day? The Americans are arch-villains on this score.

To proceed, the sound distracted the dog's attention, and I was able to retrieve my cuff.

''Bye, darling.'

''Bye. See you tomorrow.'

The car drove away at what seemed to me excessive speed (I have a Morris 1000 Estate which is quite enough for my needs), and the American, looking pleased with himself, set off at a leisurely pace across the network of Squares, Places and Gardens that form the hinterland of the King's Road.

I followed, imperceptible as the gathering shadows or as the wisps of cirrus which gleamed richly over Chelsea in the last rays of the sun.

From the Bird in Hand, which is one of my favourite hostelries since it boasts a garden you can sit in when summer permits (I myself live at the western end of the King's Road near the hideous new skyscrapers), from the Bird in Hand which is what one might call mid-Chelsea to Cadogan Square where the American ended up is, I suppose, at least half a mile, you could walk it in ten minutes, but he was so pleased with his leisurely stride and his executive suit and his Robert Redford moustache (he looked not unlike that darling of the screen in a dark-haired fleshy sort of way) and the favourable interview with his lady love that he dawdled all the way home.

He even, and I report this with shame at my sex's inconstancy, looked at other girls, going so far as to speak to one who seemed undecided about an address in Draycott Avenue. You could sense his eyes busy all the time he talked.

But he finally made it – a tall red-brick block of flats in that most exclusive of residential areas – and I had to look sharp to see which flat he made for, Number 11B. That done, I was able to gather his name from a list displayed in the deserted porter's cubbyhole: Mr and Mrs A. Richmonde.

I confess to being somewhat disappointed at this piece of information. There was something infinitely English about the name. 'The Lass of Richmond Hill' had been one of my mother's favourite songs. I should have preferred him to be called Bock or Bechstein or Vyszinski or even O'Shea. Still, with that American tendency never to leave well alone, he had added a thoroughly regrettable 'e' to his perfectly good English patronym. I could deplore him for that alone.

'Yes, sir? Can I help you?'

It was the porter emerging from his basement with a mug of tea.

'Oh, thank you,' I replied, quick on my feet, 'I'm looking for a Mr Vyszinski with a z. I'm almost sure it was this number.'

'No one here of that name,' he said, sloshing his tea almost deliberately it seemed on to the brown ceramic tiling floor. 'Might try next door. There's a Yugoslav professor on the third floor and a School of Reincarnation in the penthouse.'

'Thank you,' I said. 'Most kind of you, I'm sure.'

And after a courtesy bob into the house next door in case of suspicion, I walked smartly down to Sloane Square for a bus back to Driffield Street.

Since Isobel passed on, I have been, I must confess, something of a solitary. I cannot seem to find my place any more. I am only forty-six but it seems to me the world has pursued a direction which, both by upbringing and inclination, I do not feel very much inclined to follow.

As an only child, I was brought up perhaps conservatively by today's lights. My father owned a large hardware business in Fulham, with a chain of shops in both Fulham and across the river in Putney, and he was by local standards prosperous. My mother and he were amateur singers in the locality.

I was sent to the local Choir School, St Theodoric's (I

had a pleasant treble and slightly less enthusiastically received light baritone when my voice broke), where I was a studious if not significantly successful student. I played the trumpet in the Orchestra and obtained the requisite number of 'O' levels, which were not sufficiently convincing for me to go into the Sixth Form. So I left school at sixteen, worked in the shops for a couple of years, and then went into the Army for National Service with the Royal West London Regiment, after basic training being posted overseas to Malaya.

It all seems very far away now, but in those palmy days we were pitted against CTs, that is Communist Terrorists in the jungles, fighting for a freedom to eat hamburgers and listen to raucous music from a million loudspeakers.

Subsequent to a two-year spell in those tropic parts (I extended my service for an extra year), where I learned stalking, ambuscade and the trade of death, I found myself at the age of twenty-two back in London with no training in anything else, and nothing for it but to serve in the hardware business again, though it had been quite clear, even from my forays before the Army, that I had no particular aptitude for the calling.

'You're a dreamer, Roy,' my father would remark, discovering that I had once again got the grouting mixed up with the tile adhesive. And it was true.

I could not seem to find any meaning in life after my jungle experience. Yes, I had killed men. Not that I had enjoyed it, you understand, but I knew what had to be done. Britain did not grow great by shirking such decisions. In a curious way, I found regimental life suited me, and I even toyed with the idea of becoming a soldier, but my father contracted Bright's Disease and I was needed in the shop.

People now don't realize the Fifties were the last time England was actually English, the patch of green and gold before the blight set in. I was quietly happy in those far-off days. They still made British motorbikes then – indeed I had a green BSA Bantam, a superior 125cc two-stroke machine (who says the British can't make small bikes?), a reliable little thing that could have shown a thing or two to the yellow perils. What happened to the BSA Bantams, I should like to know. Vanished along with so much more that we cherished.

My Bantam and I soon became familiar figures in the Fulham Palace Road and over Putney Bridge as I drove between my parents' house and the shops. My mother, I must confess, was anxious for my safety, but I was young and craved excitement, and this was my undoing for, turning right in front of a large lorry that was sitting winking in the middle of the traffic, I failed to see the Hillman Minx that was overtaking it on the inside lane, and collided with it to my disadvantage (these were the days when it was considered cissy to wear crash helmets).

'WATCH OUT, CUNT.' I can still hear the lorry-driver's warning cry, not a pleasant thing to have ringing in your ears as you dive face-first into pressed steel.

My jaw was fractured in three places, a vertebra in my neck was cracked, my collarbone was a virtual write-off and my leg was broken with various lacerations and bruises.

Of course, my leg and things healed in time, and my features (I was never an Apollo) approximated eventually to their previous unremarkable conformity. Even my jaw finally knitted, though I still get neck ache. The main effect of it all, though, was to put me out of action for almost a year, giving me time to reflect and observe the changes that were beginning to sweep over the country. Perhaps it was simply my natural temper, but I am sure the accident increased my powers of observation and perception, making me feel curiously at a distance from things. Anyway, I could see quite clearly that we were all heading for something regrettable and unpleasant: the Gadarene swine were gathering momentum. Perhaps we all need a bang on the face to bring us to our senses.

'WATCH OUT, CUNT.'

I am still, as the lorry-driver urged me to do, watching out, and I do not like what I see.

I think what with my father's illness and the worry about my accident, it was too much for my mother. She was never strong, and seeing me in intensive care did nothing to increase her hold on life. She died later in the year, and my father followed shortly after. One thoughtless turn down Munster Road and I had changed the course of several people's lives.

This left me in the early Sixties (I had no other near family) with a house in the Fulham Palace Road and a chain of stores which my then weakness and congenital unsuitability rendered me totally incapable of directing. The shops I promptly sold, resulting in a capital sum of considerably over £200,000, a fortune in those days. It did nothing to assuage my feelings of guilt and loss. I shall not dwell on the unhappiness of that lonely time.

I now had enough money to do whatever I wanted, and I decided to devote myself to study. I did a great deal of reading, mainly the classics of our tongue, but I also set about discovering the English countryside – for some reason, perhaps as a result of my training in Malaya, perhaps because I enjoyed the solitude of such places, my particular interest was the English Forest, that verdant ocean which once covered three-quarters of the surface of our island, but which today only exists in random scatterings – Savernake, Dean, Arden, Sherwood, Wychwood, the names read like a roll-call.

So, while the priests of pop ranted and raved, and miniskirts flew ever higher and the King's Road, erstwhile haunt of artists and writers (Belloc and Whistler, where are you now?), became the Mecca of Swinging London and tarmac garden of the Flower Children, I was treading the ancient forest paths of Buckenham and Sherwood, and crackling the beech-mast above the Chiltern hollows.

It was late in 1969 that I met Isobel.

I was trying to locate a road that used to run between Oxford and Kingham through the fastnesses of Wychwood (a lovely forest named after the Saxon Hwicce tribe and covering some 4,000 acres in 1750, now sadly diminished), when I chanced on a young girl, she couldn't have been more than eighteen, sitting on a tree-stump, bitterly crying. It was autumn and the afternoon air was chill.

I was naturally surprised and concerned, but I am naturally reticent, especially with the fair sex, so it was a little before I approached her and asked her what was wrong.

'Oi lost moi way, aven't Oi?' she replied.

'Where do you want to go?' I enquired.

With that she started to cry again. I repeated my question, although on first enquiry it had not achieved an altogether encouraging effect.

'Oi dunno,' she sobbed.

It was clear she was not an educated girl. I was temporarily nonplussed, but I do not like to see a lady weep and I proffered my Milletts anorak, which seemed to help quieten her down.

She told me that she was an orphan living with her auntie and uncle in Chippingham. They didn't want her and she didn't want them, so she'd left and had cut across country just in case they came trying to look for her by road. She supposed she was making for London. She was over eighteen, she said, so they couldn't force her to go back.

I was moved by her tale, and offered her a lift. She was a delicate little thing with a fine bone structure, almost violet eyes and straight up-and-down hair with a butterfly slide.

I had not had many dealings with girls before, and my solitary life had left me unprepared for the casual banter that so often passes for male conversation with the fair. On the way back I tried her on forests, but she seemed to have formed a bad impression of our island's glory. Literature also was a closed book to her. Most of the time she just stared out of the window.

When we arrived at the Hammersmith Flyover, I enquired where she wanted to go now.

'Oi dunno,' she replied, the violets filling up again.

The upshot was that I took her to the house in the Fulham Palace Road, gave her a cup of tea, and tried to talk some sense into her. It transpired that she had nowhere to go, she knew no one in London, but she was not going back to her auntie. Lest worse should befall her, I decided to let her stay with me for the night. I gave her the little room at the top of the house, that used to be mine – my father had installed a bathroom en suite – and made sure she had everything she needed. She made a bee-line for Jacko, my old felt monkey.

Next day, she asked if she could stay until she had found her feet.

The weeks that followed were like the sudden coming of spring. My headaches went. I had not realized that I had been so lonely. She was bright as a button, and almost immediately started on the house, which I must confess had got into quite a state. She put up new curtains, spring-cleaned the place from top to bottom, cooked me meals of surprising quality and variety, and I do not think I saw unhappiness on her face from the moment she came down to her first breakfast with me (I enjoy a traditional breakfast with all the trimmings).

Perhaps the thing that touched me most about her was the way she wanted to involve herself in my activities. She wanted to learn. So, almost from the start, I set out to show her everything I knew – Dickens, Jane Austen, Somerset Maugham, we read them all. She even showed evidence of interest in forests, though that came a little later. And, as time passed, I noticed her somewhat rough-hewn Cotswold accent was becoming less and less pronounced.

Once or twice, naturally, I suggested she contact her aunt, and tell her she was safe.

'I'm nothing to them,' she said. 'She's not even my real aunt. My mother adopted me.'

Well, she was eighteen and it was her life, but I did think she should have someone to provide for her, to give her money to buy clothes and suchlike, and I was able to persuade her to let me contribute.

The next thing was, she wanted to go to elocution classes. I was delighted to see her pride in herself; she didn't intend to be a sponger.

'Or secretarial if you wish, I'd be glad to pay for you,' I said. 'You'll be able to type my notes on the English Woodland.' (A treatise I had in mind, but which would doubtless never see the light of day.)

'Oh no you don't,' she said. 'I'm enough drain on you as it is. I'll work evenings in a restaurant.'

This threw me into consternation. The next thing would be she'd be off altogether. I suddenly realized that for the first time in my life I was in love.

'No, look,' I said. 'You cook for me, wait on me, do the housework. You get nothing in return but a bed in the attic.'

'And Jacko.'

'I concede Jacko. But even so, I would prefer you to allow me to pay you wages, as my housekeeper.'

'But I can still go to elocution?'

'If you wish. Of course.'

'Oh, that's wonderful, Barnie.' (She said for some reason I reminded her of the barn owls back home.) And she got up from where she was sitting and gave me a kiss.

It was ridiculous, of course. There was I, already well into my thirties, infatuated with this slip of a girl. But the thing that totally undid me was that she seemed to love me in return. She had a way of looking at me with her head on one side; like a canary she was with her fair hair.

'Old Barnie,' she would say, 'am I your field-mouse?'

Oh my canary.

'Do you like my new dress, Barnie? My haircut? . . .'

She introduced me, you could say, to life again. To make my happiness complete, she consented to be my wife.

It was only then, when we were dealing with the formalities, that I discovered that she had not reached eighteen when I had first met her. But I readily understood and forgave her innocent deception. She had not wanted to be returned to the hated auntie. In fact, I blessed the hour she had not made me do it.

Nothing physical, apart from a chaste kiss, took place between us until our wedding night. We were married in the Registry Office opposite Chelsea Town Hall, not perhaps the romantic spot I might have chosen, but she said she did not want a fuss.

There followed a year of what I suppose life is like for some people all of the time, but which for me was a glimpse of paradise. She had, in the little space of time that I had known her, grown into a lady with all the graces – conversation, dress sense, flower arrangement, excellent managerial ability. She would have made a Personal Assistant to some City Managing Director, although she did not fancy typing, and I had her all to myself.

If I could have had her for a day, I should not have thought my life ill-spent, and I had her for twelve months.

Then, suddenly, she was taken from me.

2

As a little girl, she had been encouraged to think she was plain. Her auntie used to hold her face against the mirror in the bedroom.

'Wicked little girl. Just like your mother. The ugly face of sin.'

Her auntie never let her forget that her mother had run away from home with an agricultural salesman, and got herself into trouble in Solihull.

Her auntie went to Chapel twice on Sundays. Indeed, the house was full of Chapel every day of the week, but it didn't stop her uncle, a year or two later, feeling up her frock when she was doing the Christmas decorations. She had stuck him hard in his trousers with a drawing pin, his face was a picture, but he couldn't yell because auntie was in the next room playing 'On Jordan's bank, The Baptist's cry', very softly on the harmonium with only the Celeste stop out and no bass at all so she could hear everything that went on for miles around.

All that was years ago and in the country anyway, but lately she had been noticing that, even by London standards, she could more than hold her own (and if she didn't, the boy in the butcher's shop told her, there were others that would).

It finally encouraged her to pack a suitcase one afternoon, put on her prettiest dress, slip out of the house, and take a Number 14 bus down the King's Road, where she went into a pub, had three Bacardi and Cokes, and picked up a very young trainee banker who had a basement flat in Tite Street.

She stayed with him for a month, though she wouldn't sleep with him – she had already developed a useful trick of selective chastity – while she set about finding herself a job.

After several negative encounters, she met Chrys, a Polish girl married to an Englishman she never saw, who worked all day in a cheap Italian restaurant. It was here they chatted over a special House Pizza with extra ham and cheese, which ended with Chrys fixing her a job in the restaurant, but it was really hard work, you always smelt of frying however much you had a bath, and the Italians were such babies, always trying to put a hand up your knickers.

She stuck it for as long as she could, moved in for a time with Chrys in her one-room basement flat in Notting Hill, then (answering an ad in a tobacconist's window) found a room all to herself in another basement flat, this time off the Earl's Court Road, which she shared with a part-time model and sales-promotions girl called Maudie but whose real name was something else, and who – when there was nothing doing in exhibition and trade fair work – took employment as a topless hostess in a club called Chestertons in Bayswater. £50 a night, Maudie told her, everything you could drink so long as it was short and the punters bought it for you, and you didn't have to sleep with anyone unless you wanted to, in which case you could earn a whole lot more.

£250 or more a week, tax-free, seemed like wealth beyond anything the Chippingham Secondary Modern had equipped her to anticipate or indeed compute, especially when you had no training whatsoever and no friends to paper over the gaps.

It would be a waste not to, Maudie said, after she had seen her undressing one evening, you owe it to yourself, and it leaves the days free to do what you want.

Maudie didn't seem to do very much with her days except read paperbacks, watch old films on television, occasionally have lunch with a more presentable punter from the club, and wait for evening, but her new flatmate told herself that if she did embark upon this not altogether satisfactory course, she would go to secretarial school, take elocution lessons, and later perhaps learn to cook, drive and fly.

And so she found herself one evening forming up with Maudie outside the club's premises in a little low street somewhere near Paddington with a multi-storey office block dominating the skyline and shrouding the mean little street in a sort of perpetual twilight. From its exterior, it could have been a minor debt collector's headquarters, with its trimly varnished cedar door and its array of surveillance and scrutineering aids mustered by the lintel.

Maudie pressed one of the aids, announced her name, and the cedar swung open.

The aroma that wafted out dispelled any illusion that the place might have nursed a den of Rachmans. This was not the unacceptable whiff of capitalism, no scents of tawdry filing cabinets, copying machines, slightly burnt bakelite lampshades, alsatians, stale cups of instant coffee, and masculine reeks of shag and cheap half-coronas filtered past her. This was the acceptable bosom of humanity. The odour was compounded of scent (not necessarily cheap), cigarette smoke, armpits, liquor slops, antiseptic and ancient not-quite-cleared vomit.

It was an aroma that, however long she lived with it, she could never quite become accustomed to, finding its way like Italian frying, on to her clothes, her shining locks, her skin, her fingernails, and eventually (she was told) even her pubic hair.

She stood for a moment in the entrance as the savoury draught played around her like ghostly executive hands. She was tempted to turn round right there and go home, but a voice spoke briskly to her from the gloom.

'Don't stand there like a fossil, dear. Come in if you're coming in. This isn't the gates of hell, you know. Shut the door one way or the other, the cat's not been shut up yet.'

She was fond of animals. Any place that had a cat in it couldn't be all bad. She shut the door, her eyes accustoming themselves to the twilight within, and found Maudie chatting to a button-faced brunette of around forty, recently pretty, wearing a tight black dress. Maudie beckoned her forward, and then herself retreated through the swing-doors at the end of the small reception chamber, leaving her with the button-face.

'I'm Cheryl,' button-face said. 'Thank you, Maudie. And you are . . . ? Maudie's told me all about you. Got your tights and chiffon scarf? Good. I'm afraid you will have to have another name. It is our first rule. Every girl must have another name. It avoids confusion. What about Chloe for convenience? It has brevity and style. All right, dear?'

'I like Chloe.'

She had previously suggested it to Maudie, who had no doubt passed it on.

'That's settled, then. I can see we are going to get on famously. What else? I would wear good strong panties. The gentlemen will no doubt try to clutch at them. Strong but small. We do not want unsightly ridges. Our rules are few but insistent. Here by 6 P.M. Change into your costume and wait by the bar. When the gentlemen arrive, ask them if they want you to sit with them but do not pester, we try to keep things civilized here, and do not squabble with another girl over whose customer someone may be, it is undignified and leads to friction. I shall be arbiter if a doubt arises. Get the gentlemen to drink up, and always have wine or something short yourself. Lager makes you gassy later in the evening. If you can encourage a gentleman to order champagne, it will be to your advantage to do so. You get a bonus of £2 a bottle. On this floor, it is just drinks and the bar. You may sit on a gentleman's knee and he may kiss you if you think it will help him to order champagne, and he may even lightly brush your chest, but I do not wish any heavy petting. It interferes with the drinking, looks distasteful, and makes the upholstery smell.'

Cheryl paused for breath. It was clear that she gave the talk regularly. Chloe was impressed, not so much at the certainty and briskness of the house-mother's tones, as at their refinement. Maudie had warned her, just because it was a topless bar, she shouldn't expect the place to be full of scrubbers; but she hadn't anticipated quite to what an extent showing one's breasts had become a polite occupation. Cheryl was more like a Sergeant Major greeting Officer Cadets than a low madam. She sipped minutely at a glass of white wine, and continued the indoctrination.

'Upstairs, you will discover a restaurant with a small dance floor. This is where you must try and get your gentleman to take you. Here pink champagne is obligatory, and here again you get a bonus of, this time, an extra £10 per bottle. Do not eat a large meal. The food anyway is no great shakes but it *will* make you drowsy, and sleeping on duty is viewed most gravely. If the gentleman wishes to dance, you must comply and dance as closely as he wishes, but I have to stipulate against rubbing. Similarly, if he wishes to cuddle you at the restaurant table, I permit more extensive petting at the restaurant table because the lights are even lower, the booths more discreet, and the chairs are covered in washable polyholstery, but I must insist on a certain level of decorum. I do not countenance open zips or lowered tights. Hands may be used on breasts with your permission but not on the more intimate areas, it is not nice at table. When you see some of our regular gentlemen, this stipulation will come as a relief. I have to confess to you that on the whole we do not cater for the flower of our youth here. Chestertons closes at 3 A.M. You are not to leave with any gentlemen. This is where awkward scenes may occur but Ricardo and Piero will assist. Any infringement will be met with dismissal or worse, since our licence is not invulnerable and there has already been some slight difference of interpretation between ourselves and the local constabulary. A car will be waiting to take you home. What you do when you are off the premises is, of course, another matter. On the whole we try to discourage external liaisons between our girls and our gentlemen. Here at Chestertons we are in the business of magic. As in the words of the poet, we are a flower that opens but at night. The illusion is perhaps destroyed if we are seen by day. Welcome to Chestertons. We hope you will be happy. Iona? I wish to speak to you for one moment.'

A whey-faced brunette of around twenty, intermittently spotty and preternaturally slim, admitted by buzzer, and making for the swing-doors at the back of the reception, stopped at the summons and grew perceptibly paler. Sensing unpleasantness, though smiling at the girl, Chloe picked up her carrier bag with its cargo of nylon and chiffon, and headed for the odorous recesses of the interior.

Inside, as the doors flapped listlessly behind her, her eyes took a moment or two to adjust to the subdued lighting, but finally focused on a scene unlike anything she had ever witnessed. Although the house-mother Cheryl had not attempted to disguise the nature or function of the place, and graphically though Maudie had outlined the general scenario, nothing could have prepared her for the curious juxtaposition of imagery that greeted her.

There was a bar. That was familiar enough. There was an Italian-looking barman and waiter. She had seen ominous-looking latins around before. There were conventional tables and chairs. What made the whole thing astonishing was the impact of the assorted naked bosoms sported by the twenty or so girls who stood draped around the bar or reclined, smoking, on a couple of shiny-cushioned sofas against the far wall. Breasts glimmered and winked in the gloaming like strange white underground fruit. Even the coloured girls' bosoms – and there were African, Malaysian, Chinese and Indian varieties –

seemed to Chloe to have been cultivated in the same hothouse cavern by the light of artificial moons, nocturnal, troubling and forbidden.

When she had recovered a little from her astonishment, she noted that her entry had occasioned no great burst of enthusiasm or camaraderie. An early client lounged at a table with a couple of girls beside him. The Italians, in white shirts with black bow-ties, eyed her professionally but said and did nothing. One or two of the girls looked at her figure in a way that was more commiserative than competitive, but that was all. Nobody made a move.

She stood there, feeling exposed, clothed though she was. Maudie had disappeared. She had an urgent instinct to get out while she could. The barman poured her a vodka, as if heading off her thought, and slid it across to her.

'You drink that, ha? First night, ha? Cheers.'

She sensed he slept with some of the girls but more for exercise than pleasure.

'Thanks.'

Maudie came up behind her while she knocked it back. Maudie was now dressed in the regulation wisp, looking rather beautiful. Her breasts were small and friendly.

'Dressing-room's over there,' said Maudie. 'Cheer up. It's better after a few drinks, and when you've got your first money.'

'It's all right for you,' Chloe grimaced, 'you can't smell it.'

Maudie had something wrong with her sinuses and couldn't smell a galloping Brie if you placed it right under her nose. 'You'll get used to it,' she said. 'Smell's like love. The nose only responds to change. It soon ignores the familiar.'

Maudie had read Sociology at Sussex, but not finding a job in keeping with her training and intelligence, had opted for baring bosoms at Chestertons rather than profaning her education by becoming a secretary.

'The mind's more important than the body,' she used to say. 'They may put a hand on your tits but they can't touch your mind.'

You couldn't blame her but you sometimes thought she ought to be doing better things.

Chloe went to the Black Hole on the landing they used for a changing room, took off her shirt and jeans, and undid her bra. Her breasts, she'd always thought, were a little on the heavy side, but they were well-shaped, and her nipples, neither too big nor too small, were on the paler end of pink, as if they lived in a shell and only came out after dark.

She could sense the weight of her breasts as she bent to adjust the chiffon in the regulation microskirt over the silkiness of the over-expensive tights she'd bought for her first night, and she felt both vulnerable and curiously excited. This was definitely one of the wickedest things she'd ever done, and she thought of her school back in the Cotswolds where the headmistress had instructed them that their bodies were God's temples.

She was aware of her temple, now, trembling a little. This was terrible, she couldn't go out like this, people would notice. She'd have to get dressed again, and go home and be a secretary.

The door suddenly opened. It was Maudie.

'You all right? I thought you might've got your chiffons in a twist.'

She didn't seem to notice her excitement. Indeed, Chloe learned later that dormant nipples for instance were frowned on by the management, and many girls whose responses were inclined to be sluggish actually sprayed theirs with stuff to make them stand out, or rubbed them unobtrusively against the ice buckets, because a stiff nipple could be worth an extra fifty quid a night.

'You'd better come and have a drink,' said Maudie. 'That bloke was looking at you as if he wanted to eat you when you came in. There's at least twenty quid waiting for you there. When he asks you over, tell him to order champagne.'

Chloe stepped out, adjusting her wisp.

Half a dozen media salesmen and a couple of Arabs had come in and were distributed around the room. A very small executive with glasses was serving as a cushion for a massive negress with aureolae the size of dinner plates.

The man Maudie had mentioned did indeed seem to take notice as she came down the stairs, and she soon found herself sitting on his knee and pouring Moët et Chandon.

She earned £60 that night with nothing worse than a pinched bottom to show for it, and the address of a good-looking if haggard young commercials film-producer to call if she felt like earning £50 more. Though the evening had not increased her respect for the male sex, it did seem, all in all, money for old rope.

Returning home with Maudie as dawn was breaking, under a sky as shockingly pale as the brunette Iona who, it had turned out, had been caught shooting smack in the Black Hole, she felt so keyed-up and excited by the night's experiences that when they were in the kitchen having a last drink with their coffee she kissed Maudie by way of thanking her for looking after her, and when she felt Maudie's mouth respond, it didn't seem strange to pass her hands by way of friendship over Maudie's small and friendly breasts – she had seen so much of them that night, she felt she knew them quite well – so then she had to stroke them because it seemed a waste not to, and Maudie murmured in a way not at all like the poised graduate with a mastery of high-rise statistics, and took her to the bedroom.

Later, in the dark cloudlight of the Earl's Court morning, they fell asleep still nuzzling each other like minnows.

3

After she passed on, I withdrew completely into myself again. I could not bear to live in the house with its memories, so I sold up and bought a little place near the World's End. The name appealed to me. I changed my way of life, my habits, my haunts; even my appearance underwent a metamorphosis. I had been inclined to plumpness since boyhood, but now I grew thin and my hair, hitherto an undistinguished dark, was soon, like the autumnal beech, tainted with the hues of mortality.

In the despair of those early days, I let myself go, and grew a beard; this I subsequently kept. I also found I needed glasses for reading, which I arranged to have adapted as bifocals (with a plain glass upper lens) so I could wear them all the time if required.

The total result was that even the few acquaintances I had known in Fulham now failed to recognize me when I passed them in the street, and my solicitor himself had to ask my name when I was talking to his clerk outside his office. This gave me a strange satisfaction, and the notion grew in me to encourage the changes which Nature and her sister Fate had thought fit to bestow upon my person, altering the style of my clothes and the very manner of my gait.

I now wore leisure wear, rather than the formal suits I had favoured before, and reverted to a more casual bearing which would have made my former Sergeant-Major's eyes pop out of his head. Even my voice reflected the change. I now affected a more relaxed enunciation whereas before I had been punctilious. It was all in keeping with the laissez-faire attitude of the times.

I genuinely believe my own mother would not have

known me. I had always been brought up to be careful of my outward and visible signs.

Thus, when I began to formulate my plan of action with regard to the American, Richmonde, I already possessed a well-developed instinct for disguise, for camouflage, for being, though not obviously, anybody in a crowd, and for pursuits which I shall touch on later. This oblique approach to life was my response, if you like, to the disappointments and sufferings I had experienced when venturing head-on into the fray.

But to the matter in hand.

The morning after my adventure with the American, I awoke feeling both keyed up and refreshed. I customarily rise shortly before dawn, and after a good English breakfast of porridge, eggs and bacon, my first for many months, I walked in leisurely manner down to the Thames and watched the houseboats nudging each other like bumpkins at a procession in the rising tide.

The whole of Battersea Reach lay shimmering at my feet. The morning stretched before me, golden with opportunity. And yet I still hesitated. Why had Fate, previously so treacherous, so sapping to my spirit, suddenly decided at this point to offer me a transfusion of fire?

I stood there on the steps, minutely perusing the dimpled water and the swirl of splintered crates and plastic beakers as if for a sign, locked in the most profound inner turmoil. The argument, like the lap and tussle of the water below me, broke and flowed and ebbed on the reaches of my consciousness. Could I grasp this sudden lifeline that had been offered to me? I had become accustomed, you see, to the dun-coloured routine of my days. Even hopelessness becomes tolerable with habit. Was I strong enough to start living again, to throw away the familiar bromide that had become my norm – it is, after all, the way most people spend their lives?

I stood there for a full hour looking intently down at the

filling river, so intently that a trio of charwomen who passed, concluding that I was nerving myself to leap into the stream, approached me with conventional expressions of solace.

'There, there, dear,' exclaimed the first, 'can't be as bad as all that.'

'I'd rather cut me throat than jump into that stuff,' concluded the second, less romantically, with a meaning look, and the third launched into a long diatribe about her sister's son who had contracted hepatitis in some Mediterranean resort – caviare for the general, I thought, but did not let on.

However, I had to agree that the water did look singularly uninviting at that moment as a large condom swam past with an irregular gait that was strangely lifelike. Sex has been the ruin of our civilization: in one generation we have exposed what it took a thousand years to obscure.

'Thank you, ladies,' I felt like saying, doffing an imaginary hat, 'your solicitude has won me over. Are you perhaps not what you seem? Clotho, Lachesis and Atropos, perchance, whom men know as the Fates?' For indeed their intervention was timely.

I do not believe that I actually spoke, but they looked askance. I have that effect on people if I choose.

My levity was perhaps forgivable, for it came to me now that I had, in some part of my mind, been contemplating self-destruction. It would have been at least a decision, putting me beyond the reach of loneliness and doubt. But the robustness of the old women's response braced me like a douche of tidal water, and suddenly there I was cracking jokes and committing myself to the undertaking in hand, lead where it might.

Before you could say 'Sunray Minor', I was halfway down Royal Hospital Road, destination Cadogan Square. The air was soft, my step was springy, I had found the soldier's swagger. I caught myself humming 'The Middlesex Maid', quick march of the 121st Regiment of Foot, composed by Charles Dibbin (1776–1832), who also gave us 'Tom Bowling' and 'Wapping Old Stairs'. New Intake had to learn such details in those far-off days in Acton Barracks.

Mr Tony Richmonde with an 'e' was evidently not an early riser, since I had to wait until after half past nine before he showed up in the doorway of Number 46, talking to my tea-slopping acquaintance of the previous night.

Sighting him, I rose from where I had been inconspicuously reading a newspaper on a bench beside the railings that skirt the Gardens. (I had taken the precaution of buying the *Daily Telegraph* – both because it is my customary newspaper, still upholding as it does some of the standards that made our country a byword for decency, and because nobody who reads the *Daily Telegraph* can easily be suspected of dark designs!)

Casually folding my journal, I strolled unhurriedly past Number 46, and managed to catch a few words of their conversation.

'Oh . . . Oh, and by the way, there, uh Mike, Hooper's are sending over an extra case of champagne some time. Let 'em in, would you? They can leave it in the kitchen.'

'Very good, Mr Richmonde. Certainly, Mr Richmonde.'

Three bags full, Mr Richmonde.

'Thank you there, uh Mike. Have a good day now.'

I detest that meaningless benediction, don't you? Do they really care what sort of a day you have? Of course, they do not. If they really cared they would give you £5 and have done with it. As for their habit of using your Christian name almost before they have met you, I can only say that I do not want my name handled by strangers.

While I pondered this tendency to over-familiarity, and put up a silent vote of thanks to the gods of English reticence, I made my way with practised imperceptibility up past the Gardens towards Pont Street, where I paused again, turning to watch the American bound with an unnecessary display of vigour (there was no doubt the man was a jogger) down the steps and make for a garage set in the corner of the Square, from whence he proceeded to extract the inevitable shiny black motor-car the size of a mews cottage. Our streets are not made for these behemoths.

I had been toying with thc notion of following him to his office, hailing an obligingly passing cab and tailing him to discover his place of work and manner of occupation, but another idea had struck me. I stopped at that telephone kiosk on the corner of Pont and Walton streets, and looked up Hooper's (Wine Merchants) Ltd in the book, trying to ignore the smell of stale urine (these people are no more than animals) and the instructions enjoining me to telephone Trish and friends, Sue, Pamela and Chrissie for unspecified revelry.

Sure enough, there they were, hardly a cork's pop away in Draycott Gardens. So far, so good. I dialled their number – the machine was by some miracle of providence still in a state of operation – and a young assistant's voice answered. This was yet another good sign. Had it been a man of more mature years, the proprietor even, he might have been on familiar terms with the man Richmonde and my little ruse would have had to be abandoned.

'Uh . . . uh . . . Hooper's?'

A remarkably good stab, I thought, at the American's twang.

'Yes, sir?'

'Uh . . . I ordered uh a case of champagne . . . Mr Richmonde here. Cadogan Square.'

'I'll just check, sir.'

There was a pause which gave rise to a moment of self-doubt. Though versed in camouflage and the skills of the Iban (tattooed Dyaks from North Borneo or Sarawak attached to every regiment as trackers, their instinct was uncanny), I had never so far launched into impersonation.

My heartbeat must have been echoing down the wires like a jungle drum.

'Yes, sir, that's right . . . a case of Roederer.'

I had passed muster.

'Well uh see here. Cancel the order for the moment, would you? Change of plan.'

'Certainly, sir. The van hasn't gone out yet. I'll take it off the list.'

So that was the first stage safely over. The next was the more dangerous, for it would involve a live encounter and a degree of illicitness if not criminality, which I had hitherto, I am sure, avoided in my pursuits. There is no law against following people.

I returned to my house at the World's End, extracted my Morris 1000 Estate or Traveller, drove straight to Drayton Gardens where I found a Resident's Parking space, and strode as bold as you please into Hooper's Wine Merchants, purveyors of fine wines, spirits and cigars to the nobs and bobs of the neighbourhood.

'Yes, sir?'

It must have been the assistant I had spoken to on the telephone, a harassed-looking youth with lacklustre hair and red eyes. Presumably he had not been shedding tears over the American's cancelled order? I would soon, in that case, give him cause to rejoice and set him totting up his commission on the calculator I saw peeping from his breast pocket. Whatever happened to the basic skills of arithmetic so assiduously dinned into our thick skulls at St Theodoric's, I should like to know?

'I'm looking for some champagne,' I said.

My voice was a few thousand miles east of my earlier conversation tone with the gangling lad – Knightsbridge would, I think, be the word for it – without being in any way over-memorable.

'Certainly, sir. What did you have in mind?'

'Something rather good.'

'Well, we have the Dom Perignon, of course. The '73 is

very good. Perrier Jouet . . .' he indicated the shelf where the bottles roosted in comfortable abundance.

'Good, good . . .' I encouraged.

'And then, of course, there's the Roederer. That's very popular.'

'Good God, man, don't say popular,' a voice bellowed.

A stout, bullying sort of man with black hair, red face and a pinstripe suit with a carnation in his buttonhole, appeared, reminding me more than somewhat of Major Gilliatt of B Company.

'Popular? This isn't a popular place. We don't sell popular here.'

The stripling quailed. I felt I could discern the source of his miseries, and I must confess my heart went out to him, though at the same time experiencing certain twinges of discomfiture on its own behalf. The last thing I wanted was an altercation at this stage. A quick in and out would have been more my line of country.

The large man in the suit (I assumed it must be Hooper himself) advanced upon us as though he would crack our heads together.

'That will do, Glebe,' he said to the youth, whose expression had graduated from wan to extreme dismay. 'Now, sir . . .' turning on me a smile like an eruption. 'Fine wines, vintage ports, cognacs, armagnacs, eaux-de-vie, almost every malt whisky distilled on Speyside . . . All these I can offer you, sir. Name your choice.'

It was quite clear that the man was a toper of the first water, his ruddy features playing host to a positive Irrawaddy Basin of little veins. He was now practically on top of me. I backed away against a shelf full of claret bottles.

'I have here, for instance, a rather special vintage from a little estate just behind Château Beychevelle. It would make, if I may say so, sir, your mother's milk smack of malt vinegar. Or what about this '72 Chambolle Musigny? I understand every other case has now been bought up by the Elysée Palace. I truly believe it'd corrupt an anchorite if you happen to have one you wish to suborn. Yes, sir, I swear Stylites himself would descend from his pillar for a snifter of this little number. I could probably get you fermented yak's milk if that were your desire. The distinguished . . . yes . . . the excellent . . . yes . . . the rare . . . yes . . . the noble, yes indeed . . . the eximious, the recondite, the eclectic, yes again. But don't please, sir . . . I don't think we've had the pleasure of your custom before . . . don't come in here asking for the popular, because by God, sir, if that's what you're after, you'd better clear out right away and cut along to the supermarket round the corner before I say something I might regret. Popular my backside.'

Well, I had to admire the man's sentiments, even if I did not like his tone. It is good to know that there are still sticklers about at this time of fallen standards and national decay – we seem to have had Elm Disease in our tree of state for longer than I care to think about – but just at that moment I was anxious to avoid confrontation, and by the way the man narrowed his little piggy eyes and glared at me I was only too aware that my cloak of anonymity was in danger of being ripped off like a corn plaster.

I summoned my military bearing, restrained but adamant, stiffened my shoulders, and pointed firmly to the upper reaches of the champagne shelf.

'A case of Roederer, if you would be so kind.'

'A case, sir? That's Roederer '71. Twenty pounds a bottle.'

'I said a case.'

'That'll be £240, sir. You have the transport? Mr Glebe, take a case of Roederer out to the gentleman's car. And now, sir, would you be good enough to fill in this questionnaire – we are doing a survey on our customers to try and keep our service in line with their requirements. May I ask how you propose to pay?'

'Cash,' I said, 'naturally.'

I saw his piggy eyes widen as I peeled off the notes. Clearly not many customers paid up like this, but I was anxious not to provide any trace of my origins. As for the questionnaire (which I regarded as a gross intrusion, no doubt to be fed into the central computer which oversees all), I filled it in with reckless levity, using the name of Arthur Ransome and giving details of that old yarn-spinner's cellarage which would have done credit to Silenus himself.

Luckily the assistant Glebe, as he struggled up the street to the Morris, looked too preoccupied and ill-used to bother about taking registration numbers. Finally, when he had successfully deposited the liquid gold in the back, received my thanks and trudged glumly off again, I was able to sit in the Traveller for a moment and wipe my palms on the Kleenex I always keep handy.

You might perhaps have imagined that after such an encounter any sensible man would have thought better of his madcap scheme and returned home to put his costly prize on ice. The man Hooper had given off a powerful aura of danger. But, though shaken by his proximity, I was curiously elated. In the primary forests of Malaya, I had experienced the heady effects that danger had on my system. I now felt nerved for Phase Two of my Plan.

When I was satisfied that my deportment could be taken as being suitably casual, I started up and headed for Cadogan Square once more, right at the Fulham Road traffic lights and then first right again into Walton Street, thoroughfare of little restaurants and health food shops (only the rich can afford the simple these days), right again into Pont Street ignoring the primrose path that leads to Harrods, and finally third right into the Cadogans.

I parked round the corner so the porter would not notice the absence of the Hooper's van, and humped the crate up the steps to the man in the cubbyhole.

'Order for Mr Richmonde, Flat 11,' I breezed.

He was sitting, mug in hand, goggling at the centre pages of a daily newspaper (not, need I add, the *Daily Telegraph*) upon which a young lady pranced in an attitude of licensed indelicacy, and I could see he was disinclined to stir. For once in a while, I had reason to appreciate the depths into which Fleet Street has fallen.

'Oh yes,' he said, without enthusiasm, 'Hooper's, isn't it?'

'Don't worry,' I replied serviceably, 'I'll take it up. Give us the key and I'll put it in 'is 'allway. Nice and easy. No need for you to move.'

I could see he knew he should not, but he agreed, and I soared aloft with my precious cargo and a fistful of Ingersoll and Banham mortice keys. I had gathered from the American's conversation the previous night that his wife was in the country, so I anticipated no interruption once I was in the flat, and in this I was not disappointed. The whole thing was a piece of cake (no doubt from the wholefood bakery up the road). The door yielded obediently to my hand. The place was unoccupied. Even so, I remembered the disciplines of Mr Parsons, our Platoon Commander: appearances can be deceptive, fools rush in, and he would give examples, with many an instructive anecdote from the Korea hostilities, of untimely haste.

'Hullo,' I called, 'Hooper's here. Your champagne, Mr Richmonde.'

No reply. It was as still as a deserted Terrorist camp.

I placed the champagne on the deep slightly grey-mauve carpet, and proceeded to make a swift recce of the terrain in a manner which Mr Parsons himself would have endorsed, pausing only to take a cast of the front door keys.

I wasted little time on the hall, kitchen and dining-room beyond noting that they were expensively furnished. It irritated me to see the way he had amassed our English antiques and Victorian pictures, but I did not let it show in my rapid professional movements. Resentment could come later.

I made a cursory inspection of the lounge which merely confirmed my impression of the previous rooms. However, a photograph in a heavy silver frame showed a woman in her early thirties, with large teeth and too-long hair and wearing a kaftan, whom I supposed to be his good lady. There was a baby grand piano also prominent in the room with music by Gershwin resting upon its stand whom I particularly detest. No doubt he serenaded his inamorata with Rhapsody in Blue while she sniffed cocaine in a corner. The thought gave me an idea.

If I searched I should almost certainly discover drugs on the premises, knowing what these people are like if report is to be believed.

I hastily investigated a likely-looking lacquer cabinet and did indeed unearth a small screw of tinfoil containing what I took to be cannabis, replacing it carefully so that my discovery should not be noticed, but not before I had mingled into the brownish matted stuff a considerable quantity of fluff from the arm-pieces of the sofa, purely for the mischief of the thing.

I had no idea what I should do with the information at that moment, but one never knows – in preparing an attack the ground must be thoroughly covered. This is what one learns on the banks of the Menlik.

I hastily proceeded into the main bedroom, aware that however capacious the charms of the delinquent on the centre spread, the porter could not be counted on to glare at them all day. The bed was unmade and there was, in spite of an overlying aroma of deodorant and American toothpaste (the Viet Cong used to aim at it in the jungle, I am informed), a stuffy sort of smell of pyjamas and unopened windows. The hairbrushes on the dresser were in a sorry state. My poor mother would have given them short shrift.

I cast a rapid eye over the chest of drawers (a bow-fronted piece, possibly reproduction) but could find nothing more revealing than a pair of female panties in among the jockey briefs, whether suggesting carelessness or quirk I could not fathom.

The trouble was, of course, that I did not really know what I was looking for. There was material here for a painstaking turnover by seasoned agents, but I did not have the luxury of time.

Beside the bed there was one of those American sagas of witchcraft and vampirism which do so much to disturb the young. It told me about the man but it was not what I had come for. My heart was beating fast. I had been up in the flat for over ten minutes and I was beginning to feel the way I used to during mathematics tests at St Theodoric's, a sense at once of urgency and constriction.

The only remaining door turned out to be that of a second bedroom which also appeared to double as a study. This was more promising. I proceeded at once to the desk with eager tread. It proved to be a treasure trove of information too much for my limited period of inspection, more suited to the leisurely mole with his micro-camera.

There were letters upon it, some of which seemed to relate to the American's work. His company was Craxton & Kuhne, with offices in Soho – not my favourite part of London. They were in the Video and Security business, whatever that might be. I jotted the address down and urgently scoured the desk for any other item that would give me something to work on. On one of those chichi businessmen's cards was written 'Chloe, Ground Floor, 44 Prosser Street, W 11'. Finally, there was an electricity bill addressed to Mr A. Richmonde at Mast Hill Cottage, Cowden, Nr Henley-on-Thames, Oxon.

Cowden, near Henley . . . I remembered, with a sudden surge of longing for the forest, those steep rounded slopes alive with murmuring beeches off the old road from Henley to Oxford, all those quaintly-named flint-dashed villages, Nettlebed and Christmas Common, which now, it seemed, were alive with loud-voiced Americans.

Just at this moment, while anger vied with memory and I

frantically scribbled addresses in my Nature Year notebook, I heard what I had been half-expecting since I entered the place, a sound of scrabbling keys at the front door. Who could it be? The man's wife? The porter? The girlfriend? The police? The situation was rife with possibilities, none of them welcome. I froze, and my fingers tightened automatically on an invisible sten gun.

It was this jungle training that stood me in good stead. When the need arises, I can still be as cool as a cucumber. Others might have secreted themselves and been humiliatingly flushed out, but I had been taught in a hard school to improvise, adapt and extend. The youth of today does not know what it is missing.

I launched myself like a Piat missile into the hall and ripped open the case of champagne, assuming an air of casual inspection as the key-holder finally negotiated the third lock and the door swung open.

There was a pause and a spate of heavy breathing. I did not look up but continued lovingly to unwrap the bottles from their tissue, laying them on the shag-pile and bracing myself for whatever recrimination, query or janitor's curse might be my portion.

My task completed, however, I finally ventured to glance at the looming newcomer. It turned out to be a large shapeless woman, cousin no doubt to my acquaintances of Battersea Bridge, considerably out of breath and wearing an unseasonably heavy coat with an air of martyrdom. Before she could register surprise or misgiving – and it was clear that any such registration would not occur in a flash but gather by degrees like the threat of rain – I forestalled.

'Thought I heard something clinking in there,' I said. 'With bottles at twenty quid each, I don't like to deliver a wrong 'un.'

I liked the wrong 'un, don't you, with its smack of complicity? The very word conjures up a cheeky grin. Such is the power of language, and so it was now.

'Ow,' she said. 'Now. Don't want to do that. Hold the door would yer, ducks, while I get me doings?'

I complied with willing grace. It seemed she had been expecting my presence in the flat, warned by the ogling janitor. She never used the lift, she confided, she had a fear of coffins, so she carried all her equipment up the stairs herself at some inconvenience.

'Twenty quid a bottle,' she observed, as she lugged in the industrial Hoover that served the block. 'It's more than I make in a couple of days. It's all right for some.'

I had some sympathy for her case, but I was not going to embark upon a discussion on the pros and cons of market economics with the good lady, so I agreed with polite expressions of solidarity, swopped details of my heartburn with the incunabula of her fallen arches, declined an offer of tea, and made my escape in leisurely manner while she shuffled about the kitchen filling the kettle.

Gurkhas could not have vanished into the oil-palms more imperceptibly than myself as I slipped past the porter, this time occupied with a racing journal, and out into the well-heeled anonymity of the Square.

Mission completed. In the absence of a superior officer, I congratulated myself on my performance.

4

For three months, the novelty interested her. For another three, she didn't much care either way. She stuck it for four. Then the old restlessness started again in earnest. It was well-paid, yes, but in the end you had to admit that it wasn't getting you anywhere.

The hours, of course, were awful – you expected that. But could you be blamed for not predicting the effects of sitting up all night drinking shorts, in a badly-ventilated smoky room, messing around with foreigners and the lower sort of businessman? Maybe you could. Anyway, in the end, finally it got to you, leading at the very least to pimples and pasty faces and at the worst to all manner of unpleasantness and eruptions. Even Evadne, the giantess from Guyana, who had never had a day's illness in her life, had to take a week off with boils.

As for the daytime, when she'd felt she was going to be able to do all sorts of things, like typing and learning about interior decorating, somehow you never seemed to have the energy. She'd been surprised originally that Maudie didn't do more, but it was as if the place were a sort of Dracula, sitting there in the shadows even on the brightest day waiting for the night to fall, to sink its teeth into you again.

Maudie did a sociological survey of it.

If you took the average complement of two dozen girls, she calculated that at any given time there would be two girls with TB, two with some kind of plumbing problem, five with some form of VD (including of the mouth), four with boyfriends who beat them, two breakdowns, one eventual suicide (either during or subsequent to their career at the Club), and four alcoholics.

It made you think.

Cheryl herself, it was rumoured, would leave if she could think of anything else to do, but she was keeping her mother in an old people's home in Folkestone which was reputed to cost an arm and a wobbly leg.

Not surprisingly, there was a high turnover at every level of staff; even Piero got a nasty wound in a fight outside, and had to go back to Catania for restyling. At the end of the year, only about a third of the original complement were still working. The rest had gone their way – though sometimes they would resurface for a stint after a love affair, walkabout, or spell in hospital, prison, or both.

The other thing was that Maudie was growing possessive. Though Chloe was fond of her, she knew that there was no future in an affair with a girl. That it was a sin was exciting, beyond even auntie's scale. That it led nowhere was the punishment.

For the future, however much you pushed it out among the Earl's Court dustbins, wouldn't go away. It was always there, ruffling the edges of the mind like the breeze in the basement curtains. In between even the most delectable embraces, she could always sense those parsnips of position, influence, security, insistently there, steaming away, waiting to be buttered.

The only way to deal with the future was to keep moving, not to stand there waiting to be hit.

She had been seeing something of an American smack dealer (though she didn't hold with hard drugs) called Willis, who was a friend of the thin girl Iona. He'd been attending a course in business management at Summer School in Cambridge, and he now had to make a trip back to the States. He suggested that she and Iona should go along with him for the ride. It seemed like a good opportunity.

There was a tearful scene with Maudie, who understood why she was going but still didn't much like it, and a memorable farewell to Chestertons.

She went out in fine style on a flood of pink champagne, ingeniously rearranging her costume to disclose a pair of large pale eyes painted on the upper slopes of her backside so that it looked like a rude man peeping out. The effect was both striking and popular. Cheryl, though officially disapproving, was forced to smile. Chloe had become her favourite hostess.

'It is the end of an era,' said Cheryl, handing over her final wages and bonus, from which she had deducted almost nothing for misconduct. 'America, is it? Tell me about the amniotic baths. I hear it is all the rage. A postcard would suffice. I daresay you will be back. There is always a position here, you know.'

Chloe promised her a report, and flew next day to Los Angeles, from there moving on to Venice, California, where everyone seemed to be on rollerskates. It proved to be a confusing though memorable trip for a girl who had never been further from England than a weekend in Normandy with the television producer and a fortnight in Lindos with Maudie.

From the moment they arrived in Venice, before they had even booked in, Willis was out. He was out in the morning, he was out for dinner, indeed it seemed that he was not even sleeping in his room.

Iona and Chloe were left to their own devices.

As it happened, they didn't have to devise for very long. They soon realized that they were being followed everywhere by a not-very-new cream Rolls Royce which might or might not have to do with Willis or his friends, or his enemies, but the fact that it was a Rolls at least made it seem in some way reassuring.

It eventually disgorged a polite half-Japanese half-Cherokee (at least that was what he said he was) who introduced himself as Yannick, complimented them on their style and beauty, bought them lunch, and over a couple of bottles of Napa Valley Cabernet Sauvignon explained that he was a terminal therapist working for a millionaire who had only three months to live. It was his job to ensure that his client had everything he craved before the final painful stage began, and what he craved was his therapist in bed with two girls, recorded on video, so that he could play it as a kind of celebration of procreation, a song of renewal, a meaningful affirmation of life in the cruel days ahead. There would be five hundred dollars apiece for them in recognition of this act of charity.

Since they were running low in funds (there seemed every possibility that Willis had done a vanishing trick), and the half-Japanese half-Cherokee was really rather tasty, and they were running on that irresponsibility that affects one in sunny foreign countries, and everyone seemed mad here anyway, and they had by now consumed a great deal of Cabernet Sauvignon, they agreed. It sounded crazy, but there it was, what else were they to do, the story was so corny it had to be genuine – a dangerous assumption in America, but they were newcomers.

The Rolls took them to a villa a little way out of town, where they were shown by their guide into a large bedroom containing an outsize bed, a video camera and monitor, and a director's chair on wheels. The therapist opened a cupboard door, and brought out some Californian champagne. They all got into bed and started to drink it.

At this point, a door at the other end of the room opened, and a little old man with a wrinkled face and impeccably pressed white suit entered, shook hands politely, asked if they were enjoying their trip, and stationed himself in the director's chair so that he could view the action as well as the monitor screen.

'The reality and the image,' he confided obscurely, 'this is where existential actuality and fantasy meet.'

The girls didn't like to ask him if he were the millionaire, or simply the director of the song of procreation, and the therapist who had been smoking since they left the restaurant was too high to give any kind of coherent reply, and simply giggled.

'Action,' said the little old man.

'Pardon?' said Chloe.

'I think he means us,' said Iona.

'Hahahahahahahaha,' said the terminal therapist.

He was a fine figure of a redskin but he seemed inclined to do little except wave himself at the camera.

The director was active for such an elderly person. He would leap up, peer at their bottoms, run back, check the screen, and sit on the edge of his chair looking from existential actuality to image so fast it made your head spin just to watch him. Then he'd jump up again, readjust their positions, run back once more, twiddle the zoom lens, check the light, scratch his balls, and all the while issue a stream of staccato imperatives.

'Hold it,' he would urge.

'Hold what?'

'Left labia. There. There. So . . . Finger on anus . . . So . . .'

'So?'

'No no.'

'So?'

'No no no. Lower lower. So.'

'Ah. So. How're you doing down there, Iona?'

'So so.'

'No talking, ladies, please. Save your breath for the task in hand.'

It was only afterwards that they discovered he wasn't a terminal millionaire at all but a blue film-maker too mean to pay proper prices. He just combed the streets looking for likely-seeming visitors. He had learned, he said, that if they believed the therapist story, they'd never make trouble. No one would ever want to admit to being that dumb.

They turned to the therapist. He had stopped laughing and was now pulling out a pocketbook from which he peeled a thin wad of notes.

'There you are, ladies. Fifty dollars each.'

'My left tit. You said five hundred.'

'You must have misinterpreted. It is easy in strange country.'

'How low can you get?'

'Twenty-five dollars each?'

'We'll take the fifty.'

Some years later, Chloe actually saw the song of procreation being played at a media salesman's palazzo in Sunbury-on-Thames. The episode in which she and Iona had taken part formed a sub-plot in a so-called Swedish epic called *Cunning Lundquist*. It was surprisingly well filmed of its kind. Clearly the little man's hyperactive camera-work had paid dividends, as had his method of casting: there was an incontrovertible freshness about the performances. No one recognized her. Much of the material was shot in extreme close-up, and what longer vistas he had allowed himself was in fashionable soft-focus. Chloe only identified Iona by a rather distinctive little strawberry naevus.

The rest of the trip was a medley of not dissimilar experiences, though they took care to be on their guard against therapists. It was not that the girls were promiscuous. They were simply short of cash.

For a sizeable bet, Chloe had a professional footballer in an inter-State Boeing's washroom with the stewardesses eagerly refereeing through the 'Engaged' sign. She sold waterbeds or 'flotation support systems' for a company called Ecologee Furniture Inc, encouraging potential (male) buyers with explicit lolling, until it went into liquidation. She was hired as a single in a Mainly Married orgy near Santa Barbara, but a combination of tequila and Quaaludes allowed her to sleep right through it.

In an effort to break out of the horizontal, they agreed to take some cocaine across the border to Canada, but it scared them so much they put it in a public postbox, and then took refuge with a draft-dodger in the hills near

Vancouver for a month because they thought they were being followed.

Finally they got so bored that even a vengeful pusher would have seemed a cheery change, but it turned out they weren't being followed any more, so they went down to Hollywood, where they met Willis again and stayed with him and a hit-man he seemed to have with him, in the hit-man's apartment, helping to get the hit-man off Willis's back, where he half seemed to be, which was nice of them after everything Willis had put them through. And so it went on. Sun, drink, killing wasps, snorting a little coke now and then, and wickedness almost only when you felt like it.

Finally, at a poolside party, she met a large tanned industrial chemist who seemed to have paradise within his grasp. He told her about amniotic baths. She had forgotten them in the general throng and press.

'But you should not forget,' he insisted. 'It is the ultimate physical experience. All sensation is maximized. You float in a saline module, warmed to blood heat, concentrating exclusively on your genitalia.'

It sounded neat.

Like so much else, however, it wasn't all it was cracked up to be, because when she entered the module with the chemist – she wouldn't let him sleep with her until he arranged it – she found that though the initial experience was delicious, as he had indicated, when he entered the final straight the supreme sensations were replaced by the most exquisite agony as the heavily-salted water bit into the delicate membranes. She uttered a piercing shriek, and the chemist dropped off her like a pybuthrined housefly.

Someone had got it wrong, and she sent Cheryl a typically incisive telegram:

'AMNIOTIC MY FLAMING ASS.'

It was received with acclaim. 'Just like our Chloe,' said Cheryl. 'What a nerve. And hasn't she gone native? Ass, indeed. In the old days, the Post Office would never have allowed it.'

Maybe it was the salutary effect of the saline, or the fact that she'd now been away six months, or that she yearned for fish and chips, or that Iona had gone off with a real estate executive to Florida, but Chloe suddenly decided she'd had enough. She persuaded a reproduction furniture manufacturer to pay for her ticket back to London, promising that she'd be his agent for him there – she was learning to live a little more on her wits now – and straight from Heathrow she took a taxi to Cheryl's flat in Maida Vale.

'There you are, dear,' said Cheryl. 'I knew, once we got the telegram, you wouldn't be far behind.'

Chloe made the toast while Cheryl opened the Gentlemen's Relish, and over a pot of Earl Grey they had a good long talk about Chloe's discoveries.

'I can't get over it,' she said, 'the way they treat sex. It's like paper underwear. Easy and intimate, but not much fun.'

'It's a terrible thing, dear, when other people treat your body as casually as you do yourself. It's like outsiders criticizing your mother. You may criticize her yourself but it doesn't mean that they can. To be honest, I think my Stimulette de luxe takes a lot of beating.'

Cheryl had always been an advocate of do-it-yourself. She said you met a nicer class of person.

'But,' Chloe countered, 'it doesn't take you round America for six months!'

'Maybe not, dear, maybe not. But I always say the most important discoveries are in yourself.'

5

It was a sine qua non when we were fighting the Communist Terrorist that all aspects of the terrain, all possible diversifications of his behaviour in the field, had to be considered before any action was undertaken. After six months I thought I had seen it all, but I was still brought up short on one occasion.

There was this operation east of Penang when Lieutenant Parsons, Lance Corporal Farleigh and I actually went native, living with the Malays alongside their chickens and pigs for a week while we studied every avenue, every approach path, every possible piece of cover in anticipation of a small squad of CTs (they only travelled in limited numbers) that we had received information were on the move. They used to come and terrorize the villagers into giving them food, shelter and information, much to the natives' disgust, but their hands were tied (and sometimes worse).

We knew they were coming an hour or so before they arrived. The headman told Mr Parsons that he had received word, though goodness knows how – the CTs moved quieter than the little green krait.

I had found what I believed to be the natural escape route from the compound, and stationed myself with the bren, concealed in the doorway of a hut. Sure enough, the CTs arrived just as the headman had predicted. First one came slipping through the wire like a shadow out of the forest, then another and another until there were five of them, a large party for their manner of business.

It was careless of them to group together like that. I suppose they thought they were secure, but Mr Parsons shattered the peace with an anti-personnel grenade which killed two of them outright, Corporal Farleigh got the other two with his sten, and the fifth, some kind of bigwig, because he had a star on his tunic, came scuttling down the compound like all get out.

And then he saw, or rather I should say sensed me, standing there in the doorway.

'Don't shoot. Take him . . .' I heard Mr Parsons shouting.

It seemed the CT had some command of English. He paused for a fraction of a second, smiled, and started to walk away at right-angles as cool as you please, looking over his head at me as he moved towards the forest.

I called out in Chinese: 'Halt or I fire,' and then, in Malay: 'Berenti. Saya tembakh.'

The Terrorists were almost all Chinese we had trained to resist the Japs. Ironical really.

He just went on smiling. I called again. I had to do something, he was almost away.

'Fire . . . Fire dammit . . .' I heard the Lieutenant yelling.

He had changed his tune.

I squeezed the trigger of the bren, five seconds rapid fire, and I shot the CT in two just above the waist, and this is the extraordinary thing. He actually ferried himself with his arms across the last yard of compound, through the wire (it was cut so he knew where to go) and into the trees like one of those hideously mutilated cripples you see in Calcutta.

I remembered, strange isn't it how at moments of shock it is the trivia that come to mind?, a film I had seen in Kingston called *Freaks*, and there he was, a freak of my own, still grinning and scuttling and fountaining blood.

When we ran to look, I promise you he had disappeared in the jungle – it was thick round there. Only his blood and legs remained like the other half of Ozymandias, king of kings.

Now, I ask you, you can't get stranger than that. No

amount of planning will prepare you for that sort of caper. But at the same time, there was a horrible kind of logic to it, like a place you recognize that you have never seen before.

You see how I occupy my time when I get home to the World's End, no switching on of 'Crossroads' or filling my ears with the packing-paper that passes for radio. Instead there is a tendency to muse upon the past, to rove in the territory of dreams.

Unhealthy, you could say, and my mother would have gone along with you. 'Be off with you,' she would say, 'get some fresh air into your lungs.' And off I would go, out of the house, out across Putney Bridge, and down along the waterfront to see the skiffs and dinghies bobbing in the wake of the steamers and barges, or away on my push-bike to feed the ducks at Barnes. Days that can never return.

I have always maintained that the past is more satisfactory than the present or the future. The past is made. The rest is raw material. You can take the lid off the past like a Hornby Dublo, and, if you're lucky, get a look at the moving parts inside.

For an hour or two, I sat at home and rested. I had forgotten how exhausting it was, the pushing and the prodding, the tweaking and the wrenching, the heaving and the shovelling that goes into the making of fact out of the base metal of the Future. The Present is the production line and it is hard graft.

At length, however, I roused myself, it was by now almost midday, overcast but still warm, and caught a Number 14 to Shaftesbury Avenue.

From the top of the bus I marvelled once more at the change that has come over our historic city. Newspapers flapped listlessly in the gutters, refuse bulged like chunky foreign sausages out of the taut black skin of rubbish bags – there was a dustmen's strike in Westminster as usual – and talking of black skins there was hardly a white face to be seen on the top floor. I am not bigoted. I had the greatest respect for the Ibans, who were as dark as the coming of thunder – at least they were before their tattooist got to work on them – and the bravest little fighters you could ever wish to see, but one likes to feel at home in one's own capital.

The sensation was even more displeasing once I had dismounted. I have recourse to come to Soho but seldom in the normal course of events. Oh, I have kept one or two chappies under observation, out of the sheer need to keep my hand in, who have frequented these parts but on the whole I try to give that sort of character a miss. And now, walking up Wardour Street past the Queens Theatre, the sense of outrage choked me. This old Georgian quarter where Chippendale and Sheraton created their masterpieces, where Handel strolled with his amanuensis John Christopher Smith, was now more ablaze than ever with Amusement Arcades full of electronic death-guns (give the little gangsters a spell in the jungle south of Yong Peng and they'd be wetting their Y-Fronts soon enough), strip shows, erotic cinemas advertising Explicit Acts, demi-monde bookshops emblazoned with magazines featuring buttocks and worse, Gay (the Americans deserve worse than death for having debauched the adjective) Clubs and Clubettes, and Marital Aid establishments (a euphemism) in which rubber dolls lounged with mouth agape and thighs at the ready and monstrous things with prickles on like cricket gloves wagged insistently from every window. It was like a midden crawling with dung beetles most of whom, I have to report, looked foreign. Thank you for nothing, Mr Mintoff.

It did not bode well for Mr Tony Richmonde. I was becoming more and more incensed by the minute. Was it for this I risked my life and limb in the bug-infested swamps of the Lower Bertan? True, I could not accuse him personally of having debased my native city, but its decline had clearly been contemporaneous with the growth of American influence.

What, I asked myself, had we got in return? A higher incidence of iced popsicles in the corner shops.

Craxton & Kuhne, it turned out, were established in a glossy modern glasshouse at the Oxford Street end of the street of dreams. A discreet brass plate outside the building proclaimed their name and, inside, in the main hall, another notice pointed the way upstairs to their offices on the first and second floors. In addition to giving their name and location, it added cryptically (at least as far as I was concerned) Video Hardware and Software.

I considered the phraseology deeply offensive. Besides, what did it mean? With my background in the hardware trade, I found 'software' the stuff of nightmares, like boneless women or elastic chisels. However, I had to take myself in hand; if I were to do any kind of mischief to the man, I had to know the nature of his occupation. Yes, you see, already I had set myself on causing a little more than local nuisance. I could not let this kind of person get away with it.

I approached a melancholy-looking security man in a black quasi-uniform with a weeping moustache and bulging eyes who was sucking barley sugar (at least I assumed it was barley sugar, it could have been Love Sugar) behind a sort of counter in the corner with a little white plastic pyramid in front of him that said L. Thwaites.

'Hullo,' I said, going up to him like a museum visitor, 'L. Thwaites.'

'Mr Thwaites,' he replied. 'L. to my friends.'

I saw at once that my approach was too familiar. I have a British tendency to have my little joke which sometimes comes to the fore in moments of predicament. 'I wonder if you could help me,' I said. I had no wish to antagonize the man, or to render myself more than passingly imprinted on his memory. I should no doubt be coming this way again.

'Don't suppose so,' he said without regret. 'What would you be wanting to know?'

'What is software?'

I could hardly bring myself to speak the word, my father would writhe in his grave.

'You an industrial spy?'

I did not like this drift so I became playful.

'My mother used to say I was naturally inquisitive.'

'You know what curiosity killed, don't you?'

'I do not hold with animals in London.'

'Oh well, you look harmless enough.'

And indeed I did. I had donned (forgot to mention) my city suit, gold-rimmed spectacles and mildest expression for the outing.

'Video software is what you put on your video cassette machine, programmes and such. I have a machine myself, the wife gets restless the hours I work in this job.'

'Yes, yes,' I said, anxious to avoid revelations of a family nature. 'Anything else? What sort of thing?'

'Feature films, of course. Home improvement programmes. Teach yourself Zulu if that is your fancy. Sport, Games. Info. Porno. That's still the big growth market. They've serialized the Karma Sutra I see. It will be a boon. Whether they do that sort of caper up there,' he rolled his eyes heavenward, 'is another matter. Very reserved. They have a publishing interest, that I know, their fingers are in many pies. Care for some Love Sugar? I am told the effect is perceptible.'

I declined with some dignity and reviewed the conversation. If I asked more questions it would look suspicious. Besides, I had learned enough for the moment. It would not do to let L. Thwaites sense the quite extraordinary surge of excitement and distaste that his disclosures had aroused in me – more, I am certain, than a whole course of fructose could provoke; it is a symptom of our age that we need these surrogate fillips, a well-turned ankle was enough for our forefathers – so I bade him good day and continued about my business.

I wandered, lost in thought, down the frowsty bazaar that is now Oxford Street scarcely noticing the throng of doomed loiterers from all the corners of the earth who seem to congregate and drift eternally along its windy purlieus, up to Marble Arch, down Park Lane, where my pace quickened past the Playboy Club, the Arabian Dorchester and the crass snout of the Hilton, all in the dusty swirl of the light spring breeze that had sprung up in the lunch-hour, and into Knightsbridge, where I hopped aboard a Number 14, finding myself, after the customary inconveniences, back in due course at the World's End and the conducive gloom of my little study.

Here I pondered a while, made tea, nibbled a Chocolate Bath Oliver (my only luxury) and prepared my mind for the rigorous enterprises of the evening.

6

Chloe sank back into the routine of life at Chestertons easily enough. It was a relief not to be waking up in strange rooms. Cheryl's flat was comfortable, she had a room to herself, and there was a bathroom with bidet and jacuzzi en suite. It was almost everything one could wish for.

Almost a week after she had started at the club again, Maudie turned up, and seemed anxious to bury whatever hatchet had been raised. She had found a new friend, a little French girl with a face like a wicked pixie and a gymnastic ability in bed, it was rumoured, that made Olga Korbut look like Babar the Elephant.

Chloe was glad she was happy. Indeed, on the face of it, everything seemed fine, but already she knew that the worst of her old problems still remained. What was she going to do? Before the old Dracula got to work again and inertia set in, she had to find something else. And yet what else was there? She needed that £400 a week tax-free. She needed to dress. She wanted to run a car, have her own flat. Nothing came immediately to mind. But with the impetus of her trip still upon her, she enrolled in a smart secretarial, cooking and modelling school, located in a large Edwardian building in Kensington, that specialized in turning geese into swans (between whom, the madrigalist tells us, there is an imbalance). She had taken little courses in the past, elocution and things, but this was the genuine article. She began to acquire habits of social confidence.

Chloe would never have been able to afford it, or as Dracula bit deeper, endure it, without Cheryl's help and support, and she was more than duly grateful to her, but the day the course finished, she knew she had to be on the move again. So one morning when Cheryl was out getting her hair done, she packed her case, left a tender note on the minipiano next to the photograph of Cheryl's father in his RAF Warrant Officer's moustache and uniform, and booked into a small service flat behind Harrods. From here, she felt, she could navigate upstream.

It wasn't quite as easy as that, though. She knew no one, and to break into even the middle of echelons of London society you need some kind of contact. None of her fellow students at the school in Kensington would do. They had either not wanted to know her, or were in the same boat. And the clientele at Chestertons were hardly the sort of people you met in polite drawing-rooms or the better sort of reception area, or if they were, they would certainly not wish to recognize *you*.

She was on the verge of thinking seriously about taking a temping job and working in advertising agencies, which would have been lowering her sights drastically, when she happened to walk past a Private View in one of the Fine Art galleries that abound in the hinterland of Harrods. Some instinct prompted her to pause and look through the window at the pictures on display – mainly angular nudes in a style she could recognize (thanks to the once-a-week lectures on Living with Art that she had attended at the college) as Modern. The sight of the linear posteriors made her grimace. It made you ache just to look at them.

'Don't fancy 'em? Quite right too. If I had a backside like that, I'd sell it for dogfood.'

She turned and saw a man in his early thirties, sun-tanned, slightly built, tousle-haired, sloppily dressed and unprosperous-looking, but with that indefinable something that her experience told her was class, and an air of thinking about something else which made you want him to concentrate entirely on you.

'Are you going to come in?' he said. 'Or shall I take you out to dinner?'

She had gone to some pains with her appearance that day. She wore a simple blue dress and simple blue shoes, and with her newly-trimmed shrewdly flowing blonde hair and residual Californian tan, she looked healthy, half-innocent and a little wild. She was also hungry.

Over dinner, he told her that his name was Robert and that he was a glass-maker. He'd previously been a moderately successful architect but eventually he realized, he said, that architecture was another of those things caught in the trench created by the rival drifts of capitalism and socialism.

'A pox on both their houses,' he announced rebelliously, changing imagery as he sprinkled cheese over the fettucine.

She didn't know exactly what he meant, though she knew about pox, luckily not at first hand.

'Glass-making is badly paid,' he said, warming to his theme, 'but it doesn't press upon the spirit like a twenty-storey block.'

Instinct made her refuse to return to his flat for coffee (though she would have liked to), and prompted her to resist inviting him into hers when he walked her home. There were times, Cheryl used to say, when a pleasure delayed is a pleasure improved. But he didn't agree.

' "Tis madness to prolong a pain,
But to defer a joy,
Believe me, gentle Celimene,
Offends the winged boy.",' he said, obscurely, gently kissing her cheek.

He took her out a dozen times after that, to the theatre, to exhibitions, to concerts on the South Bank, to a little pub that sold Sancerre and smoked salmon sandwiches, hidden in the woods near Hurley, spending more money than he could realistically afford, before she let him kiss her properly, but when he did she felt her heart was going into Fast Forward.

He had taken her that evening to a little restaurant in Wandsworth where the proprietor, an ex-Greenjacket major, had made them giggle until they were nearly ill with his litany of the menu: 'A plump white breast of Dorking fowl cooked in its own stock with white wine and a little cream, and then waistcoated with a mousse of mushrooms before a final overcoat of choux pastry whipped up with white of egg and a hint of mango gratinée, presenting us with a strangely gourd-like taste . . .'

The laughter, as she had found in the past, had a curiously arousing effect upon her, and sitting drinking brandy in Robert's flat (she had decided finally to relax her rule) above his warehouse in Putney, they laughed about the restaurant again.

'A Scottish soup made of capercaillie drumsticks spiked with wild garlic and just a hint of sporran . . .'

And then suddenly their mouths were together, and his hands were touching her ears, her neck, her back and finally her breasts, so lingeringly, so treasuringly that she felt that no one, not even Maudie or the chemist with those first caresses in the amniotic pool, had ever remotely come near to her before. They went to bed and spent much of the next six months in the same place. His business, which was at a delicate early stage, suffered but it didn't seem to matter for a time.

He had been shy with women of his own background in previous encounters, always being more anxious to prove himself than to give them pleasure, but she was able to take him beyond silly anxieties of performance. Funny that someone so goodlooking could be lacking in confidence. In his turn, as well as providing the happiest (if not the best) time in bed she had ever known – it had always been something between a sin and a giggle before – he gave her a social plausibility that was a passport to an altogether new range of possibilities. It was true she only understood about half of what he said – his mind was like a butterfly's – but the cross-purposes didn't seem to worry him.

'We misunderstand each other perfectly,' he said.

There came one day, however, when a letter from a creditor and another from the bank pulled the whole thing up short. There was no more money. He would either have to leave London and set up in some distant and inexpensive workshop, or return to architecture where a place was still kept open for him. The situation was further depressed by a maintenance order he was having to pay his ex-wife, which he hadn't told her about: he didn't want to worry her, he said.

The upshot was that he could cash no more cheques, and couldn't even take her out for a consolation meal at their favourite restaurant, so she urged him to go back to architecture because being without money seemed far worse and more shaming than working for a prostituted profession – which was, after all, an over-dramatic way of looking at it, and certainly a great deal better than working in a topless bar (though she actually didn't mention that).

He looked at her with a sad reflectiveness in his eyes that she had not seen before.

'Men and women,' he said, butterflying, 'spring from the two great branches of the dinosaurs. The ornithischians who flapped along, trying to get into the air . . . men, you see, and the world of ideas. And the saurischians, lords of the Earth, Tyrannosaurus Woman with her feet on the ground, and hungry.'

She saw now what she had sensed before but it hadn't mattered, that she was stronger than he was. He was not so much a rebel as a misfit.

It was the beginning of autumn, and the slight chill you notice in the early mornings seemed to have crept into their relationship. They lived with each other for another six months. He went back to his old office. And she saw the butterfly turn into a moth. They had a terrific holiday in Sicily, some wonderful meals round town, took on a company Porsche, moved into a new flat, and ran out of conversation.

Then, at a party given by a friend of his, a PR man, the inevitable happened. She was talking to a swimming star who was urging her to let him teach her the crawl, when a voice from the past spoke behind and slightly below her.

'Haven't I seen you somewhere before?'

She turned and saw a very small man with scurf and glasses, smiling up at her in a manner which suggested she could sit on his face if she liked. She had indeed seen him before – pinned under the girl from Guyana with breasts like steamer-fenders, a couple of years or so ago at Chestertons.

'I don't think so,' she said sweetly, 'or were you at Vanessa's party?'

Robert had come up behind her with a drink, she noticed, and was listening intently, wondering whether to intervene. The little man was swaying slightly, and clutched again at her elbow. She panicked. She had never spoken to Robert of her earlier career, simply that her parents had died when she was young, and she had had to fend for herself from an early age. The nature of the fending had not been specified.

'Go away,' she hissed at the small man, but he was fatuously drunk.

'Chestertons, wasn't it?' he said. 'I never forget a nice frontispiece like yours.'

This was too much.

'Push off,' said the swimming celebrity.

'". . . And sitting well in order, smite the sounding furrow . . .",' said the little man, who obviously had something up top besides dandruff.

'Hold on,' said Robert, stepping in. 'Chestertons? What's Chestertons?'

'Tits,' said the small man, 'Bristols, knockers and thanks for the mammary. Chestertons . . . Savvy? Not the poet Chesterton to whom we are indebted for The Rolling English Drunkard' – he slewed round and grabbed an armful of Robert – 'but the Chestertons where beautiful ladies serve you drinks without any tops on. Not you without any tops. Them,' he said earnestly, anxious to avoid any possible misapprehension.

'I think you ought to teach her the breast-stroke, don't you?' said Robert to the swimming star, and walked away.

She stayed with the swimmer for that night, and several nights more, and never saw Robert again. She heard later that he had got engaged to a merchant banker's daughter. It seemed he was making a great deal of money designing shopping precincts, and drinking a bit. And then one evening, after working late at the office, he drove his Porsche into the lift well on the fifth floor of a multistorey car park but omitted to notice that the lift itself, for some reason, was still on the ground. There was no indication that it had been deliberate, the coroner said, but Chloe knew she had helped to kill him. If it hadn't been for her, he would still be alive and happily turning out not very good goblets.

And yet, she had had to be honest with him about going back to architecture, hadn't she?

She remembered suddenly a passage from the New Testament that she hadn't thought about for years, but which her auntie had quoted with more aggression than the text merited when she'd snitched a slice of cake. She looked it up now in her mother's leatherette-bound Bible which she never read but carried around as her one piece of inherited property:

'Lay not up for yourselves treasures upon earth, where moth and rust doth corrupt and thieves break through and steal. But lay up for yourselves treasures in heaven where neither moth nor rust doth corrupt and where thieves do not break through nor steal. For where your treasure is, there will your heart be also.'

It was the day she noticed two tiny little lines, you could hardly see them really, running in the tiniest of lace-maker's hand-stitching at the corners of her eyes.

7

Following people is a considerable art, there is no other word for it: like a virtuoso getting his hands on a piano, there is an immediate rapport between artist and instrument, the very keyboard seems to achieve an extra dimension in the presence of genius, and I do have this unmistakable affinity for the shadows which it would be absurd to gainsay. I will dog a man for days on end for no other reason than the sheer delight of stalking, I truly believe MI5 or the Foreign Office would be happy to call on me in a crisis. Even the Iban would be hard put to it, in London and the Home Counties, to equal my instinct for fieldwork.

Partly, of course, it stemmed from my long months of idleness after my dear Isobel was taken. I needed something, anything to do to take my mind off the solitude, and the nearest to hand was my old military craft, so hard learnt in the far-off forests of Johore. It was good to have a skill, good to exercise the old disciplines. I truly believe it saved my sanity; grief is not the soldier's way.

But there came to be, I cannot deny, an element of power in my pursuits. This or that person, going about their business, totally unaware that they had an observer of their nights and days, privy as much to the broad outline of their public face in their daily rounds as to the quirky, grubby little peccadilloes of their private side. I have seen a company director pick his nose and eat the end result in an underground car park. This is what I call humiliation.

On other days, I would find not so much exercise as comfort from gazing into the lighted windows of other people's lives. There was a small comfortable man with a little round wife – he was a clerk in a mail order company – and whenever I felt really low, I would go round to his house, he had one of those little railway cottages in East Sheen, and stand by the thicket hedge looking in on his domestic harmony. He had three fat children and a rolypoly dog called Conker, and I am not surprised they were all on the plump side, for her cooking was absolutely Al. A session by the thicket hedge did me more good than a whole pharmacy of boosters.

Occasionally too, I would work a prank. Not, of course, on Mr and Mrs Purkiss and Conker, but upon those who I felt could take a little ribbing. That too would lift my spirits. You may perhaps have wondered when you lost a key, did not have your papers delivered, discovered unexplained toads in your patio, lost milk from your doorstep, found your bicycle with its handlebars the wrong way round, whether you were not perhaps the victim of some malign but hardly significant aberration of Fate, and the answer might well have been no, your little troubles stemmed from an altogether more deliberate finger, yours truly's.

I followed a detective once. I knew he was a detective from the way he wore his mackintosh. He was following someone too, so I pursued them both (his quarry was a small sallow man of Italian appearance), and I was so tickled by the picture we must have made in procession, all three of us dodging and lurking, that in the end I outflanked the detective, told the Italian what was happening, and he insisted on taking me to his bedsit where he gave me wine and a substantial chunk of cannabis fortified with, so he told me, resin – which was a mistake because I do not hold with drugs, the Sixties were Babylon in this country – so then I had to double back and mention him to the police (by telephone, of course, otherwise they waste your time with a hundred and one questions), which was doubtless why they were following him in the first place, a conclusion of classical circularity worthy of the greats.

I confess, though, that if you were to ask me for a

percentage figure in terms of my chosen pursuit, I should have to submit that at least sixty per cent of my subjects were women aged between sixteen and fifty.

To follow a child seems to me to smack of unfairness, not playing the game or shooting pheasant when they are sitting. To follow old folk likewise, there is no sport in an old fowl. But for the rest, I have ranged freely across the field, and what a field it is.

I read a book once which suggested that originally, before recorded history, men actually came from Mars. I cannot vouch for the truth of the assertion, but the argument continued that women were a race apart dwelling on the planet Earth or Tellus. Long ago, we men were cast out of the irrigated Garden (see the Martian canal system) for some undisclosed misdemeanour, and despatched to till the fields of Tellus by the ordinance of galactic creatures. How the two separate races propagated before the conjunction was not revealed in my edition.

Be that as it may, I have always regarded women as persons of another realm; mysterious, highly-strung, down-to-earth, far-fetched but magnetic. I suppose you could say that I did not so much follow them as permit myself to be pulled along behind them: try as I might to hive off and inspect a sports model or pop into the Roebuck for a pint, there they were always tugging me along at the last with their unremitting North, the clickety-clack of their heels like the crackle of static in a force-field.

Of course, I am of that school that was brought up to regard women as finer beings than us men. They have subsequently descended from that position, their own choice, and yet what have we all gained? Has the world improved since women got the vote? The question is rhetorical. Armageddon stands bulging in the wings. No longer do men stand up for women on the buses, because men know that women have shorn their locks, like Samson and Delilah. What would Shakespeare say? Take but degree away, untune that string, and hark what discord follows . . . strength shall be lord of imbecility and the rude son shall strike the father dead. Only it is not the rude son, it is the rude daughter. And you remember what happened to the foolish king who gave his throne away to his girls. It is too desperate to contemplate.

Oh, the females I have followed. Smart society women in furs with little dogs and Harrods habits, though you would be surprised at the things they get up to when they think no one is looking – I have seen a Countess shoplifting. I have observed little shopgirls after work when the sun has made the Park lazy with leaf-light, stretching out on the grass and saying the most coarse things to each other, it would cure the moonstruck. I have seen housewives admit salesmen to their boudoirs, and the most licentious acts have been mine to witness between madam and cleaner. I have viewed a well-known television personality being obliged by her dog, a King Charles spaniel of the best pedigree.

But please do not think that my tours of inspection, my patrols on the fair sex, have ever been used by myself for anything other than observation. I have always kept myself scrupulously clean. There is no place in my canon for deeds of shame.

I do, it is true, have dreams, one cannot help dreams. My dreams are legendary, real shockers, so lifelike you would not believe. Strangely enough, they always seem to involve forest or woodland, or perhaps not so strange considering my interest in the subject. I remember one about a girl, a blonde she was, full of the beauty of her youth. I saw her in a clothing store and I tracked her back all the way to her home, a little mews cottage in Hampstead – I have never cared for north of the park, have you?, I feel positively disoriented – and I waited for her outside.

Finally she came out again and climbed into what I had previously decided must be her car, a sporty little Italian job (why won't these people buy British, we still make sports cars, don't we?), and just as she was fumbling with the starter, I snatched the keys, showed her my kukri, and made her drive me out of town with all the speed at her command.

Strange things, dreams. You remember the details so vividly. She had only 8,568 miles on the clock when we started out, and just 8,651 when we finished.

I made her drive down to one of my favourite forests, Ashdown in Sussex, what a noble sweep of greenwood that must once have been. It is still extensive. I instructed her to stop at a quiet spot up a track where the pleached boughs made the pathway darker than nightfall. I still had no idea what I wanted to do. I seemed propelled by someone other than myself, as is the way with dreams.

'Get out of the car,' I told her. 'Please do not make me have to do something I would regret.'

'Please,' she said, 'please.'

And I marched her into the woods with my kukri at her back the way I used to deal with the CT prisoners. It seems ungallant as I narrate it but that is the way it unfolded.

We had walked perhaps half a mile into the forest when I made her stop in a moss-covered clearing where it seemed there might once have been a well or shaft of some kind. The trees were mainly oak here with a smattering of ash and the occasional clumps of sallows. Harebells and wood anemones adorned the scene, and I believe I even noticed St John's Wort in one corner.

'What do you want? What do you want?' she kept saying.

'Take off your clothes, please,' I said, not unkindly but firmly.

She was wearing only a light-blue summer frock with a pair of blue panties underneath. She obeyed me silently and stood with some dignity, pale against the trees.

I was overcome with the beauty of the scene. She

seemed like a dryad of the forest, or England, pale and defenceless but still noble, with the shadows before her, all round her. I remember suddenly pausing, aghast, as the realization of my country's vulnerability swept over me.

As I wept, she hit me inaccurately with a lump of rock that she had plucked from its mossy bed, making my neck wound start and throb.

The shadows gathered at a rate of knots.

I must have struck my head against the bedpost in the night, because when I woke there was blood on the pillow-case.

I wept again because the girl in my dream had had the face of my poor departed Isobel.

What strange confections the unconscious can serve up to delight and disquiet the spirit.

8

She had given up her flat to save money, when she had been with Robert, but that hadn't been successful either. She was now seriously short of cash again. Mindful of the lesson she had learnt from the long-memoried little executive, however, this time she did not resort to Chestertons. She did call up Cheryl to ask if she could stay for a while, but even Cheryl seemed to be away. It was a very low moment.

Finally she found a room in a tall house in Knightsbridge whose lease was owned by an urban landscape-gardener called Julian. He had a very simple system. If you slept with him, you got a rent rebate.

She slept with him rather a lot.

Meanwhile she moved in and out of various temping jobs which paid lamentably little money, not nearly enough to buy her decent clothes let alone purchase an escape from the sticky-sheeted Julian, so she took a part-time job with an escort agency. This was hardly more satisfactory, from a party conversation point of view, than showing your breasts to businessmen, and though better fed, it was less well paid. The management of the agency appeared to pocket all the profit, leaving out of a fee of say, £50 a night, a mere £20 for the girls.

You could earn more if you slept with the client, but even so the management sometimes seemed to sense what was going on, and wanted to get in on the act. 'Special Introduction' commission, they called it. It smacked too much of the game. Showing her tits and sleeping with who she liked for money occasionally was one thing, but she had never seen herself as a trollop.

She changed agencies, in spite of some threats from the first. Her occasional private understandings with some of the clients were not, this time, marked up by the management, but then the inevitable happened.

He said he was a Turkish statesman over dinner, which meant that he was almost certainly something else. He spoke French to the waiter at La Cocotte, if that meant anything. He had been quiet, attentive, respectful, and seemingly very rich. She was beginning to find him highly attractive.

They had discussed at some length the role of women in society, and after dinner, she had agreed to go to a nightclub with him, but first, he had said, he must go back to his place to collect some more money. It was the oldest trick in the business, but he had seemed so well-behaved and reserved that she had fallen for it.

Once in his North Mayfair flat, he had given her a brandy while he busied himself with a briefcase, and he must have mixed in something else when he poured it. When she recovered consciousness, she was lying face-down on the bed, with hands and feet tied to the corners, and he was tearing off the carefully chosen dress which she had only been able to afford as a result of sleeping with a Belgian diplomat in Muswell Hill.

She lay there in her bra, tights and pants while he looked down, panting slightly with his exertions.

He had tied a handkerchief over her mouth so she could neither scream nor remonstrate, but she had a terror of suffocation, and struggled so vigorously that the man relented and undid the scarf a little.

'The apartments above and below,' he said, 'are at present unoccupied, so even if you scream, you will not be heard. But if you do, it will be the worse for you, and this,' he indicated her scarf, 'will go back immediately.'

'Don't hurt me,' she said.

He took off her bra and squeezed her breasts meditatively.

'If you want to do whatever you want to do,' she said, 'do it, but there's no need to pinch.'

He pulled down her tights and sniffed at her like a dog, which after all his talk about women's role seemed particularly graceless. She lay inertly, frightened and incredulous. It couldn't really be happening. There was a sort of ghastly humour in the scene, scared though she was, like lying in front of a doctor, just so much meat.

She tried a ploy that she had previously thought up against the possibility of such an occasion.

'You better watch out,' she said, 'I've got VD.'

'Don't worry. So have I.'

He pulled down his trousers and anointing himself with something that smelt like béarnaise sauce, took her with a horrible sort of rough accuracy.

When at length he had finished, he put his member up to her face.

'Filthy bitch,' he said, ritually rather than maliciously, 'now lick it clean.'

She bit it so hard she could actually feel the skin shredding in her mouth.

While he rolled around the room in agony, she slipped out of the cords loosened by her struggle, and made her escape, huddling on her torn but still wearable expensive dress, and only marginally surprising a middle-aged couple in evening attire coming in from a function in Park Lane.

'Rape,' she mumbled at them, but they hurried past, quarrelling expertly – 'Arabs, punks, it'll be blacks next. Why didn't you damn well sell the place when I told you to?'

She didn't tell the police about the attack – she felt the man would be unlikely to repeat his activities for some considerable time, if ever – but she did send an ambulance round to the flat because he might have been bleeding to death for all she knew.

She was not a vindictive girl.

Strangely enough, the only enduring effect of the disaster was a perverse increase in her confidence. The worst had happened. The rape was a punishment, but it didn't encourage her to mend her ways. It merely served to heighten her determination not to be caught next time.

As it turned out, the man had not had VD. There was some justice after all.

9

I mused on these matters as the day wore on.

A week before, I could easily have believed that any interesting party, male or female, within the specifications that I have already outlined could have absorbed my attention with equal force for a spell until the fever burned out. There was no real difference in the quality of my tracking between the Golf Club Secretary and the barmaid at the Cadogan Arms. I followed them with like attention. A trimly turned ankle is, I admit, rather more agreeable to supervise than a pair of plus-fours, but I had learned, as I say, to ration myself with respect to females. I did not wish to become debased. The art was all. 'The life so short, the art so long to learn', that is the legend on my grandfather clock by J. Walker of Holborn circa 1785, and it speaks the truth with every hour it strikes. Thus I had trained myself to feel no especial emotion for my subjects. My interest was detached, Olympian if you like. Even my little pranks had no special malice in them.

The Iban is brought up to track from his mother's breast. His whole life is pursuit, even in his mating rituals there is no sentiment, it would never enter his head. Within the confines of my upbringing and nature, I had to emulate his passive expertise and content myself with the austere satisfactions of the overseeing eye.

But, yes, I had to admit, with the American it was different. This was more than a random exercise. Everything else, it now became clear to me, had been merely limbering up. If his appearance and manner, his proprietorial manner with our English girlhood, had not been enough to fill me with indignation, the discovery that he was marketing 'software' gave wings to my latent instinct for mischief. I realized, of course, that I still had considerable reconnaissance work to effect, but I confess I had already allowed my mind to wander into delicious areas of speculation. What, given the man and his position, was I going to practise on him?

Lieutenant Parsons, of course, would have been the first to put the thing on a disciplined basis.

In the old days, in the Army, we always used to have a sentence that prescribed in mnemonic form exactly the stages to be covered in any plan of attack. What was it? A humorous reference, if I mistook not, to some former notable. Hitler? Goebbels? King Farouk, King Farouk, hang your bollocks on a hook? How the old Army songs came back, like lifting a forkful of spaghetti, you want a mouthful and you get the lot. And thinking of spaghetti, that is what it was. IN ITALY, MUSSOLINI ALWAYS INTERFERES.

INFORMATION.

INTENTION.

METHOD.

ADMIN.

What INTERFERES stood for, I could not immediately remember, but I had a feeling it was not significant and related to ANY QUESTIONS or SYNCHRONIZE WATCHES.

Well then, what did I know about my quarry?

He was American, of course, coming from (I felt) a city – it did not seem possible that such a slicker could ever have known the influence of trees. Philadelphia, Pittsburgh, Chicago, New York, my knowledge of the United States is understandably patchy, I should have to get out my old school Bartholomew's.

He was in his forties and apparently in reasonable health, although there was a hint of excessive good living about his jowls. He was married. He had a flat in town and a cottage in the country where, it seemed, his wife spent some of her time. (I told myself with a sense of pleasurable anticipation that I should be visiting those leafy lanes of the sub-forest of Cowden, tributary of the ancient Forest of Birnwood, of which more later, to reacquaint myself with the lie of the land.)

He had a girlfriend who appeared to have no scruples about forming a liaison with an adulterer. (I wondered whether his wife knew about the affair – it was clearly an area of promise for the mischiefmaker.) He was presumably well paid, though I somehow sensed a whiff of money about the wife – don't ask me how, I have an instinct for these things, perhaps a reflection, in this case, of her independent modus vivendi, or, as our American friends would put it, her life-style, though the nib splays as I write the word.

What else came under INFORMATION? Oh yes, his job, marketing something still not completely specified by L. Thwaites, a closed book but one which I would prise open in the fullness of time. I do not like a challenge to be too easily resolved, so it must have been for the questers after the Holy Grail: if they could have found it at the shop round the corner literature would be considerably the poorer. However, it seemed to me, though darkly, that I could sniff the promise of some sport amid the business men and the video moguls.

He drove a quarter of an acre of black Cadillac. He wore Westchester After-Shave balm. So much for info. for the time being. The file was open.

On to INTENTION.

At this point, I was pulled up short again. What exactly *did* I have in mind? A flurry of diverse emotions assailed me like those snowstorms in plastic you buy in the Cairngorms, but I felt when I became calmer and I could see as it were the wee jock in the kilt, that the best way it could be expressed was that I wanted to take him down a peg or two. Who did he think he was, coming over here horsing around, corrupting our language and youth and behaving as if he owned the place? Call me simplistic but that was as far as I was prepared to commit myself at this stage.

'Never rush your fences, Roy,' my father used to say after I had intemperately emptied the Odd Hooks into the Trivet drawer, and subsequently Lieutenant Parsons endorsed the advice when we were pitted against a more deadly adversary than the omnium gatherum of the accessories cabinet.

All right then, I should be the American's Robin Goodfellow, his poltergeist. Had not the man himself given me the cue? A pranksome, playful spirit of anarchy would be my guiding principle, simply to pay him back for being him and being here.

There was one other thing I recalled from the military past. We *will* . . . That spirit of positive purpose that is so missing from our national character today. We *will* destroy the enemy's position next to that bushy-topped tree. I *would* bring the American to book.

MUSSOLINI. As for Method, the military options open to the commander in conventional terrain usually devolved into left or right flanking movements while keeping up covering fire from a base position with the bren. Occasionally this might be varied by a pincer movement. In the jungle, however, all this was changed. There was no set way to do anything by the book except observe Silent Discipline, never fire until you can see your target, rub all exposed parts with cream against the bug that will penetrate the skin, lay eggs and cause paralysis as soon as look at you, conceal and position the latrine with more than customary vigilance, the CTs have noses in the back of their heads.

The science (or methodology as our American friends would say) of jungle warfare comes right down to kill or be killed. It is the oldest craft of all, the skill of track and pounce, the practice of patience, the exercise of lightning reflex, and a conversancy with shadows.

Thus, here, my Method would be: by the employment

of my former trade and my present practices, to find ways of embarrassing, irking, discomfiting and discommoding the enemy at work and leisure. I *would* do it, there would be no failure of will in this unit. I had no will to do anything else.

ALWAYS. In the matter of Admin., there seemed to be no problem at all. Transport, billeting, commissariat, all seemed well under control. I should, of course, need to give due attention to matters of camouflage and terrain. Maps would have to be issued, my make-up box would need to be topped up, but this was small beer. As for weaponry – anything from Iban blowpipe to itching powder – these would simply have to be drawn from my armoury or purchased according to the dictates of the field. Flexibility as ever was the keyword . . .

I woke from my reverie with a start to see the rays of the declining sun gilding the chromium mono-tap above my stainless steel sink and draining board unit (I always have the latest in kitchen fittings in deference to my poor departed father, though nothing flashy, he would not have wished it). It looked like an accusing finger. Glancing at my watch, I found to my consternation that it was well past five o'clock. My delicious musings and conjectures had eaten up the afternoon. I had hoped to reconnoitre the girl's flat before sundown, and I felt duly ashamed. What this country does not need at this juncture is cardboard heroes.

Perhaps I had proved that morning, in the broaching of the man Richmonde's flat, that I had fire in my belly, but I should have to watch my tendency to dreams and mental derring-do. It is a disease of the age bred of television and convenience foods. I myself view but seldom and rarely purchase agar-based whips or cook-in sauce mixes, especially eschewing any form of hamburger, but one cannot expect to be unaffected.

So be it. Though my planning procedures were top priority, and an unplanned sortie invariably ends in disaster, I knew well that I had spent too long relishing the prospect of action. I had squandered my time. So be it. The soldier does not cry over spilt milk, he learns from the sour puddle. I should spend the earlier part of the evening evolving an identity suitable for lurking outside a young lady's love-nest while she entertained her guilty secret within.

The role I chose for myself, after careful consideration, was that of a Rodent or Pest Officer, who would naturally be the sort of person you would expect to find lurking on the qui vive for rat or cockroach. No one suspects a Rodent Officer – they are like milkmen or nuns.

Having made up face and hands with a judicious application of Number 3 and Number 5 to give the outdoor urban look, I donned a convincing peaked cap, blue denim overalls and a curiously questing moustache (it is strange how people grow to look like their profession). I then selected a large canvas bag on which I stencilled PEST OFF. I was going to add ICER but I ran out of stencil as luck would have it, I would attend to that on the morrow. For the moment, though, no matter, it was simply painting the lily; it would be dark soon and no one would wish to inspect my kit too closely, it is curious how people are funny about rats.

I checked myself in the mirror and with difficulty restrained myself from recoiling. I looked curiously official, and at the same time quite unsavoury. Satisfied with the preparations, I stuffed torch, rat poison and DDT into the bag, locked up the house and climbed into my Traveller.

Because of my wasted hours, I had no specific objective tonight. If queried as to my intentions by my Platoon Commander, I would have returned an open reply. 'Patrol Duty, Mr Parsons,' I would have replied in clipped tones. 'But always prepared for the possibility of encounter.'

A man not given to displays of emotion, I believe he

would have granted me his qualified approbation. A great fair giant of a man, he moved with feline stealth in the rain-forest; he had had his earlobe shot off in Korea and never turned a hair.

10

She set off on her travels again, this time with Tania, another friend from the old days.

Tania was from South Africa, so that was where they went. They worked as waitresses in various clubs, played tennis, swam and sunbathed. Chloe slept with a Zulu, not because she particularly liked Zulus but because it wasn't allowed, and left Tania in Cape Town engaged to a prosthetics engineer. All the girls from Chestertons got engaged to people – soldiers, dentists, small-time racing drivers, drug dealers – but it never lasted.

Finally, she hitched a flight back to Europe with Willis, who turned up again in a nightclub in Durban where she'd gone with a mine manager.

'Where've you been?' she said to Willis. 'Have you had plastic surgery?' His nose was shorter and he wore a beard.

'Yes and no,' he said, and took her over to a solitary corner. He seemed jumpy.

'You in some kind of trouble?' she said, more as a statement than a question. Willis was always flirting with disaster. He could not see thin ice without an irresistible urge to be out there curvetting. It was only afterwards that the full import of what he had been doing would strike him, and he would have phases of horror, after which he would do it all over again.

'I think they're after me,' he said. 'D'you see that guy up at the bar?'

Not only had Willis been dealing in cocaine, it appeared, but he had been pushing it to coloureds. He was in a horror phase.

Chloe decided that the man at the bar was not in the least interested in Willis, but was becoming increasingly interested in her.

'Let's get out,' she said. 'Where d'you want to go?'

'Got to see a guy in Spain,' he muttered. 'You want to come along?'

'All right,' she said, 'but pay the Spanish hotel bill before you do your vanishing act.' So they flew to Marbella and stayed together for a week in the Sidonia Hotel until he settled up, said a rare goodbye, and left her with enough money to take bus and, later, boat to Ibiza where there was a job going as a disco waitress. Willis was an attractive puckish figure so long as you didn't trust him further than you could throw him. She was always both sorry and relieved to see the last of him.

The proprietor of Los Hesperidos was a prominent member of the local mafia and clearly regarded his disco waitresses rather in the same manner as Julian back in London had regarded his lodgers. His wife, on the other hand, was a wiry and excitable woman who, even when chopping garlic, did it in a manner which suggested it had seduced her daughter. She made it quite clear to Chloe that any liaison with her husband would involve a fight to the death.

Caught in this web of passion, strangely reminiscent of certain films she had seen on sneaked teenage outings to the Bijou, Banbury, she tried to escape to a small neighbouring island, but fell foul of the police, who were in some way in league with her employer in Ibiza, escaped by yacht with some Germans, found shelter with a policeman who appeared to be honest until he revealed that he too was prey to the major preoccupation of most Spaniards, but was finally rescued by Willis, who turned up in the nick of time and took her off to Italy. Landing at Salerno, they hired a car and drove circuitously to the outskirts of Naples, where she stood watch while Willis engaged in a bizarre transaction in the baths at Herculaneum under the anguished gaze of a fossilized two-thousand-year-old bath attendant.

When she finally returned home again, after a spell with Willis recovering his nerve in the South of France and finally Paris, she had acquired a sort of cosmopolitan background which in England can serve in some degree as a social credential. Instead of the too easily definable Oxfordshire–London accent she had managed before, she now spoke a passable mid-Atlantic.

She was now a pretty and superficially well-travelled young woman of twenty-six, but the lines under her eyes had not gone away, indeed they seemed to have intensified with the sun, and it was time for her to find a rich man. A rich husband might be more difficult, since husbands usually have sharp-eyed families – she wasn't putting it right out of court, she would find the right one at the right time, but a rich lover she could have whenever she wanted it, and she felt she wanted it now. She could afford to take a temping job for a month or two while she stayed with Cheryl, who had been away last time she tried her, visiting her sister in Paisley. And on her third assignment she spotted her big fish, the Marketing Director of a toiletries company. He was called Horace, he was fifty-five, married, with three children, and he fell in love with her as if he had been a schoolboy. It seemed men behaved over their last chance with the same headlong enthusiasm as their first.

After three days, he took her to dinner. Then he took her to bed in his hotel, and within a month he had established her in a trim little maisonette near Olympia where he came to visit her most afternoons, neglecting both business and family. She gave him a nice time in bed because she was grateful for the house, and he had never known anything like it (his wife, whom he had married when he was very young, regarded the act of sex as a form of hoovering), but in the end it became too much for him. He was so besotted with her that he talked about divorce.

She tried to dissuade him because she only really wanted the maisonette for ever, not him as well. She still had notions about marriage. Meanwhile his wife was threatening suicide and his employers were contemplating superannuation.

He solved all their problems by having a minor heart attack (luckily for Chloe not at the maisonette but over a business lunch), and he was sent home under doctor's orders, to lead a quiet life in the family home near Norwich. Chloe tried to contact him to say she was sorry he was ill, and she felt in some way responsible, but she guessed his office was monitoring the mail.

'Perhaps I was too much for him,' she said to Cheryl.

'Don't worry, dear,' Cheryl comforted her, 'it's not the sex that exhausts them, it's the guilt.'

But guilt seemed to work both ways because it appeared he had told no one else about the maisonette – no one, anyway, suggested she should give it up – and for this she was grateful. It was the first real home she had ever had, and she worked devotedly on it. But she still needed money to run it.

'Don't worry,' said Cheryl, 'pecker up, mustn't mope. A friend of mine's just opening a croupier school. What d'you say to casino life?'

'Is the money good? Better than Chestertons?'

She had always been assured that the hours were terrible and the money indifferent.

'Not at first, dear, but a lot more if you play your cards right. You have to take the longer view. You mingle with a richer class of person in a casino. Some of it's bound to rub off.'

Chloe enrolled. It was expensive, and she had to dig into the very last of her savings, but it proved to be a profitable investment. With her good looks and natural quickness she had a talent for the job, and on graduating from her course she was taken on by first one and then another gilded establishment where she found she earned better money than she'd expected. On the other hand, Cheryl had definitely overstated the likely availability of the clientele (casino managers, ever on the watch for a fiddle, were more severe than Chestertons in their treatment of fraternizers).

At all events, the immediate financial problem was resolved, but the question of the future remained. Someone, somewhere, sooner rather than later, would have to remove the burden of her earning a living. In terms of market value, she knew her capital was decreasing. It wasn't that she wanted a family – the thought of having children made her feel quite ill – but she did feel the need for some form of security and centre.

She bought a dog, but it still didn't quite fill the gap. Who was she to choose? The question gave her many sleepless days. The English, on the whole, if they were rich or clever, could still see right through her. And if they weren't rich or clever, she didn't want to know them.

It was at this point that she noticed, one night, a thickset good-looking man with a Robert Redford moustache ogling her energetically over the roulette table.

11

The girl, if the address I had spotted in the Cadogan Square flat was anything to go by, lived in a part of London that I rarely visit, that warren of little streets which squirm and wriggle in odd whorls and dead-ends as if distorted by the vast gravitational bulk of the Olympia Exhibition complex. She could not, I deduced, be a lady of substantial means since she would not, in a position of affluence, have chosen the eastern reaches of Brook Green for her place of abode, but I suppose these days, even out there, the price of property is prohibitive, forced up by the international bankers, Arab princelings, spivvy developers, gambling racketeers and pop stars who have taken over our erstwhile mighty metropolis.

I arrived at the address – Ground Floor, Number 44 Prosser Street – approximately a quarter of an hour before the American was due to appear, and drove the Traveller slowly down the street, inconspicuous but noting everything.

My luck was indeed in. The light was already failing – it was now 20.06 and the spring twilight, mingled with the dust that seems endemic in those parts, was thickly bestrewing the circa 1840 villas that composed the streets – but I observed that Number 44 included a garden level or basement floor with an open gate and steps leading down to a tiny area which promised fair for my investigations after dark.

Better still, I saw that the house next door had a For Sale notice outside it, with curtainless windows, which indicated a welcome absence of witnesses from that quarter. And round the corner I discovered that there was an alleyway for dustmen that ran all the way behind

Prosser Street with a high rickety wooden fence interrupted by sagging doors leading into the residents' rear gardens.

It could have been made for my purposes. My estimation of the area rose.

I parked the Traveller down a sidestreet next to an old pink Vauxhall with no wheels, and proceeded down the alleyway, turning upon every detail my most rigorous scrutiny. It ran for a distance of some 100 yards. It was paved with crumbling macadam and lined with sickly-looking plantains, dandelion, couch-grass or squitch as they call it in Oxfordshire, and (rather surprisingly) what looked like ragwort, but in the beam of my blackout torch I could not swear to this. There were only sporadic numbers on the doors, and some of them appeared to be either locked or rusted fast on their hinges, do not ask me how the dustmen coped, but I managed to get a bearing with Number 38, which had a nice set of Spanish ironwork numerals for which I gave the owner my silent benediction, and I was just limbering up to try the door of Number 44, three along, when a voice nearly made me jump out of my overalls.

'What you doin', man?'

I turned in a controlled manner – in the jungle one learns to take the unexpected as commonplace – and saw in the gloom a vast black man, darker than Erebus, with a hound of nightmarish stature straining at the leash beside him. They had emerged, it seemed, from Number 40. I would rather have confronted a whole squad of CTs.

'Pest Officer,' I answered, quick as a flash, stifling my misgiving and turning my incomplete stencilling away from the inquisitive torch. 'Were you the gentleman that reported a sighting?'

I showed him a small official-looking pass that I had constructed out of my National Trust membership card. 'Rats,' I said, noticing an expression of puzzlement settle upon his outsize features. 'Rats and cockroaches. They are my meat and drink. Although we also handle lice infestation. You rang?'

'Hell no, man, we don't have lice, what do you think we are? Savages?' he replied, seemingly bent on trouble. 'If we see a rat, we set Tory on it, don't we, Tory?'

The dog dribbled an eggcupful of saliva and wagged a knobkerry-like tail.

I could not help feeling that its name could have been more respectfully chosen but I elected at this stage to refrain from comment. There are some people who are clearly impervious to the common decencies.

I thought a more official line might now be in order seeing that he appeared to have fallen for my ruse hook, line and sinker.

'Did you or did you not report a rat sighting?' I enquired severely. 'I have not got all day.'

'No, man.'

Why they need to keep affirming one's gender I shall never know.

'Drat the girl. It's the night switchboard,' I explained. 'They will not remember the simplest rules of procedure. Just Prosser Street is not enough. I need a number. Prosser Street is an extensive thoroughfare. Thank you for your assistance, sir. I will just make an inspection of the locality, paying special attention to basement areas and garbage disposal facilities.'

'Well, while you're here, man, you better come and look at our kitchen. You mentioned cockroaches. You see, Tory don't eat cockroaches.'

This was disastrous. I cursed myself with having been so open with the man, but there was no recourse now but to follow him into his yard, with the hound gambolling round me licking his lips like one of those generously proportioned Queen's Beasts you see outside the Tropical House at Kew, the Black Dog of Richmond without an 'e'.

I had never entered a black man's demesne before, it is not one's usual lot, though I have followed people of that hue, particularly in the nursing profession, and I had to steel myself as I stepped across a patchily sown lawn some fifteen yards long flanked by sickly-looking rose bushes and spindly creepers which somehow contrived to make the chipped latticework over the walls look like an encrustation on a scalp. The tropical diseases you saw in the rain-forest could turn your stomach if you dwelt on them.

My guide led me down a narrow flight of wobbling concrete steps towards a pair of ill fitting double-glazed French windows of a type my father would never have set his imprimatur upon. What is this craze for double-glazing in this country anyway? Another symbol of decadence and foreign character-erosion. Britain's greatness was not founded on stuffy salons or blood-hot boudoirs, a little draught and damp never hurt anyone – indeed many would say they help to inculcate the spirit of Leonidas – but now every Tom, Dick and Harry has to have his aluminium perma-vent twin-frame and his slim-fit micro-bore radiators. It is good for the hardware trade, no doubt, but character-formation has to come first.

Inside, the house was as dark as Sin itself, and the black man and the dog Tory were swallowed up in the gloom as I hovered at the lintel. An odour of sweat, chilli and ancient okra assailed me, not unlike certain establishments we used to frequent down Boogie Street in Singapore, though I always kept myself clean, confining my activities to a glass or two of Tiger Beer and a noodle.

'Hold on, man, I'll put on the illuminations,' my host announced.

I was tempted in the darkness to repair hastily whence I had come, but I was tethered to my post by considerations both of duty and prudence. Not only would a retreat at this stage have impaired my cover but – fast as I might move, and I was renowned for the speed of my evasive action – I felt that Tory could doubtless move faster, and I had no desire to feel those sabretooth incisors making tickertape of my denims.

Suddenly, my debate was resolved. Light blazed forth from a single bulb over a laminate-topped kitchen table, revealing an electric stove liberally curded with the remains of ancient soups and sauces, bright yellow walls, red and blue curtains, a diamond-patterned green and blue vinyl floor, and a disaster area of washing-up piled upon a greasy sink. To my poor mother, it would have been a vision of Hell.

Even as I watched, two big brown cockroaches scampered cool as you please across the floor towards a cupboard beside the cooker.

'Caught in the act, man,' said the householder exultantly, pouncing on the errant orthoptera and cracking them like brazils. 'That's why I waited so you could be sure of getting a good view. Didn't want to blow the scene by turning on the light too soon. They're cunning as demons.'

He was right about Tory. The dog cringed in a corner.

I extracted my little book and pretended to take notes, aware that even now the real object of my visit to Prosser Street would be arriving with his flowers and his bottles of wine and his noisy expressions of uxorious bonhomie. I swallowed hard and licked my pencil.

'Well, man,' the fellow said, noting my impassivity, 'ain't you gonna treat 'em?'

His attitude indicated, I felt, an all too prevalent dependence on Authority. Public services, I have always maintained, are a privilege and not a right, but then I was not of that generation spoonfed by the Welfare State.

However, not wishing to precipitate a scene, and sensing that speedy action would be the only way to obtain egress, I extracted my flacon of DDT (topped up with talcum powder, I was running short), stiffened my sinews and advanced upon the cupboard.

I am not fond of the insect world. For me, it is the only blot on the woodland landscape. Look at the elms: if they had voices, which I sometimes believe trees do, I am sure that we would hear them concur. Talk about genocide, we have stood by and let eleven million of them bite the dust, their gaunt arms still haunt us in field and hedgerow.

No, I am not fond of crawly things, but most particularly am I not fond of them in larder cupboards of dubious cleanliness full of lumpy objects seemingly stored in coarse cotton stockings doubtless obtained from mine host's concubines unwashed and then used to contain what might have been home-made coarse-ground sausages or equally pickled organs from Bluebeard's pantry. It is this kind of thing that must make the genuine Pest Controller's life more a Hieronymus Bosch fantasy than a local government Grade Three pensionable occupation.

I ordered the cupboard to be cleared of all foodstuffs, and stood back while Mr Fitzgibbon (such was apparently my companion's name) piled all the little drab mounds on to the table, saving one or two that had been the subject of intensive depredation, which he gave to the attentive Tory.

I noticed with misgiving that while I applied my lethal dust to the cupboard in question, the man Fitzgibbon was busy emptying out other niches, drawers, shelves and even a disused pram (at least I supposed it was disused) in the corner. Soon the whole kitchen, and shortly the whole house, seemed to be awash with little muslin bundles from which cockroaches clambered with the clumsy alacrity of old men caught in a bomb scare after dinner at their club.

It was after midnight by the time we had finished. I had exhausted my stock of quasi-DDT and was now very considerably out of patience. Fitzgibbon explained to me threateningly that he and his wife (of whom no evidence was to be seen, a possibly sinister twist) supplied genuine Jamaican sausalitos to half the expatriate population of North Kensington, and if I breathed a word to my superiors of the night's work he would either make me into a sausalito all of my own or put a particularly nasty voodoo curse upon me, possibly both.

I was not afraid of his truculence and braggadocio, though one learns out East that there are more things in Heaven and Earth than can be breezily anatomized by the comperes on late-night television chat shows. I have seen the monks dance on red-hot coals and a headman sicken by the curse of a Bomo almost before my eyes, but at that particular moment I had bigger fish to fry.

'Come,' I said. 'It is late, Mr Fitzgibbon, your home is now cockroach-free. I give you a clean bill of health.'

'You're damn right you do.'

'I must now be on my way. Mr Rat is abroad. I have a night's work to attend to.'

'OK, man. But remember, no blabbing to the Authorities or . . .'

And he gave a very creditable impression of a Kenwood Chefette.

'Quite so,' I said, backing out of the kitchen towards the double-glazing, 'quite so. But I fear I might be rather strong meat for your customers.'

I have supped on monkey, it is rich and tough.

For the first time in the entire evening, he smiled. It was a mirthless rictus not unlike a pre-Roman carving I once came across on my rambles beside a well in the woods near Chapel-en-le-Frith, there is England's music in the name, and the dog Tory slunk whining into a corner under the mincing machine.

'I wouldn't be too sure, man,' the fellow said, 'I wouldn't be too sure.'

'Quite so,' I replied with a nod, achieving the garden steps, 'quite so. I have heard of these delicacies. Good evening to you. Bon appétit.'

And I hurried faster than a cockroach on castors, towards the safety of the alleyway.

'Hold it, man.'

I froze as the hound came bounding towards me, claws scrabbling on the concrete, drool flying in all directions.

'What is it now?'

I was in no mood for a further round of toxification. Surely he had not already discovered another nest of the creatures?

'I got a present for you, man.'

And he thrust something dank, fibrous and putrid-smelling into my hand, slapping my back in a gesture of malicious farewell.

Something in his manner made me reluctant to refuse or give expression to my sense of revulsion, but in the safety of the alley, and by the light of my blackout torch, I was able to discern the unmistakable features of a Jamaican home-made sausalito from which, even as I watched, a cockroach dropped, tumbling into the rank squitch-grass that flanked the path, and headed straight back towards the kitchen, like a drunkard to his bottle. Deciding to dispose of the unwelcome gift a little further from the scene of its inception (and its creator's possible chagrin), I stuffed it into the pocket of my overalls, merged into the shadows, and gave thought anew to the matter in hand, what we call in the military a sitrep.

I realized, of course, that my earlier plan had to be considerably revised. I had hoped to catch a glimpse of the proceedings at Number 44 before the curtains were drawn, watching unnoticed but attentive to every gesture within, in the grey Olympia nightfall. Now I should have to take pot-luck, peeping through the chintz like a vagabond. (It is amazing how the gaps are never in the right places.)

The gate of Number 44 was unlocked, which did something to mitigate my mortification at the earlier setback, and I coaxed it open silently with the deft hands of one who has served a long apprenticeship in Locks and Catches. Who says Hardware is not a training for Life?

Inside, the garden (from what I could discern by the fitful dusty glimmer of the quarter-moon and the light from the downstairs toilet) was considerably better kept than the sausage-maker's sparse patch. Patio flagstones with tubs, white trellises and a small green shed completed the picture.

I advanced to the main window (this too was French) and scrutinized intently but could see only the vaguest suggestions of outlines through the coarsely textured drapery. From within emanated a low music which I did not recognize, no doubt more Gershwin, it was not anything to write home about. Heaven knew what they were doing in there, but whatever it was they were sparing in their movements.

I was just considering going round to the front for an inspection of the area when a tree-like shape arose from one of the blobs within, swiftly followed by the uprearing of another shape from the same spot. The two dendriforms thereupon appeared to wrap their branches around each other, clumped, disentangled, re-clumped and separated again, upon which the first shape advanced rapidly upon my point of vision and turned on the instant into the object of my pursuits and author of my disapprobation.

I could have taken him with one extended burst, but this is not my way.

12

She had always known when he was around.

There was a sort of clammy prickling at the base of her neck like damp ultraviolet, and she knew that if she were to inspect the crowd on the pavement, or the bus-shelter down the road, or the shrubbery in the park, or the gently billowing net curtains in the empty flat across the street (View by Appointment), she could more or less pinpoint the precise spot where he'd be.

He had tracked her down within hours of her leaving the Fulham Palace Road. She had half expected him to come up and speak to her, to try and persuade her to come back home, even to molest her in some way, but he had simply followed.

For almost a year, there was hardly a moment, save inside her flat or at Chestertons, when she hadn't sensed his nearness, or didn't know that his pale little tracker's eyes weren't bent unswervingly in her direction – 'I drink in your every gesture, Isobel,' he used to say when they were together.

It seemed he had become addicted.

The funny thing was, to start with she hadn't particularly minded. At worst it was a punishment she deserved for having walked out on him (though you couldn't say she didn't have good reason, sleeping with him had been a nightmare) and at best it was sometimes almost comforting to have an overseeing eye watching out for you when you spent the time she did working in the night-life business.

If he wasn't going to fuss her, she didn't mind him tagging along. She was glad he couldn't see some of the things she got up to, because while she couldn't bear to live with him any more, she was grateful for what he'd done and didn't like to be cruel. On the other hand she hadn't asked him to spy on her, so if he didn't like what he saw that wasn't her fault, was it? As Cheryl said, if you can't take a joke, you shouldn't sit in the front row.

And so it had gone on until she made her trip to the States. He didn't follow her there, and after that she had had so many changes of address and different jobs he must have been thrown off the scent. A fortnight or so ago, though – it had to be sheer bad luck, he couldn't have known she would be there – she had practically bumped into him at that Chelsea pub. And, since then, shopping or going to work or, like now, sitting in the lounge after dinner with Tony, she'd kept having that old sensation again, clam on the back of the neck, and it had suddenly annoyed her. What did he think he was playing at? This was her place, she was all right now.

With the anger came an urge to inflict pain. She suddenly wanted to show herself to him, pull her skirt over her head, wave her legs at him as she lay abandonedly on the furry white Greek carpet, so he wouldn't come round and bother her any more. And, though she hadn't slept with Tony yet – following her old principle – she decided that this should be the moment when his patience got its reward. You could usually tell who would be good in bed, it was something around the eyes and mouth, and she rather suspected that Tony might not be. (If she were honest, it was another reason why she had been delaying the experience – a shame, since he seemed so suitable in almost every other way.)

However, with the thought of the peering face outside which Tony didn't even know about, she became quite enthusiastic about the idea. She could picture Roy now, his feet set well apart in approved jungle posture, breathing perhaps a little faster than usual, patiently waiting, not even allowing himself to admit he was getting a kick out of seeing his princess behaving like a swineherd's daughter.

She waited, playing with her coffee, spinning the situation out, building up a delicious expectation, answering Tony without listening to him as she toyed with her anticipation. Why was it she preferred her sex not quite on the straight? Women, of course, knew how to please you, but the average man's idea of sex was a bristly kiss, a tweak at your nipples, a heavy hand up your panties, and they reasoned they'd observed the social niceties of foreplay and could get on with the heavy stuff. At which point, they thought that if they stuck it in, and pumped it up and down until they came, you'd explode like the Molnar Dam and shout confirmation of their virility halfway across Olympia.

Really, girls were better, except in one important matter. In spite of the more progressive women's magazines, dykes weren't respectable. Soixante-neuf between girls was definitely what Tony would call left-field. Cock-sucking, on the other hand, which she wasn't much into, was socially acceptable, and could be discussed at executive dinner parties.

Meanwhile, there was Roy behind the curtains, and Tony looking meaningful and trying not to peer up her skirt too obviously. She went out to the bedroom and took off her knickers.

'Let me not to the marriage of true minds
Admit impediments,' Robert used to admonish them.

She returned to the lounge. Tony had moved to a better vantage point actually on the rug. Roy was still at the window.

She lay down beside Tony, pulled up her skirt, pointed her knees at the curtains, and spoke in her best Brooklyn accent.

'C'mon, c'mon, d'ya wanna screw or don't ya?'

She had been right about Tony, he wasn't particularly brilliant, but it was even better than the Dambusters, like that picture of the Flood in the Tate that Robert had taken her to see, with the lions hanging on with their paws to the tree trunks, the moment he was inside her, and he (mistaking her lust for desire) felt flattered that he had so obliged her, and loved her all the more for it.

The curtain trembled for an instant; a faint breath of air, like a sigh, exhaled from the miasmas of Brook Green, twitched the tasselled lampshade by the French windows; time itself seemed to hover like marsh-mist; finally, she lit a cigarette.

Sex, it seemed, made Tony energetic. He poured a drink. He wanted to talk about their lovemaking, but she did not encourage him. He finally gave up, and sauntered into the garden, pleased with himself.

Chloe felt vaguely irritated. She got up and started clearing glasses and ashtrays. The rug would need a good sponge, she reflected, but it seemed a small price to pay.

Why did she always have to think of Robert when things seemed to be going well?

13

There was no cover to speak of in the garden, so I was obliged to take shelter in the shed. It was clear the man Richmonde was emerging. The curtains were drawn, the doors were opened, and out stepped the enemy wafting aftershave mingled with the sweeter fragrances of another's toilette. Aromas of roast fowl, scotch whisky and cigarette smoke also, it seemed, had been jostling for supremacy in the close confines of the maisonette, and streamed exuberantly forth like wealthy revellers into the mean acridities of the Olympia night.

This sudden whiff of luxury living gave my nostrils, poking through the inch-open pitch-pine door, a taste of better things which reacted powerfully upon my stomach. I had not eaten since lunchtime, planning to be home for a snack in good time after my investigations, an omission I should have to put in my report.

One of our National Service subalterns, a Mr Lovegrove, I recall, used to suffer from hay-fever on summer exercises, and would be brought up short in the middle of an attack, trumpeting like a bull elephant and completely giving away his platoon's position who were theoretically destroyed to a man. So it appeared now would be the case with me. My stomach started to gurgle. It seemed to me as loud as the diapason of St Theodoric's organ, a mighty reed.

The American (there was an oppressive larger-than-lifeness about him) emerged clad only in shirt and trousers, looking well pleased with himself. He drew deep breaths, making an excessive amount of noise and fuss (which at the time I had to be grateful for), limbered a little, ran on the spot, then stopped and gazed at the moon, now free of cloud, which rode high in the west somewhere over Hammersmith Flyover, no doubt reflecting upon the chunks of American hardware that were littering its surface.

The girl, who had been clattering in the kitchen, now came to join him, and they stood arm in arm gazing out upon the queen of the night.

I found it hard to credit that they could do this and still be unaware of the tolling of my digestive processes. It could not be for long. A soldier's training took over. I clenched my stomach, I twisted myself to left and right, I touched my toes, I pressed my belt, I thought of Muster Parade and the RSM who would have our guts for garters (he was welcome to them now). Nothing availed.

At length the couple stirred. I could almost see the thought-processes elicited by my internal Maori National Park forming in the American's mind. He had never heard anything quite like it before, so it would take him some time to frame his conjectures into words, but speak he would, investigation would ensue and I would be exposed. I was prepared to sell my anonymity dearly.

At that moment, a small dog emerged from the house and stood barking in the pool of light by the windows. There seemed to be a surfeit of dogs in these parts, one of my pet hates in our cities, no wonder the dandelions looked sickly.

'Be quiet, Gaby,' said the girl.

Hardly a name for a Yorkshire terrier living in West Kensington, I think you will agree.

'What's got into her?' then, louder, 'Who's there?' said the American.

It could only be a matter of moments before my position became public. In some instinctive movement of self-defence, I put my hands into my pockets and touched something so intrinsically loathsome that even in my predicament, I could scarcely repress a cry of distaste. Fibrous, nodular, it was the Jamaican sausalito, now sent, it suddenly dawned upon me, as if by a divine providence. Quick as a flash, I extracted it from my denims, tore off a generous hunk and extended it to the marmot-size hound, which instantly ceased its clamour and advanced upon the vile excrescence busily wagging its tail.

The couple, either through fear or indolence, still had not moved, and now, reassured by the dog's silence, they began to wander back towards the comforts of the house.

'She's probably found a moth.'

'Gaby, Gaby,' called the girl, but her heart was not in it.

'I'll go get her,' offered the American officiously.

'Don't bother. I'll leave the door open for a minute. She likes a good sniff round.'

The animal was, I noticed, making a snuffly sort of noise but it sounded, not that I am expert on our canine friends, none too healthy. I looked down, and in the dim light, dog and sausage appeared to be locked in mortal combat. The beast was trying to swallow the object in one gulp, clearly not the best way to tackle the feast but there it was, I was not in a position to try and instruct it in the rudiments of moderation. From where I was standing, it was hard to tell whether it was in its death throes or simply enjoying itself, but I daresay that is true of all of us.

Judging that this might be the moment to withdraw, I stepped over the tussle – the dog was now completely oblivious of my presence – inched through the door, glided into the darkness, slipped through the garden gate and traversed the alleyway as easily as if I had been demonstrating jungle procedure to a bunch of newly arrived rookies back at Tampoi Barracks. I could not resist stuffing a potato I had prudently brought with me in the PEST OFF bag up the exhaust pipe of the Cadillac before I left the scene, more of an incidental gesture of defiance than a tactical objective, but satisfying nonetheless.

I had finished on a stronger note, but as I regrouped at home over a cup of Bournvita, I reflected that my night's work would not look good in the Report. No amount of glossing over could conceal the bungling of the cockroach affair, nor the near-disaster of my empty stomach. It was madness not to have eaten before a Night Op; Mr Parsons would never have sent a patrol out without a mess-tinful of Army-issue hash, and he would rightly have had me up on CO's Orders so fast my feet would not have touched the proverbial.

Strange, was it not, that when the moment of crisis arrived in the form of the dog Gaby, my digestive system should have quietened down upon the instant without so much as a peep. The effects of danger upon the gastric juices have not to my mind been sufficiently investigated by the medical profession. I extend the thought for what it is worth. Man can walk on the moon but we still do not know all about our organs.

But to the matter in hand.

The poor showing I had made gave me cause for serious review, and when I looked down at the hand grasping my Edward VIII Coronation mug, I saw that the knuckles were blenched. I was indeed more involved than I had realized. The consideration both excited and alarmed me. Alarm, because for pursuit one needs an ice-cool nerve and all the patient attributes of the lynx. Would passion cloud my judgment? I gazed into the dying embers of my smokeless fuel fire, trying to remember the precepts of my military days.

Some passion was surely in order. Hate could be efficacious. I recalled charging with fixed bayonet at those sandbag dummies swinging in the wind under the eye of Sergeant-Major Mathieson.

'In . . . twist . . . withdraw. It's not your partner at the Fairy Ball, you horrible little man. Don't prick it. Hate it. Do it as if it was me, you cumbersome soldier.'

And, later, there was something else Mr Parsons used to tell us.

'Hate the enemy, yes, but never despise him.'

What he required from us was controlled loathing. He was the only officer in the Regiment the men would follow into the jaws of hell.

I made a note, next time I went out, to include aniseed in my hold-all.

PART TWO

14

I had not taken the road out of Henley that skirts the river on its cattle-fringed route to Marlow for many months, not since I had my dear one with me, and we would bowl out for the day with picnic basket and Thermos flask, my heart singing like the larks on Remenham Hill.

As I drove now past the farm with the Guernseys on the left and the Catholic Seminary on the right, the cows, the Catholics and the trees fringing the road all seemed to pause in their morning's business and pay a silent tribute to the lost things of the world. I was visibly moved.

Two miles out of town, a lane straggles up the hill into the trees towards the village of Nutley. Thick with bluebells the woods are in May. You skirt a hazel clump and there between the trees in a clearing, or carpeting a ride, the ground shimmers like the vault of heaven itself. Many was the time we lay on my old tartan rug with our soup and sandwiches, caught between two skies we used to say. I suppose you could call us fanciful but there it was, we lived only for each other. Even now, second day of April, you could sense the trees fizzing with the sap.

At the top of the hill there is a junction which leads either to a dead-end on the right, unless you are looking for the comforts of the church (Early English with Norman pillars in the North transept and possibly Saxon font with carving said to depict the miraculous life of St Rumbold, grandson of King Penda of the Mercians, he only lived three days but he got through more than many would in a lifetime), or else past the Mulberry Bush if you take the road to the left, which refreshes poor sinners with Morrell's noted Oxford Ales.

As I have had occasion to note in the past, I am a sparing drinker but I enjoy a half-pint of real ale from time to time, and I bethought me now to stop and sample mine host's cellar once again as in the old days, painful though the memories might be. We used to sit in the nook by the fire and hold hands, doodling on our beer mats or reviewing the other customers shrewdly but without malice the way lovers do.

In our day, a young couple ran the pub and kept a good house with tasty bar snacks if our sandwiches proved insufficient, and a little grill room at the back, but they had gone, I discovered, like so much else, and there was now a jukebox playing while a couple of black-jeaned youths slouched at their table drinking whisky and Coca Cola, occasionally twitching to the music, if that is the word, or giving sudden unaccountable loud guffaws. It was conceivable that it was open day for the local Home for the Retarded, in which case I was more than prepared to make excuses, but there again it was more than probable that this was the regular clientele enjoying its rustic heritage. It is to these depths that our lusty yeoman stock has declined.

'Good afternoon,' I said politely to the assembled company.

One may not like the look of things but there is still such a concept as manners. The youths gave me a slack-jawed glance and returned to their truculent semi-coma. The barman, who was new since my day, was buried deep in the racing results and showed no signs of enthusiasm at my advent. Well, that was all to the good. It may not have been good for England but it was at least conducive to my mission. The less that I was noticed the better. They were used to strangers here, visitors to the Nature Reserve at Cowden, strayed revellers from the river; it was unlikely that I would be remarked if I kept myself to myself, maintained the civilities and held my temper in check, just another birdwatcher or agricultural insurance salesman. Well, today as a matter of fact I was an amateur botanist and looked the part with my field-grey anorak and my Keble Martin Book of Wild Flowers. There are some rare sub-alpine plants in the woods around Cowden, a fact not widely appreciated, and if you are lucky you may find a Birdsnest Orchid.

'Half of Murrell's, please.'

The 'o' in Morrell's is thus correctly pronounced, but the barman had obviously not studied the niceties. He drew a foaming beaker and handed it over, even as his pencil sought the while a likely winner for the two thirty.

''Arf of morals, there y'are.'

It was at least comforting to note that the beer had not changed, and as I sipped the nut-brown brew I reflected that there are still some things that we do incomparably better than other nations if only we could stop this Gadarene rush down the slope of trans-Atlantic replication. Alas, a forlorn hope. Soon, no doubt, they would be serving pastrami on rye, whatever that is, at the Mulberry Bush with a can of Schlitz to wash it down. O tempora, o morals.

There was a sound of tyres on gravel outside, and I looked out casually over the top of the Keble Martin to see who would be joining our little party, and experienced a sensation in my stomach not unlike that when, instructing recruits at the grenade ranges, I had seen Private Gregory 903, drop his grenade backwards among my crouching squad rather than forwards over the defences. Luckily, it transpired that he had also forgotten to take the pin out, but it was some moments before we ascertained that the bomb was harmless, and Lance Corporal Stott was meanwhile having problems with his denim trousers. How we laughed.

On this occasion, I was not to be let off so lightly. The source of the gravelly crunching was a shiny black chunk of Americana half the size of Madison Square, and the driver, now striding weightily towards the pub, was none other than my adversary Richmond with an e.

Curses, I had forgotten it was Saturday. It may seem strange perhaps that anyone should make such an elementary mistake, but my mode of existence was not normally ruled by the exigencies of office life. I came and went as I pleased, and no man called me master. Still, it was slack of me not to have checked, and I cursed my lack of awareness. I might have known that the American would come past the Mulberry Bush on his duty-run from Town.

I hurriedly rose and went to the Gents to ponder this new development. I could not remember an alternative exit, but I had a good look for an escape way en route and found nothing. All I was faced with were glazed urinals, a slot-machine selling contraceptives, another one selling Aspro, and a whitewashed wall covered with scrawled attempts at wit: 'Virginity is like a bubble – one prick and its gone.' Such must have been the obiter dicta in the Cities of the Plain.

This little flush of anger, however, gave me the will to brazen it out. After all, the American had only seen me once and had probably not noticed me at all. Even if he had, it was unlikely that he would connect the obscure clerk from whom he had asked a light in the Bird in Hand with the fringe-bearded botanist that I now represented.

When I returned to my seat, I realized that I should not, in any event, have been seriously perturbed. The American, with his jowl in a Hofmeister Lager – not a patch on Tiger Beer in my humble opinion if you have to drink fizzy stuff – was in full flood.

'Hang on in there, Wallie,' he was saying.

It is a phrase I have always found particularly repugnant. Hang on in? One would think it would be more at home within the portals of the Royal Zoological Society encompassing the behaviour of Megatherium the Giant Sloth. (As it happened, the barman's manner of lassitude tinged with indolence did give something of an impression of the animal in question, but that was incidental, it still did not excuse the use of the double preposition.)

I steeled myself to listen to some more language assassination behind a particularly beautiful drawing of the humble Wall Pepper. It appeared that the American's comment referred to the village cricket team's match on the morrow, and pendulous tenacity was Richmonde's recipe for success, a formula I am bound to say not advocated by old 'Thwackers' Pettigrew, our sports master at St Theodoric's, but there you are, no doubt in America things are different, or so they are always telling us.

'Will do, Mr Richmonde. Will do. You coming to watch the sport? First match of the season. Always a bit of larking around.'

'Uh well uh, Wallie, I've got to see how Joanie's fixed. You know? She has a girlfriend staying and she's no doubt got a whole schedule waiting to go just as soon as I arrive. You know ladies.'

Wallie, it appeared, was well acquainted with the sex. He nodded cumbrously. Another thought appeared to rise in his west and slowly moved across his mid-heaven.

'You're late today, Mr Richmonde. Business keep you in town? Big deals and such?'

'Shit, no.'

I sat up straight behind my Wall Pepper illustration, a mild sense of triumph suffusing me. I knew what was to follow.

'Some uh asshole,' the American continued, 'some asshole put a potato up my exhaust pipe last night. Would you believe that? You don't think that kind of assing around would go on in the middle of town. I had to get the breakdown service to come fix it this morning, and that's what they found. I felt like a clown, I can tell you.'

That 'asshole', much though the soubriquet rankled, was yours truly. I had drawn my first blood. It felt good to be alive.

While the barman murmured ritual sympathy, though no doubt reflecting that in the country up your pipe was the first place you looked, and what kind of a city slicker did you have to be not to be aware of that old caper, I buried myself deep in the vascular system of the Lesser Celandine to conceal my jubilation, and almost missed the American's next move.

He had polished off his lager at the double, the gaseous swill made him barely stifle a belch, and then suddenly, with a studied wave to the barman smacking of over-familiarity if not ingratiation, he was out of the door in a brace of shakes, leaving me wallowing with at least half a glass unattended to. Always on the move, the Yanks. They should learn to stand and stare like the rest of us. I for one am not taken in by all this febrile activity. Does not the hymnographer advise: 'Cease then thy foolish ranges . . .'?

'Ciao, Wallie. See ya around.'

'Bye, Mr Richmonde. Maybe see you later.'

Well, there it was, it now behoved me also to be on my way. I had brought along my Ordnance Survey map of the area, so long unused, so I knew where his cottage lay; it was not fear of not locating the enemy position that drove me to follow the man hotfoot, but I wished to be as prompt upon his estimated time of arrival as possible, to observe the manner of his greeting and catch the flavour of the moment.

I adjusted my field-grey anorak, drew deeply on my glass of swipes, wiped my lips, closed Keble Martin, and stood up.

'Thank you,' I said to the barman, who was desultorily

rearranging a wall-hanging dispenser of Porky Scratchings. 'The Hellebore calls.'

'Oh yes?'

I was stung by his indifference to the rarities of his native woodnotes wild, and would have paused to remedy such a glaring nay wilful omission, but out of the corner of my eye I saw the great black bulk of the Cadillac edging out of the carpark and squeezing away down the lane.

I gathered up my book, and left the man unfolding a bar-top display of Pepperoni snackettes. The nickelodeon droned on. The delinquents juddered listlessly. 'Willa warby baby tonight.' The prevailing wind from the west had twisted the Mulberry Bush out of all recognition, like those firs you see gnarled beside the Severn Sea on the very edge of Exmoor.

I was not sorry to leave.

The road down to Cowden leads through some of the loveliest wooded countryside I know. Of course you may say it is tame compared with the grandeurs of Dean or the awesome contours of Teesdale, but on a comforting and companionable scale I would maintain that there is nothing to beat it.

The old maps do not indicate that the ancient Forest of Bernwood extended as far south as Cowden, but it depends of course on the date one is talking about. I have seen no records prior to Domesday, and the term 'forest' has always been a loose one.

There does seem some evidence to suggest that the Saxons referred to the whole swathe right down to the Thames as Bernwood or Birnwood, though later of course it contracted as the clearings spread. If one takes other charts as gospel, compiled in the great stocktaking just after the Black Death, one may assign these woody reaches to the fringe of the Forest of Brill, which, of course, was later incorporated under the general terminology of Bernwood anyway.

Whatever the historical apportioning of the region, however, it seems clear that for countless centuries the predominant vegetation has been the beech.

The beech is a noble tree. It is aloof but civilized, disdaining the usual scrambling brambling bric-à-brac that clutters the floor of other forests. You can walk freely across the crispy carpet of beech-mast. There are, naturally, parts of the wood where lesser trees, sallows and birch, elder and ash, festoons of ivy and old-man's-beard work their lesser magic and trammel the traveller, snapping at his face and clawing at his bootstraps, but on the whole, of all the woodland, the beech forest is the most hospitable.

Again, I love the flintstone you find in these parts. There is a magic about that too, taking us back perhaps to the days of our ancestors when it was source both of fire and weaponry. As a child, I loved to break a flint, look at the strange inky-milky crystal inside, and smell the smoke upon the stone.

We had a collection in the garden, Isobel and I, of fantastically-shaped flintstones which we had found on our rambles in these hills, frozen relics of long-dead infernoes, long dead like lost happiness.

And that, of course, is the other thing about these parts, now I touch upon it: the hills. Steep round slopes, deep-bowled valleys which make the trees seem to leap and soar and plunge like the wild sea horses of the main. True, it may be in the Home Counties with London only thirty-five miles away, but there is an excitement here that is as primal as any place I know.

On a military note, because of the open pathways, suddenly interspersed with clumps of dense undergrowth, it is a place made for ambush and surprise attack, and though the arboreal species may be very different, it is not so far removed in this respect from the primary forests above Johore Baru.

Mast Hill Cottage lay in its own little clearing at the edge of the wood, a quarter of the way up the hill from which it took its name, backed and sided by trees but with a view of field and pasture in front. I could see its chimneys and a glimmer of windows as I parked the Traveller in a fresh-leafed niche at the side of a one-track metalled road, and investigated the rutted lane that leads up to the Nature Reserve, from which another smaller lane runs up to the cottage.

I knew at a glance that the direct approach would not pay dividends – it seldom does in my line of country. Though the American had not so far shown any great signs of fine-tuned awareness, it might just give him cause for reflection if the botanist he had seen drinking beer in the Mulberry Bush should now stride up his drive and ask for a beaker of water. No, my way had to be the route of stealth and obfuscation. I would work my way round the side under cover of the hedgerow, and debouch upon the rear of the cottage where I could observe the goings-on through my naturalist's fieldglasses.

As it happened, the terrain favoured me more auspiciously than I could have imagined. A narrow neck of hedgerow and shrubbery stretched from the cottage garden right up to the wood at the side, and I was able to leopard-crawl my way forward into a tactical position where I could not only observe but actually overhear what was transpiring on the terrace in between the house and the greensward.

A rustic table, surrounded by knobbly garden furniture, supported a tray of salad bowls and a glass jug of what looked like whey, and around this collation were grouped three persons. In my walk of life you get used to the eccentricities of the human animal, the waywardness, the staggering self-absorption, the comic disparateness between the individual's sense of dignity and his or her ludicrous appearance or predicament, but one of the most enduring sources of wonder if not mirth is the ability people have to group themselves with others who on the face of it have nothing whatsoever in common with them. Thus we have pretty girls with gross escorts, austere curates with fleshy wives, tax inspectors with boon companions who turn out to be used car dealers, the litany continues, but seldom have I witnessed such a heterogeneous trio as presented themselves, albeit unwittingly, for my present inspection.

First, there was of course the American, who had now taken off his jacket – the warm sunshine would have put a flush of colour into even Keats' pale features – and was reclining on a rough-hewn wooden armchair, looking at once relaxed and restless, a peculiarly American combination.

Next to him on a bench was a large woman in some kind of quasi-oriental robe plus obligatory sandals. She was making some conversational point and stabbing the air as if it were gingerbread dough to emphasize her line of reasoning. I hazarded that this imposing figure was the American's wife.

The other participant in the feast was a short tumbling-coiffed kittenish young woman with a mouth perhaps overfurnished with teeth – it is something to do with the quantities of milk and steak in their diet – dressed in a light summer frock and wearing an expression of rapt delight, as if she were forever hearing the first cuckoo.

I could have taken them all where they sat with an anti-personnel grenade, they were lamentably clustered.

Dogs? None that I could discern. I had taken the precaution of bringing a small supply of aniseed balls upon this occasion, but as it seemed I should not need to call on them, I popped one into my mouth, mindful of the dangers of an empty system, the sharp nutty taste reminding me of my mother's seedcake and the land of lost content.

'It's great to have you over here, Margaret,' the American was saying to the small furry woman without any real enthusiasm, 'just great. Say, uh, just how long will you be able to stay?'

The two women saw no need to answer his question. He had only just arrived and no one was making a fuss of him. This was the kind of information I had come for.

'I could almost feel jealous of the Movement for keeping you, I know it's selfish of me but I could,' said the wife Joanie, rolling her eyes and agitating, I noticed, a quantity of chin.

She was a substantial woman. It was clear that they were old friends.

'Sweet of you, that's really darling of you. I have to get back next year of course, but Sea Watch got off to such a great start they said I could take a sabbatical and look around what was going on in Europe. Do you know the Vice-President made a reference to it in a speech the other day in Miami?'

'No? Really? You have to tell us all about it, doesn't she, Tony, just every little bit.'

The man's enthusiasm was restrained, I thought, but the women were too taken up with their topic to notice.

'Did you hear the latest findings on the porpoise's IQ? They're as intelligent now, at this moment in time, as Neanderthal Man. Did you know that?'

'How about that? How about that, Tony?'

'And they're gaining fast. At this rate, they'll have passed us by the year 2500.'

'Isn't that just fascinating, Tony? And involving?'

The American made noises of involvement, though one could see his heart was not in it.

'And yet they're still clubbing them off the fishing grounds in Manila.'

'My God, isn't that shocking? Isn't that shocking, Tony? Yes or no, are you man or machine? He has a cash register where his heart should be. Sometimes one feels ashamed to be human. It's kind of like genocide.'

'I think I'll get a beer,' said the American, responding with ill-concealed loathing to the taste of the whey. 'Beer, Margaret dear? Beer, Joanie?'

'Don't let me stop you,' the woman Margaret announced, 'but I've given up alcohol. Did you know that one measure of vodka dropped in a porpoise tank can cause serious disorientation?'

'Well, uh, no, uh, Margaret, I didn't know that.'

'It's the kind of thing that ought to be more widely publicized. But there's a lobby of course, the liquor barons are paying to have the information suppressed. If alcohol can do that to a porpoise, think of the trauma we're inflicting on our already poisoned systems.'

'My God, Margaret, is that true?' said the large woman. 'But that's terrible. That is absolutely terrible. Pass me my nucleoproteins, would you, dear? And cancel the beer, Tony.'

The American heaved slightly in the manner of one who is accustomed to having his own way but sees temporary reasons for self-discipline, while the kittenish young woman plunged into a lengthy exegesis on porpoise and indeed human physiology, referring to obscure glands as casually as if they were old friends, and not hesitating to name parts which caused me, even where I was concealed among the laurels, to blush to the roots of my moustache. She had one of those low insistent voices which can drone on endlessly if unchecked, and it was quite clear that the older woman was not the one to administer any conversational disciplines to her guest.

While the breeding habits of the porpoise were examined with an intimacy which, had I been of porpoise kind, I should have regarded as rank invasion of privacy, and accelerated my development, on the instant, from Neanderthal to Jacobean (our tongue's Golden Age) the better to express my sense of outrage, I at least had ample opportunity to examine Mrs Richmonde in detail, and to note that she was wearing solid Inca-like chunks of gold around her wrists. She had a look of wealth in her bearing, her eyes bulged with substance, and I deduced that she was the source of capital in the family. Richmonde himself merely had income, which gives a man all the sense of security of standing comfortably for an unknown term on top of a trapdoor.

'They opened it up and its liver was like, you know, the size of a squash, and you know, suppurating . . .'

I concentrated on the man Richmonde. So that was what he was doing, a duty weekend of salads and buttermilk, and then back to the fleshpots. He had got it all worked out, he needed the secure foundation of his marriage the better to cut his capers. I understood him now, but to understand is not to love.

Even so, though I deplored so many things about him, I must confess it gave me cause for conjecture – while they tucked into the raw vegetables and cracked wheat – to see how a man like that with his tastes and his fleshy good looks could endure, even for a weekend, so preposterous a tribe and so unattractive a diet. I reflected it was not the first time that money had played madam to such strange bedfellows.

Honey-cakes were brought out. The women talked on. My head began to ache. After lunch they rolled cigarettes which I took to contain the scourge marijuana, no wonder Vietnam was such a shambles, and went to sleep in the afternoon sun.

Something had crawled down my collar and was now negotiating my sternum, a mere nothing to one who has patrolled the scorpion-infested hinterland of the Ulu, but nonetheless irksome. It was time to do a preliminary recce in the woods. I had seen enough of Mast Hill Cottage and its denizens for the nonce, but I should be back, I had not concluded my business by any manner of means.

Retiring from my position posed no problems. The trained soldier always keeps his line of retreat open, although a certain stiffness in the limbs reminded me that Time had inflicted more damage than Communist Terrorists had ever been able to achieve: the danger is always from within.

Out of sight of the house, skirting the hedgerow, I decided to make a brief foray into the unknown territory the other side – instinct prompted me, the soldier's sixth sense – and there it was, the outsize motorcar, sitting shimmering like a big black glasshouse in a hazel-fringed parking bay. I do not normally like letting tyres down – the smell of mackerel that emanates from the inner rubber is always distasteful – and there is nothing subtle or distinctive about the act, any green boy could do it, but on this occasion I was able to stifle my squeamishness and press my index finger over the stamen of the valve.

This second minor assault on the car would, to the American, be more than coincidental but less than conclusive. Enough to unsettle but not sufficient to disturb, and I was congratulating myself on the delicate nuance of my tactics when, just as the huge wheel settled slowly like glistering Titan on to the horizon-wide curve of the flat, something happened which I confess had not entered into my calculations. The car started a raucous honking in a manner that, when I had leisure to ruminate on the matter, reminded me of the elephant park at Kuala Lumpur, but which at the time, being so completely unexpected, temporarily bowled me over backwards – the soldier is trained to fall. However, since it is also his art to recover without panic or post-mortem, assuming he is not dead, I picked myself up at the double and took evasive action behind the hedgerow.

I should, of course, have known, and the lesson would not be lost on me. The American, piqued by the matter of the potato, was evidently taking no chances, and had activated his burglar alarm – he was more security-conscious than I had bargained for. All well and good, we cannot create without making mistakes.

Confused drowsy sounds from the cottage followed in my wake.

'What the hell . . .' from the American.

'Is that your automobile making that hideous noise? You know what that sound is doing to the wildlife?'

I was convinced, such is my fieldcraft, that they had not seen me, but I lost no time in reaching the bottom of the lane, for it was clear some kind of sortie was being organized.

The element of surprise, that goddess to whom the soldier must ever make sacrifice, was however on my side, and I was able to achieve the wheel of my faithful Traveller without impediment or loss of security. As I swung the car with practised dexterity along the bosky lanes to Nutley, I reflected that I could report at least eighty per cent success for this operation. True, I had not penetrated the actual woods for the recce which I had promised myself, but that could wait for another day. At least I now knew enough about the American to propose a specific plan of research and investigation which could be mounted in the months ahead, and from which I could base a proper operation in the summer.

'Fools rush in' was one of Mr Parsons' favourite dicta. 'Get your planning right, rehearse your attack, and then rehearse it again. If you barge in like a bull in a brothel you'll get your balls shot off.' He had a ripe turn of phrase but his equipment was always spotless.

As I drove across the succulent bowl of Cowden valley, I could still hear the melancholy hooting of the behemoth, like a dinosaur prescient of race-death. I could imagine the American swearing as he grappled with the circuitry, and the women disassociating themselves from the disturbance as best they could.

'It's uh like some kind of uh aural pollution . . .'

The noise ceased as suddenly as it had started, and as I crested the lip of Nettlefold Hill the valley reverted from the honking swamps of late Cretaceous to the chalky silences of a Chiltern spring.

15

'Nobody likes to kiss spots.'

Tony Richmonde settled himself more comfortably into the swivelling captain's chair behind the heavy tooled-leather desk with the brass lamp and the executive pen-set that looked like a veteran automobile, and made a note on his Gucci executive memorandum pad, more for the sake of making a note on his Gucci executive memorandum pad than in the belief that he would ever need to read it. He prided himself on his retentive memory.

He was running through a selection of commercials which might be suitable as Natural Break fillers in a projected new video-cassette series on 'Personal Improvement', and at the same time giving himself a status report on his situation as at that moment in time. He liked to give himself status reports. They provided a sense of continuity.

Video publishing was not the basis of Craxton and Kuhne's business activities, but it was taking up an increasing amount of his planning hours. His brief was to diversify into the video business, and video was very much the flavour of the marketing month. Studios were sprouting, series were shooting, little corner shops in frowsty High Streets were selling all the equipment they could lay their hands on. It was a passion that affected the whole socio-demographic spectrum, from ABs to Ds; everyone felt life was passing them by if they did not have their cassette machine and monitor to record and review something with.

Craxton and Kuhne's real business was the hardware and software of surveillance, but, for one thing, Tony felt it was against the confidential nature of their image to have Security looming too large in their shop window; they needed a front. And, for another, the field was becoming increasingly competitive. Surveillance had been the flavour of the month a couple of decades back, a big boom industry given an enormous boost by the wave of kidnappings, bombings and hijacks of the Seventies, but like so many other growth areas it had been hit by the recession and by the proliferation of cut-price competition, often offered by quasi-criminal backstreet organizations.

For both these reasons, Tony (with a reputation for marketing wizardry in New York) had been taken on to extend and develop the business in London, a capital that with its Arab and Common Market contacts was rapidly expanding as an important world centre of terrorism, surveillance, and video production – a happy combination of interests for C & K and, as it seemed, for Tony.

Smart operator that he was, he had been reluctant to commit venture capital to any random 'blue-sky' production project of his own, after all neither he nor C & K had real experience in the area, but he had hit on the notion of acquiring the advertising time in any series being made, and selling it to advertisers who would thus have a prime audience for their products – garden equipment manufacturers would advertise in gardening series, skin-care companies in beauty series, and so on. This would not only help producers amortize the cost of production but would put a great deal of money into the coffers of C & K without their ever having to dip into their own pockets, a classic marketing stratagem which could conceivably lead to a Profile in *Business Week*.

To assist him in the project, he had hired the services of a young Englishman, Hugo Bracewell-Smith, who sat facing him now, public-school-educated, trained in the music business, suave, glossy, sleek as a stag beetle, a born salesman and instinctive sniffer-out of opportunities. Tony had employed him personally, simply notifying Bidwell, the caretaker head of Craxton & Kuhne (UK) Ltd, that he was going to do so, and had made it quite clear to Hugo that he, Hugo, owed allegiance only to him and to no one else in the company. They understood each other perfectly.

'We're two of a kind,' he had said to Hugo last week.

'Two of an unkind,' replied Hugo with a cheeky grin.

Tony was not sure that he altogether trusted him but he let it rest. He could outsmart any Englishman in the business, and why waste time worrying when the pickings were good? The whole field of video, with all the various producers from giant corporations to tiny entrepreneurs, all tending their furrows – from porn to poetry, from politics to Pelmanism – lay becomingly before him. All it needed was somebody to come along and take the cream off the harvest, and he saw no reason why it should not be Craxton & Kuhne.

Of course, he projected, when he had developed it to the stage when he could see an assured revenue, he would rip it off Craxton & Kuhne and run the thing himself. There was no point in handing the thing to old Kuhne on a plate. Meanwhile, he would do his job, write reports on his progress, and develop the main part of the business as best he could in a shrinking market situation, promoting security aids and systems, and building his own future at C & K's expense.

The scheme seemed to have no flaws. To invent a whole new advertising medium . . . it was a marketing man's eldorado.

Existence in Britain, which he had viewed with some misgiving in New York, had turned out to be really quite reasonable. For a start, it had given him the opportunity to be away from Joanie during the week. Oh sure, he had married her for her money, and she had married him for his drive, his career, let us not kid ourselves, it had been a deal, but she hadn't had those zany ideas about ecology and eating beanshoots every meal in those days. It was that smartass Margaret putting notions in her head.

He kind of got the feeling there was something else between them, but he didn't waste much time on it – if it made her happy and kept her out of his way, it was all right with him. And then, it couldn't be ignored, she was Old Kuhne's daughter. There was no point in rocking the boat just yet awhile.

The British, it was true, tended to be a pain in the ass, either stuffy and old school tie, or idle, inefficient, negative and slow. Or sometimes an amalgam of the lot. The idea of service was almost non-existent, the bars were shut half the time, the night life was limited, the coffee disgusting, the showers ineffectual, the climate lamentable, all the clichés about London were to some extent true. But there were compensations. The golf courses were near to hand, the sea was only an hour or so's drive away, there were some great places to stay if you knew where to look. And the English women were something else.

They had neat little teeth, their hair seldom seemed to hang in lacquered bangs, their voices were rarely strident, their personalities were developed but not assertive (like their breasts), their well-bred thighs under a Burberry skirt suggested more promise with one swish of a leg-crossing than a whole repertoire of 'Ya wanna screw or don't ya?'

Tony Richmonde was an ambitious, indeed in many ways a thoroughly regrettable man, but he was disarmingly open about his faults. 'Frankly,' he would say, 'I would do anything for money. You name it, I would do it.' People would laugh, thinking he must be honest if he were so self-damning, but he wasn't. He had simply hit on a good trick.

'What, Tony, sell your own mother?'

'Yes, goddammit. My mother, my sister, my daughter. I'd sell my own asshole if I could' (a sale he was unlikely to clinch in the present state of the market). Delicacy was not one of his strong points, but since indelicacy was the idiom of the moment, his very bluntness passed for wit.

'An engaging rogue,' they would say.

And at least in the second part of their opinion they would be right.

Old Kuhne recognized Tony as a rogue, since Old Kuhne was one too, one of the old school of American rogues which was just about as roguish as you can get. He had run a small but well-formed gang in Atlantic City just after the Second World War, made himself a pile of money, and got out just at the right moment on the hit list of hardly anyone. The few that nursed a grudge he either bought or quietly disposed of, and he had then made himself a second pile by turning his experiences (and some of his former workforce) to good effect in the new growth industry of surveillance – security, protection, recovery (goods or bodies as required), and personal insurance. True he was only a small operator compared with the big boys but, as in his earlier career, he found again that many people preferred an individual service.

The only blot on the landscape was his arthritis. He had broken a hip once during a getaway from some unexpected opposition, and it had never been quite the same. Surprisingly, for so intrepid a man, he had a dread of hospitals and wouldn't agree to an operation, and so in later years he had become more or less desk-bound, which, as contracts fell away and Europe became an increasingly important centre for the industry, came to be a considerable impediment to his business.

So when his daughter Joan announced that she was getting married to this guy Tony, some kind of whiz-kid marketing executive, it had suited him right down to the ground. He felt he needed a marketing executive in the family almost as much as he wanted to get rid of his daughter, who was manifestly a pill. In fact his only doubts about the man, apart from the fact that he was clearly a guy to be watched, was that he had in a free market elected to tie himself to someone who was, he had to say it even though she was his own flesh and blood, so outstandingly charm-free. (She had been hanging around since her mother died five years ago, on the pretext of keeping house, and it was driving him crazy: not having anything to do herself, she spent her time telling him what he should *not* be doing, like eating, drinking and playing cards with his cronies.)

His old partner Craxton, who was merely a respectable financial front and cipher, married to the daughter of a senator, had, it was true, raised a note of query, pointing to the frequent moves Richmonde had made throughout his marketing career in various advertising and recording companies in New York, but Kuhne had brushed aside his protestation.

'Mac,' he had said (Craxton's mother had named him Macready after a flirtation with stage history), 'Mac, you leave the worrying to me. That's the way it is in the marketing world. We need a smart guy to get to work on those sheikhs and drum up some new business. Diversification is the name of the game these days, Mac. This guy has ingenuity, ingenuity and persistence, goddammit that's what we need. The old ways are over. We need to sell. He's hungry, Mac.'

'Yeah, well, just so long as he doesn't take a bite at us.'

'I shall be watching him, Mac, so close he won't even know it. Do you think I as near as dammit invented the surveillance racket and learned nothing? You bet your sweet ass I'm watching him all the way.'

So Tony had been enrolled into the family and its business. At the time, though he took some trouble to conceal it from his father-in-law, he was heading for serious trouble over a rather too lavish interpretation of his expense account allowance, and would almost certainly have been out of a job within the month. He threw himself into the surveillance business with all the marketing man's powers of over-view.

He cursorily familiarized himself with the hardware – the infrared lenses, tele-microphones, trembler-sensors, video scanners, circuitry, weaponry – and the language (especially the language) with an enthusiasm that would have astonished his class-master in Bellington, Ohio, who pronounced that his attention-span was the briefest of any bright child he had ever taught. 'I shall write a paper on it,' he would say. 'Such a tiny thing should be made known. It will rank with the quark and the neutrino.'

The truth was that Tony had seen no point in attending to discussions upon matters that seemed to have absolutely no practical application or profit in them. Of what use the logarithm or the pluperfect tense? You couldn't eat them. You couldn't sell them. You couldn't screw them on the back seat of a Chevrolet.

Whereas with the software of surveillance, his next project, anything was possible. From simple automobile and property protection procedures, through commercial premises systems and wage delivery, to tailing, bugging, interception, detection, vigilance, clandestine pick-ups, conciliation, negotiation, retaliation and disposal, these were the bread, the very stuff of life, and spelt as much money and ass as a man could take on board.

Tony had served briefly in Vietnam until he had, not altogether inadvertently, contracted Saigon Rose, a particularly virulent and tenacious form of gonorrhoea, and managed to get himself repatriated without doing more than the briefest of spells as clerk to a Paymaster, but certain disciplines he now learned evoked echoes of things he had heard of during his service. Tell-tale aftershave, for instance, was to be avoided by the operative. Even highly flavoured toothpaste should be eschewed: a waft on a still night could put an entire operation in jeopardy. Tony learned more in three weeks than he acquired in three months in Saigon, apart of course from venereal disease.

When he finally emerged after his crash course, he was equipped to advise on (if not participate in) a whole Pandora's boxful of security situations. He could recommend how to snoop on your wife, he could sell you with equal facility a burglar alarm or an entire video circuit for your store (either dummy or fully operational), he could suggest forms of parley with kidnappers of your children (or enter into negotiations on your behalf to remove unwanted heirs), he could organize a team to electrify your fence, sniff out hidden explosives, provide a miniature voice stress analyser to let you know when someone was lying, equip you with an ultra-compact high-powered portable communication module, or a portable defence system to give you non-violent protection against attackers, he could introduce people who would interrogate your terrorists, shoot tranquillizing darts into hostile guard dogs and supply dart-proof coatees for friendly ones, help plan a dozen different ways for you to leave the house and go to the office every morning, do extraordinarily complicated things with photo-electric cells, and he could even whistle up a dentist who would put a microphone in your enemy's back teeth if you could bear to hear the punctuations of his dinner going down while he articulated the industrial secret that you craved . . . In short, Tony could spread the illusion of a net of total security over the rich, the powerful, and the nervous. 'The Invisible Wall,' he called it. Old Kuhne liked the expression. 'That's what I call marketing,' he said triumphantly to Craxton. The phrase became their slogan.

At this point, Richmonde was considered ready for London. C & K already had offices there run by a trusted

British operative who was, they felt, better employed supervising the day-to-day business of security rather than planning the selling strategy of the company. The plan was that Tony should go over, find his feet as head of Marketing, and develop profitable areas for diversification, leaving the operative Bidwell to supervise existing activities in the field.

The scheme nearly fell apart, however, before they left the States. Joanie met the ecological Margaret and almost refused to come to London, such was the impact of their friendship. This was bleak news to Old Kuhne, who instructed Tony to get his wife off her butt, and Tony only managed to persuade her to come by promising her a country cottage and urging Margaret to be their guest any time she liked.

Joanie finally agreed, with some surprise help from Margaret, who it seemed was anyway planning a trip to Europe and liked the idea of having somewhere to stay. Thus, as soon as they arrived in London and almost before they had taken an apartment, she was off looking for a suitable place in the country to grow potatoes and cannabis, which indeed she found with quite extraordinary dispatch (and at a quite extraordinary price, but no matter, Old Kuhne was paying for it), taking up residence with the same relentless impetuosity.

To Tony's mind, this arrangement could not have been better. The cottage, near Henley, was idyllically placed even by city-lovers' standards; it would appreciate in value; and it would keep Joanie out of his hair.

As for the office, everything was fine. It was clean, it was neat, it was in a good position. There was only one drawback: very little business. He had known it would be so, naturally, since it was the reason for his presence, but in a strange country – and by God it was strange, all the more so for speaking a remotely similar language – without a heritage of English contacts for getting things done, even Tony felt a momentary pang of self-doubt. Just how was he going to get this thing moving? He felt all the loneliness of a well-fed flea in a laboratory.

Whenever in the past he had experienced such depressive twinges – and it was seldom – Tony had always found that a night on the town produced a cheering effect.

Even Tony, prone to self-esteem as he was, had not considered that this was necessarily an original remedy. A large meal, a bottle or two of wine, these things are noted for doing wonders for morale: the very lack of originality removes any possible sense of strain or disappointment. The grateful throat, the lickerish tongue, the respective stomach, what reliable organs of pleasure they are. For though the act of sex may induce a sharper delight, it is more momentary, more dependent on a second party. A filet de boeuf en croûte never rolls over in bed, lights a cigarette and comments uncharitably on the technique of your knife and fork. Likewise the Sole Véronique does not enquire why you have been tasting other dishes. This, anyway, was the line of Tony's reasoning.

But, greedy man that he was, he was not content with the undemanding pleasures of the table. Sure, he and the operative Bidwell (a man of neutral personality, as befitted his calling) started the evening with an excellent dinner at the Brasserie in Stratton Street where Tony ate and ogled happily till eleven, but then he took it into his head that he wanted an English girl.

Bidwell, in spite of his muted manner, seemed to have the operative's repertoire of places to go, so they did a tour of two or three louche establishments, and nearly ended up with two ex-stable girls with galloping breasts in a topless bar in Mayfair, only to be put off by the final obstacle of the price – London in those days was as expensive as anywhere in the world. Not that Tony and

Bidwell could not have afforded it but it was the principle of the thing. Rip-off merchants are the last people to suffer rip-offs gladly.

So Bidwell took him on to the Mome Rath, a newly opened and nearly fashionable gambling club with a décor in the manner of Tenniel, and here Tony fell in love. They had girl croupiers at the Mome Rath, and the management had evidently gone out of its way to select a superior class of lady for the job. They were all pretty, they all seemed to have been to finishing schools in Switzerland, and they all looked at you with a gaze that was candid, polite and unapproachable. Tony would gladly have settled for any of them, but straying idly by a roulette table, he glanced across at the girl who presided, and decided there was only one croupier for him.

At this point, Bidwell's bleeper sounded, and he indicated that he would have to leave him. Tony scarcely noticed.

She was blonde, of course, he liked blondes. She was of medium height, finely featured, her breasts were definitely Ogens, and he somehow knew, even under the long black skirt she was wearing, that her legs were authentic Chippendale.

He stood for a moment, imagining the value.

She looked at him as he paused and, yes, there was an invitation in her steady blue eyes – not the brash come-hither of a hooker but a calm amusement that indicated that she might and then again perhaps she might not. It rather depended on whether she decided he was a frog or a prince and she hadn't got as far as that yet.

He was, on the face of it, not an unattractive man. A wise American would have seen quite soon that he was shallow, opportunistic, bumptious, greedy, every inch a frog, quite possibly a toad. But then a wise Englishman would have noted that the girl was not quite all Tony had cracked her up to be. The two cultures find it difficult to digest each other – like those dung scarabs in Australia that can only cope with the native marsupial turd, puffy and fibrous, and are thrown into confusion by the more solid pats of the European bovine.

'Would you like to play?' she asked, and her accent seemed pure Burberry. Tony played energetically and lost £300, but it didn't matter. He knew the Rath closed at four, so at three fifty he asked her if she'd like to join him for a drink. She replied, semi-ventriloquistically, conscious of the bouncers who seemed to be becoming interested in their corner, that she wasn't allowed to associate with customers but she would meet him for breakfast at the Cavendish Hotel off Jermyn Street.

Over eggs and bacon, she told him that her name was Chloe, and no she wouldn't go to bed with him. Thereafter, except at most weekends when he had agreed to pay duty visits to the cottage, he saw her almost every day. She was, he had to confess, something of an enigma to him, and he was astute enough to realize that this was a deliberate policy on her part. He did not try to find out more about her. He knew that in good time it would be revealed, just as, in good time, she would share his bed.

Patience was the last thing his acquaintances would have expected of him, but in a couple of months it paid off. One spring evening, after she had given him dinner at her maisonette, with the dog snuffling outside in the garden under the West London moon, she had suddenly turned down the light, lain down on the shaggy white rug in her living room, pulled up her skirt and done that neat imitation of a hard-nosed New Yorker. She was wearing nothing underneath her skirt, and insisted that he take her there, basely, on the rug.

The strange thing was that he had taken many women in his life but this was the first time he had found himself actually giving something in return. He did not realize, of course, that (among other things) she had finally decided that he was in love with her, and that she could now afford to sleep with him. Nor did he immediately register that the interlude on the shaggy rug had elicited a fatal flaw in his character. Previously, he had been an archetypal shit, but the affair with Chloe had discovered in him dangerous virtues. Thoughtfulness, a degree of constancy, even patience itself.

A little good in a really bad person puts him just about on the same level as everybody else. The totally evil man is closed, self-contained, psychopathic, cannot be breached with normal appeals to decency, love, duty, honour, or any of that insidious armoury of social guilt-inducers. But Tony was now at risk. While he attended to his unsavoury job, while he busied himself building up an empire from which he alone would profit, he was also studying ways to please his mistress and learning the unsettling disciplines of consideration. He had even started to ask himself what she saw in him, a self-questioning that had never crossed his mind before and which has unhinged even stouter souls than potential media magnates.

Part of his method of pleasing her was to spend a great deal of money, which, after a couple of months, began to introduce its own problems. He was well paid by the company but, even so, a gold bracelet, a necklace, a little Pissarro from the Parkin Gallery that someone had told him was a bargain, seats at the theatre, nightclubs, dinners, lunches at the Bell at Aston Clinton, a little gambling (not at the Mome Rath), all added up to more than mere salary could afford.

Admittedly, it wasn't all spent on Chloe. Sometimes, he had to take out other girls simply to relieve the insecurity Chloe induced in him. It didn't help but it didn't stop him doing it.

No, the only real source of income now would be the introduction of new business to the surveillance side of the operation. It would be some months before the advertising scheme could come on line. What luck or rather what forethought that he had managed to get himself on to a commission basis deal with Old Kuhne for any new business he introduced!

On this front, he had to admit, when he examined it in any kind of detail, the situation looked problematical. The selling potential of the organization had, under Bidwell, hardly been activated at all. The London office in the past had simply serviced trans-Atlantic contracts for sports stars, screen celebrities, perhaps the occasional tycoon, and one or two East Coast based companies setting up in the UK, but had missed out entirely on the European and Middle Eastern market. This he had anticipated. But he had not fully appreciated the extent to which other security organizations had already moved in.

Tony had tried a number of likely leads – oil sheikhs who were reported to be newly arrived, heads of pan-Continental consortia, Italian motor magnates, Greek shipping tycoons, German chemical moguls – but everywhere he looked, he found the contract was already sewn up. He tried the other end of the market, lunched with the IRA, drank endless cups of coffee with Iranians, had meetings on park benches with Gaddafi's people to try and get a lead on the metropolis's index of soft underbellies, but he found they were spoken for already. The Mafia were curt to the point of rudeness.

Thus it was that he found himself now tapping his teeth with his Cartier pencil – a present from Chloe, the traffic was not totally one-sided – and reviewing possible TV advertisements in an effort to hurry along the media operation.

'DermaFair Padettes take a shine to your eyes . . .'

The Sony U-matic reached the end of its reel, clicked, whirred, and ejected, leaving its viewers with a sense of surfeit.

'Watching undiluted advertising is like eating stock cubes,' said Hugo perhaps a shade over-cleverly (Tony did not like having smart-asses around him), 'rich but not satisfying.'

'Never mind that,' Tony snapped. 'How long is it going to take to get this thing off the ground?'

'I dunno, mate.'

'Well, goddammit, you should know. You're in charge of this project.'

Hugo's stage cockney always irritated Tony more than he cared to think about. Come to think about it, quite a number of things had been irritating him lately. He put it down to the end of winter.

'Had a touch of the cardiacs up at EMI this morning,' said Hugo, cockily. 'Thought for a minute they were on to our idea.'

Tony didn't like the 'our'. It was his idea.

'But they weren't?'

'Not yet. But we've got to move quick or we'll be ripped off. That's why I've organized this little presentation, haven't I?'

'Have you?'

'Well, not yet, mate, give us a chance. Only got the latest research through this morning. We'll do a song and dance to launch the idea. Slides, reels, charts, the lot. We'll ask round a select group of prospective customers, give 'em drinks, you show 'em the works, I sign 'em up, and then we take the genuine punters down to dinner at Mome Rath's. What d'yer say? We can have it all together by the summer.'

'Are we ready for that yet? You got all the information, the uh data you need?'

'It'll be ready by then.'

Tony got up from his chair and paced.

'Not Mome Rath's,' he said.

'As you wish, squire. Scarab's.'

Tony paced some more. Summer wasn't soon enough. He needed money quicker than that. And why the hell did *he* have to do it? Hugo was the executive in charge, wasn't he? In his book, he should never have to do anything. The successful manager delegates. It leaves him more room for a fallback situation. He put the question to Hugo.

'In this business, squire, it's all personality. You're the geezer who thought of the idea, you're the geezer what's got to tell 'em, ain't yer? If I looked like the golden boy, why then they'd all come to me, they won't want to know about you. Very clannish, us Brits.'

He supposed on this occasion he was right. Lucky they were so naïve. In Hugo's shoes, he'd have quit his employer without so much as a tremor, and indeed that was what he had in mind when the moment came. The more he thought about it, the more he liked the idea. There was too much hustling in the surveillance racket. Sure, the rewards were high, but he loved the notion of setting up a machine, a system for making money that would simply run. In surveillance, you kept having to start again as your clients died (whether naturally or violently), became bankrupt, went mad, or simply decided they didn't care.

And, dammit, surveillance was dangerous. One of Bidwell's London operatives, there were only six in all, had recently collected a couple of shattered kneecaps on a lousy delivery job which someone had ambushed, quite possibly a rival company who wanted the contract – luckily they were able to ship him over to Belfast General Hospital, where they had perfected a replacement technique, thus proving that the situation in Ireland was not all bad as the Brits seemed to make out – but it was indicative. Next time it might be a ruptured spleen or a hole in the head, and Belfast had not yet come up with a solution to that one.

Next time it might be him.

'All right, squire? You on, then?'

'OK, Hugo, OK. I'll put it in the diary. First week after May Day. I'll give 'em the line. Just point me in the right direction and I'll shoot. But I'm leaving the admin to you, OK? I don't want to know the problems, I just want results. You're on the line. OK?'

'Fine, squire, that's the way I like it. Leave it with yours truly.'

'You're a shit, Hugo, d'you know that?'

'It takes one to know one, squire.'

At this point, his secretary came in with some letters, and Hugo withdrew with his usual cheeky 'Ta-ra.' Tony thought it would really give him a great deal of pleasure to be rid of him, but he couldn't lose him for the moment.

He opened his mail. His credit card needed to be paid, his bank wished to point out that he was overdrawn, his wine merchant respectfully suggested that his bill was three months outstanding, and a casino manager was rather less polite. He always had his bills sent to his office – it somehow made them seem not quite so close to home – but this was too near whichever way you looked at it. Tony made a sound that his acquaintances were rarely privileged to hear. It was a sort of little sigh. In all conscience (a department he had only just opened), and perhaps more pressingly in all prudence, he could not put all his owings down to expenses for, until his probationary period was up, they still nominally had to be approved by Bidwell.

He thought of asking Joanie for a loan (not only was her father rich but her mother had been an heiress in her own right), but he knew that, like many who have not earned their money, she was reluctant to part with it, fearing that, once gone, she would never know how to replace it. Early in their married life they had had a number of arguments on the subject, and Tony knew that if he were going to benefit from her, his approach had to be oblique and never urgent.

He could, of course, have suggested to Chloe that they

lower their standard of living – spaghetti and Valpolicella, say, rather than châteaubriant and Nuits Saint Georges – but the insecurity of the lover possessed him, and he sensed that if she knew he were less than rich, she might well feel less than committed. It was a sense more of superstition than certainty but, after all, that is what love is about.

He was driven to ask his secretary to bring in the New Business file again – a folder open to all within the organization. It did not make encouraging reading. There was, at the end of it, just one fresh suggestion that had been typed upon a single sheet, which indicated an area that had not yet been essayed. It simply read: 'Query pre-emptive soften-up sample situation with ref in-depth follow-up.'

Yes, whoever it was was speaking his language. The best way to alert the attention of a would-be client to your services would be to give him some kind of scare (not letting on that it came from yourself, of course) the day before you called.

Why hadn't he thought of that before? In marketing terms, it was simply the reinterpretation of that old classic, the sampling drop.

He called in his secretary again. She was a neat girl from Muswell Hill whose only vice was potted plants.

'Laura, come in, would you? Who typed this, d'you know?'

'No, Mr Richmonde, never seen it before.'

He nodded to her and she returned to her dwarf jungle.

A mystery, then, but whoever it was had his best interests at heart. The suggestion was certainly a viable notion which he himself would put into operation, not even informing the Chief Operative of his plans (by this means securing even greater credit for himself when he brought in the contract).

As he turned the sheet of paper musingly in his hands,

his eye fell on something else. There was a second typewritten inscription on the other side of the page in what looked like identical typescript. But whereas the first suggestion earned the author maximum points in Tony's Brownie Book, the follow-up struck him as being frivolous and even irresponsible.

It simply read: 'Are you being followed?'

Of course he wasn't being followed. Who would want to follow him? And had he not sat in on the tailing course at Old Kuhne's school for operatives in Atlantic City? He could shake off more tails than a menagerie of skunks.

And yet . . . and yet . . . there had been the incident of the potato last month . . . and how about the flat tyre at the cottage? . . . insignificant in themselves but perhaps significant links in some kind of chain. And hadn't the milk left outside his door that morning, normally so innocently, so unswervingly white, today for some unaccountable and indeed grotesque reason been an intense, a leprous, a toad-like green?

Maybe someone was trying to tell him something. Or maybe he was just letting things get on top of him. Whichever way, it would never do to let the company know.

He removed the sheet from the file and locked it in his desk. Green milk? The idea was too ridiculous to think about.

16

When I returned to my quarters at the World's End, after my exploits at Cowden, a wave of melancholy hit me and carried me on in its trough for several weeks. It was as unexpected as it was prolonged.

The soldier, of course, must endure misfortune and privation, these are his meat and drink. But unless a loving heart is waiting for him at home, all his risks and escapades may seem as naught, withered may be the garland of his war, and he may have excuse at times to brush away a tear. There were no alleviating touches of a feminine hand to welcome me back to Driffield Street. It was a mood I knew I should have to arm myself against, but try as I might I could not shake myself out of it.

I spent a week or so reading *Little Dorrit*. What a master is Dickens, with his picture of bureaucrats in the Circumlocution Office 'where the great question is, why it should not be done'! Things have not changed at all, have they?

By the middle of April, I was able to leave lethargy behind, make my way over to Cadogan Square and, while the porter strolled off towards the nearest newsagent, no doubt to acquire further insight into the female anatomy – he would give himself a heart attack if he went on like that, I have seldom seen a man so out of condition – I was able to slip up to Richmonde's penthouse and introduce a hypodermic squirt of lichen dye, I have it made up myself, into the bottle of milk standing outside his door.

It turned the most satisfactory hue. Totally harmless, I assure you. You could drink it, but the colour is so violent you would not wish to.

Now you may say, and I would have some sympathy with you if you did, that transmuting a bottle of milk into the semblance of loathsome slime is hardly going to unsettle any but the most dyed-in-the-wool faintheart, and the American Richmonde did not yet by any means qualify for that category, but I must ask you to take all my actions in this matter as part of a pattern.

Imagine if you will the American, frowsty with having drunk a little too much whisky the night before while sitting up chatting with some colleague, a disagreeable taste in his mouth, eyes almost closed with blear, mouth agape like a stranded cod, aching for a cup of coffee. He totters to the door, he puts out a hand, he grasps the bottle, thumbs off the bottle top, splashes the liquid into his mug and maybe even takes a sip before he sees that what he has poured into his boon beverage looks like snakes' bile. He dashes it away from his lips with a cry of fear and loathing.

Even if it does not work out quite as I have depicted, even if it is simply an irritating, a puzzling hiccup in his morning, something the porter (prised from his splayed crotches) cannot explain, it serves to inculcate a sense of surmise as well as inflicting a passing humiliation in front of a witness.

Oh yes indeed, I have better things for you, but as with any carefully considered feast, the good chef never goes straight into the main course. Nibbles and titbits first, or as my dear mother used to say: 'You can't have your cake until you've eaten your bread and butter.'

A car tyre here, a mislaid docket there, a mysterious stain on a carpet, a smell in the drains, these are the first courses of the banquet, auguring better things to follow. And so for the next few weeks I devoted myself to these canapés.

Two further details will suffice to show the nature of my pranks. A grass-snake inserted into a newly-delivered laundry box was certainly not the most original of my inspirations, but it did serve to keep the pressure on the target. Perhaps more entertainingly, a week later I had half a hundredweight of evil-smelling coley delivered to his front door in a trunk.

Oh, of course he would arrange to have them removed but they had to sit outside on the landing all weekend until he returned, causing considerable embarrassment to him as well as offence to the neighbours, who numbered among them a peer of the realm and a pop star – strange bedfellows, but there you are, this is the pass to which we have come.

Just when he would be becoming vigilant, I gave it all up and let him relax again, the way Intelligence treated the Ming Yuan (fifth column of Chinese who worked on the rubber estates, eyes and ears of the CT) softly softly catchee coolie, some we were able to persuade to work as double agents against their own people, some we just treated the way the CTs did, nailed them up on their rubber trees – or if we didn't we said we would – they came round in the end, it is all a matter of timing.

As for the serious part of the feast, though I did not yet know exactly what shape it would take, reconnaissance and more reconnaissance had to be the discipline.

I went back to Wardour Street and kept watch on the building where Richmonde worked from the Post Office across the road. How Post Offices have changed, have they not, since the days of yore! Gone are the keen attentive youngsters and the benign old postmasters, the apple-cheeked grannies and the comfortable matrons, the helpful booths and the familiar dispensations. Now it is simply: 'You're in the wrong queue, can't you read?' though since there are no signs directing you to the prison-visitor-like grilles, it is hardly a matter of literacy, as I pointed out to someone who scarcely seemed to speak the language anyway. You cannot even despatch a telegram now (I had had it in mind to send Richmonde some piece of drollery). All is symptomatic, is it not?

However, I had not come to cavil or reminisce, and I mingled obediently enough with the pensioners and Indians East and West who now seem to be the principal customers, pretending to fill up one of the more encyclopedic forms so beloved of our desk-wallahs. Dickens, where are you now? I spent many days in this Post Office, suitably disguised as a semi down-and-out, and came to the conclusion that though always crowded, it was always full of the same people, a phenomenon ideally suited to my purpose.

I noted in these patrols that much of the traffic from Purbeck House consisted of film cans, and that these were constantly being taken round the corner to Livonia Video Studios, whence they appeared to emerge again in a few hours accompanied by small rectangular black cassettes. I followed one such consignment at a discreet distance, and it was as I suspected – a transfer took place within Livonia Studios from film to videotape. I actually heard the receptionist discussing the consignment with the youth who brought it in. Here, to the trained eye, like a broken sapling in the jungle, was an incontrovertible pointer.

Next day I dressed in the attire of an out-of-work caretaker – centre parting, dusty hair, cardigan and brown coat – and proceeded to the portals of Livonia Studios enquiring whether they might have a job of any kind, caretaker, porter, warehouseman or similar. They had no doubt received many similar enquiries in these lean times, but they were courteous enough and said they would let me know (I gave them my special poste restante address). It was a long shot, no more, but I spoke of my military service with some authority, and a big man with a beard who happened to be standing in the vicinity, signing some papers, turned round at my mention of Singapore.

'You were in Malaya?'

'I was, sir. Royal West Londons. '54 to '57. Seconded to Special Operations, Jungle Warfare Instructor at Kota Tinggi. National Service but extended to Short Service. Sir.'

'I was out there. East Surreys. '56 to '57. You might even have trained me.'

A manky mob but I did not expand.

'Quite possibly, sir,' I said, and then on clearer ground: 'It's a long way from Wardour Street.'

'It certainly is. Do you see that the Malaysian government is forbidding people out there to buy British now?'

'We should've let the CTs have a crack at 'em, sir.'

'Leave your name. We'll see what we can do.'

I left with military step, and enrolled at a Night School video course in West Brompton that same evening. Here I familiarized myself with the mysteries of a trade that to the outsider may seem as impenetrable as the secondary jungle, rife with belukar scrub and wait-a-bit thorns, but which the initiate knows may be circumvented with a little experience and a great deal of commonsense, a quality I had honed to razor sharpness under the shade of the rambutan tree.

This then was the way I laid my preparations. Though perhaps plodding and unspectacular, it is always the groundwork that counts.

By day, I continued my observation of the American, and was fortunate enough to obtain various revealing insights into his character and occupation in the course of the following weeks. One of my best sources of information was his own office staff whom I followed into cafeteria and bar. Talk about security, they would not have lasted a day up the Yum, but 'security' seemed to be part of Richmonde's daily bread, albeit, I learned, in a desk-bound capacity. Whatever they meant by it, it meant that my own security must be tighter than a Boogie Street G-string.

I also discovered that he went out with other women; the blonde was not his only peccadillo. Men, the Bard tells us, were deceivers ever, and perhaps I should have become used to the idea, but it made my blood boil to see him playing fast and loose when he already had a peerless specimen of English girlhood his apparently for the asking, as well as a kaftaned spouse. The man was incorrigibly greedy.

Speaking of his wife, I found out something about her which gave me quite a turn. One hears about these things but one never thinks it can be real, Queen Victoria was of my opinion. I would not have believed it possible, but stealing out to Cowden one night in late April to further my reconnoitres, I actually saw her embracing her friend Margaret in a manner that I can only describe as fulsome. I was observing through a chink in the French window draperies after one of my many familiarization courses of the wood when I saw it, and I am very glad to say that I could not see it all. They appeared to be scantily clad. It was not a sight calculated to refresh the spirit. After the shy grandeurs of the wood in spring to be confronted with a spectacle of such warped disnature was almost more than flesh and blood could stand. Familiarization was not the word for it. I had difficulty restraining myself from rapping on the window.

What has got into people nowadays? The aborigine I can understand. He sits with his people under the duriam tree at a certain time of year and eats the duriam fruit. It is meant to be an aphrodisiac. The smell is disgusting. He eats, he fornicates, then he passes on to the next tree, and so on until the crop is finished. Then the fornication is over. He settles down and leads a normal existence. But we, who are meant to be civilized, are more like apes on heat, all the time on heat, we are at it all the time.

It was clear that they would have to be encouraged to leave before the rot could spread.

As I drove home in the faithful Traveller, vast designs were forming in my mind which I truly believe the Little Corporal himself would have applauded.

17

Tony Richmonde, like a true marketing man (a stick-insect sort of creature with the ability to identify temporarily with whatever twig of industry he happens to have settled on), had only taken upon himself the aspects of C & K's product that he felt was necessary for the discharge of his duties. 'You don't have to know how to grow cane,' he would say, 'to sell molasses.'

It meant that, though he had equipped himself with a superficial knowledge of the techniques and gadgetry of surveillance, he was by no means up to operational standards himself. It would have been idle to send him out personally to guard your payroll or negotiate with your blackmailer because, apart from the fact that he would all the time be mentally transferring the action into chart form for presentation, it was exceedingly doubtful whether he had the requisite mental and emotional qualifications for the task, being of an impetuous and restless nature always eager for the quick return, to say nothing of the necessary courage.

Tony was essentially verbal. Reality only resided in his ability to express it. Thus, though it was possible he might some time have to put the dangerous charade suggested in the New Business file into effect, his first instinct when faced with a challenge was to explore some conversational avenue.

'What we're going to do,' he said to Chloe, 'is to have a party, very select, very ambienceful. You know? I just had a drink with one of our consultants, travels in the Middle East, he says there's this Lebanese guy, pal of his, coming to live in London . . . and he's loaded. Seems like no one else knows he's coming, and I want to get in first with a welcoming party. If I can't sell him a complete surveillance package, I'll wipe my ass with my contract.'

Chloe looked at him thoughtfully. She often looked thoughtful like that but you could never tell what she was thinking; it was one of the things he liked about her, classy, so often with girls they never stopped talking. He objected to other people opening their mouths too much, it eroded his sense of monopoly.

Yes, Chloe was different all right. For instance, he'd asked her about her family, the gracious silver-haired father, the faded once-beautiful mother always in the country house garden with the secateurs and roses, but while Chloe had smiled at his description, she had not come forward with any concrete information. It was as though she wanted to keep him out of her family group, a temporary snapshot, not something to be stuck in with paste and captioned, or silver-framed and placed lovingly on the grand piano.

'Are you ashamed of me, honey?' he had kidded, at least he thought he was kidding. 'Is it because I'm, you know, married?' It was a measure of the change that had come over him that he could suggest, even in pleasantry, that anyone could be ashamed of him.

'Uh-uh,' she had shaken her head. 'It's just that I don't like being crowded. Everyone always wants everything at once. We've got some Present now. Later we'll have some Past. And then we'll see if we've got some Future.'

There was something oracular, fascinating, about her when she made pronouncements like this, although Tony had once come across something similar to what she had just said in some syndicated story in a women's magazine – not his customary reading but he was marketing pop albums at the time – anyway it was a great line and it satisfied him for the moment. She had this ability to divert his course of thinking: an abstracted gaze, a vague answer, and he would suddenly find himself at right-angles to his conversation. She was doing it again right now.

He had told her everything about himself, everything that he could regard as creditable, there was no need to rake shit, not that he could see much of that as he looked back over his life. His small-town boyhood in Ohio, his father a drugstore owner called Reichmann who had changed his name to Richmonde in the war (Tony edited that bit out), his mother who earned extra money as a dressmaker, his boredom at high school, his Business Studies course at university, his sudden access to fame with a trainee position at a Manhattan advertising agency after winning a competition in a business magazine, and his rise to prosperity through a dozen blue-chip marketing companies (at least he said they were blue-chip and who'd know the difference?) ending with a salary now of $120,000 a year.

It made, he thought, an impressive story, and because he had told it often he told it well, but Chloe didn't seem to be all that impressed.

'Real money,' she said, 'isn't salary, is it, Ant?'

She called him Ant because of his name, his feverish business activity, and the muscular strength of his jaws, she said.

'Well uh yes, I guess you have to be right. Capital comes into it some place.'

She had diverted him again.

'Tell me,' he said, 'why do you love me?'

She had never said that she did, but even if she had, it was something even Tony knew one should never ask. 'Because you're quite rich, Ant,' she said, laughing, 'and you're going to be richer.' It was his philosophy entirely, but somehow he wished she hadn't said it. On the other hand, perhaps she was joking – you could never tell with Chloe.

Chloe, like many attractive women, was more straightforward than she looked. It was just one of those accidents of fate that men should happen to view her obliquely. For her part, she recognized in Tony a kindred spirit. Now she'd come to know him better, she saw the two of them as brightly coloured beetles, the sort she used to watch on Chippingham Ponds, water-boatmen, skimming along the surface, or maybe dragonflies, brilliant but not honeymakers.

You could call it compatibility of a sort, she reflected, but was that what was going to make her happy?

Ridiculously, she was beginning to feel restless again. That spirit of not wanting to be pinned down, having her options open, she knew it was a fatal flaw, that it was why she wasn't married now and settled down – she'd had her offers – but there she was, she couldn't help it, always looking for something, like the princess in the fairy tale, forever searching for the man who could make her smile. Ant couldn't make her smile but perhaps he could make her comfortable, and he might just be the last good opportunity she had. She was tired of working in casinos.

'What d'you think, honey?' he was saying. 'Do we have a party? Are we in business?'

'Where are you going to hold it?' she asked.

He liked that. In England, you hold a party. In the States, you throw it. If anyone back home wanted to know the difference between them and us, that was it in a phrase. They hold, we throw. Good, huh?

'Why, my place, I guess.'

She frowned.

'What is it, honey?'

'Do you really want me to get involved?'

'What d'you mean? Of course I want you to get involved.'

'Won't they think it strange, you being married to the boss's daughter, and then turning up with someone else?'

'Honey, this is business. They've never met Old Kuhne.

This guy's a rich Lebanese. He's moving out because of the violence out there, he just needs a little security, a little reassurance, a little party. He doesn't want to see my Marriage Licence.'

'Who else would you ask?'

'Well, no one from the office, that's for sure. I want to play this my way. The marketing guy I told you about is over, so we'll have him. He won't make any trouble so long as we find him a girl to sit next to – ask a friend, would you? And then maybe I'll ask that hotel chief's son, the one we met the other night with a model wife.'

'A model wife?'

'I mean she's a model and his wife.'

'Ah. Not Hugo, then?'

'For God's sake, Hugo least of all.'

Chloe brightened. She did not like Hugo. She had been taken advantage of by people like Hugo. Hugo, for all his cockney affectation, could see through to her lack of background like a laser. There was something rather comical about Tony's naked ambition, like a nude cupid, it almost gambolled, but Hugo's was so cold it was obscene.

'Ant?'

'Yeah?'

'Why don't we have it at my place? There's something about your flat, I'd have the feeling your wife might walk in at any moment. Besides, I'd feel happier doing the cooking in my own kitchen.'

She liked the idea of playing the big business hostess in the manner of an American television series. Indeed, she had devised her maisonette with intimate gracious dinner parties in mind.

'Why, you don't have to do any cooking, honey,' Tony remonstrated. 'We'll get it brought in from La Gavroche or some place.'

'If it's my place, I'm doing the cooking.'

He was almost about to say that the area she lived in might be a touch down-market for a millionaire, but he suppressed the suggestion with a crippling surge of tact. What the hell, you could never tell with millionaires, they might even think it was kind of cute.

'Just as you say, honey.'

'Do you know anything more about this man, what's his name?'

Tony pulled out his chequebook, where all the notes he felt he really might want to read again were made.

'His name is Selvan, Henri Selvan. He's a Christian, he is married, he has three children all at boarding schools in Switzerland, he has interests in oil, wine, chemicals and shipping. But his real thing's wallpaper. He wallpapers the world, would you believe that?'

But Chloe was not to be deflected.

'Anything else? Any other interests? We ought to do something special if we're going to impress him. Something to amuse him. You know? A little entertainment. More than just a dinner.'

'Max says he's into magic. Astrology and all that crap.'

'Well that's it, then.'

'What's it, honey?'

'We'll have a magician.'

'I can't stand those guys. You know? Rabbits and pigeons . . .'

'Not that sort,' said Chloe scornfully. 'Really, you are slow, Ant. A proper magician. I went to a party last year where they had a clairvoyant in a back room. All the guests went in to see him.'

'I can't stand clairvoyants.'

Tony was feeling tense about the impending Lebanese. He had to get this one right.

'They're fun. Don't be such a stick in the mud, Ant. Anyway, everyone else seems to like them. Everyone wants to know about themselves, don't they? Except you, of course. You know about yourself already, don't you, Ant?'

'Yeah, I guess I do.'

'Well, then, don't stop other people. You don't have to see him. Come on, what d'you say? After dinner, he can sit upstairs and see them one by one while you fix the drinks and I put my feet up. It'll be a talking-point. Your man's bound to be impressed.'

Tony was won round. As a marketing man, he knew the value of games and diversions.

'OK, OK, sounds like a good notion. Where do we find a clairvoyant?'

'I'll ask around. But why not get your secretary on to it, anyway?'

Tony became quite taken with the idea the more they talked about it, his mental calculator already totting up the money he was going to make. A contract with the Lebanese could mean a personal commission to him of $25,000, which would immediately more than see him out of trouble.

A further thought struck him.

'Have you ever had green milk?'

'What on earth . . . Green milk?'

Chloe laughed. He had been rather afraid she would.

'No, seriously, there uh Chloe.'

She looked at him for the first time with something approaching astonishment.

'Are you feeling all right?'

'Yes, yes, fine. But I had this green milk delivered the other day. It was like alligator's vomit. I swallowed some before I noticed.'

'You had a hangover?'

'I was sitting up late with that marketing guy the night before, that's all. I just needed coffee.'

'How did it taste?'

'Oh, fine. But the colour was terrible.'

'It must've been a joke.'

'Yeah, I guess so. But funny huh? And someone put this goddam grass-snake in my laundry. It peed on my clean shirts. And then there was all that fish. D'you think someone's monkeying around? It's not you, is it?'

It just could be, she had a sense of mischief. He was glad that he had come out with it at last. It had been preying on him slightly, he had a full plate at the moment.

She laughed again, giving away nothing.

'You're in the surveillance business. You find out. Have a word with your Bidwell.'

That, of course, was the last thing he wanted. Could you imagine the jokes in the office? Anyway, whatever its origins, the nuisance seemed to have stopped.

Chloe, though expert at giving nothing away, was irritated by his revelation. She knew who was responsible. It was the first time that Roy had stepped beyond observation into plain interference. She didn't want to tell Ant yet that she had been married before, indeed was technically still married (she had never so far felt the need for a divorce, and there was always the chance she might need alimony one day – early training had taught her never to throw away a windfall unless there was a better one just around the tree), so she thought it prudent to say nothing for a while, but it raised a whole number of disturbing possibilities.

Perhaps kicking up her legs on the goatskin had, after all, been a mistake.

18

My opportunity came, as I knew it would, out of the blue, but while always grateful to Dame Fortune for her handiwork, I would also point to the fact that I had my groundwork right. I was in the right place at the right time, the French Horn to be precise, across the road from Purbeck House, my regular lunch-hour listening post before going down to the Verde Valle later (the other centre for C & K clerical staff refreshment), when I heard the familiar tones of young Laura, the American's secretary, a nice girl with an affection for the vegetable kingdom which argued that her heart if not her occupation was in the right place, raised in some exasperation behind me.

'They've forgotten to water the spider-plant again,' she said.

It was true the landlord was remiss in that respect, but she should have got used to that by now. He did not water his beer, and one cannot suffer for the whole of Nature's kingdom. On this occasion, however, she did sound more than ordinarily exasperated.

'What's the matter, Lore? Boss get on your wick?'

I cocked my ear, while at the same time deploring the lapse in young girls' language since I was a lad. Give them a spell on the parade ground and a course in jungle warfare, and then they might have some right to swear like troopers.

'He's asked me to find him a clairvoyant for a party. Don't tell anyone, it's meant to be a secret. But, I ask you, where do I look for a clairvoyant?'

'In a crystal ball?'

I found the rejoinder apt, but Laura was not amused.

'That's not funny.'

Then, suddenly, it hit me. I almost did that trick with the amontillado down my trousers as enacted at the Bird in Hand all those weeks ago, but this time with a half of London Bitter, so great was my excitement, cool at all times though the soldier must be. Could it be that I was to be thus favoured?

It was true that my Jupiter was rising in trine with Venus that day. I had been watching the aspects closely as it happened: all seemed pointing to some major breakthrough with the Seventh House prominent and the Moon strongly aspecting my natal Sun (in Scorpio) in conjunction with Mercury the Trickster, the perfect auspices for stealth, guile and masquerade.

I nearly turned to her and offered my services there and then, but that of course would have been the act of a greenhorn – one never values what one finds too easily.

Her companion mentioned the name of an agency that supplied characters for many of the commercials that were filmed in the vicinity, and Laura made a note to call them that very afternoon. So did I.

Like many who have suffered loss and unhappiness, after my love was taken I myself turned to the World Beyond for solace. Apart from a night-school course in West Brompton in Astrology and Chiromancy, I had sat at the feet of Madame Palmyra and learned all she had to teach on the subject of reading the cards: numerology, prognostication, haruspication and the ball. Thus I was well equipped to cater for any such private function as the girl Laura mentioned, and would have no hesitation in putting myself forward. I would have to make stipulations, of course – however much I might disguise myself, I did not want to become too well known to Richmonde and his honeybee. I would insist that I only meet the guests, the aura of the host and hostess being so much part of the place's atmosphere that it would overwhelm the others'.

All this would merely add to the conviction of the thing, the more ornate the frame, the less we notice the brushwork. But to enter the enemy's kampong in person, to mingle and live awhile in his midst, only Corporal Ip, an SAS Chinaman, had ever achieved such a distinction. His feat is legendary.

Accordingly that afternoon I telephoned the agency the girl had specified, 'Plain Folk', specializing in 'real people' whatever that might mean, and told the woman that should anyone want a clairvoyant, I had both personality, appearance and experience in the art. I mentally earmarked for their files some pictures of a plumber friend of the family taken in 1954, not unlike me in a funny sort of way but at the same time different – you would never recognize me from them in my normal garb. Deception, you see, upon deception, this is what we find when Mercury is strong.

Once more, I gave my poste restante address and did not furnish a telephone number, explaining that the machine had adverse vibrations in the home. She swallowed it hook, line and sinker, and made an appointment for me to come in for an interview.

By the time this came up, three days later, I had made myself look almost uncannily like Uncle Arthur, that was his name, now deceased, with Fair Isle pullover, steel-rimmed spectacles, toothbrush moustache (I had to sacrifice the beard), brown teeth, hair parted down the middle. The only difference was the accessories: instead of wrench and blow-torch, I carried in my bag cards, charts, crystal and ephemeris, and nearly put in a toad for good measure – tools you might say of the trade.

I looked so convincing that I truly believed I could've got a job on an evening newspaper writing their daily Stars column, and indeed was offered three advertising roles, one of which I took on for appearances' sake, for a non-scratch wood-seal surface lacquer advert featuring a table-turning session. What will they think of next?

Finally, my patience was rewarded.

I was told to proceed to Number 44, Prosser Street, W.11, at 22.00 hours on Thursday, April 26th, well into Taurus but with Mercury well aspected. I need not stress the similarity between the date in question (April being the fourth month and 2 + 6 = 8) and the address, 2 being the Devil's own number, and 4 being a notably inauspicious configuration which we try to avoid in any residence. It is seventy per cent hocus-pocus, as I found at the feet of Madame Palmyra, but I little thought I would turn the ephemeral solace of my sorrows to such good use.

I repeated my stipulations regarding meeting the host and hostess. The agency said they would pass them on, and would I call later to confirm? My Venus indicated all would be well, and so it proved. My stipulations were agreed. I would be let in by a maid, and shown to a room where everything would be as I required. A guest list with brief notes would be forwarded. They clearly did not altogether trust my powers of divination, it seemed, but one takes what one is given.

I could scarcely conceal my elation – indeed, as there was no one to see it, I did not – nor a subsequent astonishment that where divination is concerned, people are so trusting. I could have been, indeed was, the most arrant of impostors. Though I knew all about the theory, I could not clairvoyant my way out of a telephone kiosk. Of course, the agency was a respectable one as such places go, but people never seem to doubt the integrity of the fortune-teller. He may be mistaken in his forecasts, or even quite unhinged, but they are extraordinarily reluctant to believe that he would ever deliberately dupe them. It is the next best thing to the clergy, and in some cases better; the aboriginal's relationship with his 'bomo' is much the same. At any rate, who was I to cavil at society's carte blanche?

I received the notes next day. They read as follows:

Henri Selvan. Lebanese, wealthy (wallpaper, oil, wine, shipping, chemicals), enthusiast re magic etc. Birthday 5.7.30. *Make him uneasy. Double your fee if you get this right.*
Mrs Iris Selvan. Greek/Lebanese, wife, gourmet, sceptical. 3 children. 17.3.37.
Mr Max Hertog. International business interests, keen tennis, sailor, girls, single. 4.2.36.
Miss Susie Wilkinson. Croupier, classical music, ballet, animals, single.2.6.58.
Mr Clement Cone. Hotel empire heir, collects esoteric pornography, married. 5.5.40.
Mrs Amanda Cone. Wife, ex-model, restless, just been to Coco Beach. 12.8.51.

It was clear what the American expected me to do, and he had furnished me with sufficient equipment to beguile the most sceptical among them – even if I had only known the rudiments of my craft, I could have convinced each one that I was the sibyl herself.

For a start, just to divert myself and give some scaffolding of truth to whatever deceits I should devise, I drew up each of the horoscopes in turn. They were much in line with the information provided, but then horoscopes always are, you can fit anything to them. The only thing I especially noted were the particularly favourable aspects in the chart of the man Selvan, but as this can also indicate death, I did not wish to make too much of it at this stage.

Strange is it not that death, so long regarded as the great enemy, is viewed by the circling heavens in a much more cheerful light? Of course, the circling heavens do not have to do any dying themselves, at least not for a billion years or so, which may account for their optimism.

Thursday came. I dressed in a sober lounge suit, selected a tie modestly festooned with the zodiac Scorpio motif, stilled my leaping heart by re-reading a short passage from my Jungle Warfare lecture to recruits, and, arriving at Prosser Street, squeezed my Traveller with some difficulty between two large foreign cars in front of the house, eschewing the vacant spaces in the lane at the side abutting onto the alleyway where the ragwort lay under its shroud of dog-turd. Although a million miles away in appearance from the rodent operative of before, I did not wish the troll-like sausage-maker to queer my pitch.

As I pushed the bell, I noted with satisfaction that my heart, if not now marching at steady Line Regiment pace, was hardly doing more than a Light Infantry quick step, and suddenly there I was, in the house, which smelt faintly of expensive perfumes and roast duck, being greeted by a little Filipino maid who with her little flat dark-brown features took me back for an instant to Port Swettenham and then into a small study-like room with a dressing-table and one single lamp stand burning upon it, ideal to my purpose.

I sat at the desk, unpacked my equipment and turned the lamp upon the door so that I was literally inscrutable, while the little maid withdrew to announce me below. The name I had given, incidentally, was Mr Frederick, Uncle Arthur's name. It seemed fitting. I recalled with a qualm that I had, perhaps over-enthusiastically, added to the latent interest in my trade by telling 'Plain Folk' that I was a research graduate in occult studies currently on leave from the University of Ghent, and no doubt they had passed this on. I doubted whether there was anybody with sufficient zeal at 'Plain Folk' to check up on me, and if they did, whether there was anyone at Ghent who could be bothered to unearth a list of graduates, but it was a gamble. Although painstaking attention to detail is everything, I comforted myself that there are still some risks which one has to accept.

The door opened.

I was prepared for evasive action if it had happened to

be mine host or hostess. With the light full on them so they could not see me, I should declare annulment of contract and leave. At this stage in the game, prolonged exposure to the principals was the last thing I required. The person who came through the doorway, however, was Amanda Cone. I could see at a glance that she had enjoyed a good dinner and was inclined to be equable, though with it she betrayed the arrogant yet diffident manner of a lovely woman who has had life pretty much her own way but has not been entirely satisfied with it.

'Pray be seated,' I said, feeling that a mildly archaic manner might well accord with my academic background.

'Thank you.'

We were off.

'Your birthday?' I asked, though I knew exactly what it was. 'I should say you were a Leo.'

She looked momentarily impressed, though she said she had the typical Leo forehead, and told me her age without, as we used to say on the ranges, aiming off for wind.

'You are restless,' I said, 'and yet you have only just come back from a journey to distant parts.'

She opened her eyes wide.

'How did you know?'

'Bermuda, wasn't it? No, no, wait, it's coming to me . . . the United States . . . I seem to get the Bermuda Triangle, though. Florida?'

She was hooked.

I read her cards, I calculated her chart, I told her she had a brilliant mind, that she under-employed her considerable artistic talent, and finally I read her hand.

The palm of a lovely woman is a very private place. There are a number of nerve-endings we do not find elsewhere. It is receptive, responsive, moist, almost like the very intimate regions of the female body which should not be talked about nor handled except with delicacy. We can walk on the moon but we do not know what it is like to have a female organ. It is a strange adventure. And stranger that a woman will give her intimate nerve-endings to be stroked by a mountebank simply in return for mumbo-jumbo and flattery, but there you are, we can never properly know them, as we can never know the flowers if we are constantly gazing at the stars.

I ran my fingers searchingly over the little lines of her Mount of Venus, telling her with some degree of accuracy what she wanted to hear, and noticing her become excited by my touch. I have delicate fingers for so active a man. It was quite shameful to see in an elegant lady; she kept shifting her seat and crossing her legs, and still she craned over and asked for more. Normally, in the throng and press, she would not have cared a tinker's cuss for my attentions, but because it was in the nature of the confessional, she yielded to my touch as if I had been Monsignor himself.

Finally, I became impatient. I had bigger fish to fry than this ornamental pouter.

'Is there anything more you need to know?' I asked severely. 'You have quite tired me out, and the night is not a quarter over.'

'Yes, Mr Frederick. Should I leave my husband?'

If she had expected any condoning from me of the breaking of the marriage vow, she had come to the wrong clairvoyant. I have made my views on the subject abundantly clear on many occasions, not to her, admittedly, but there are some opinions that simply speak through the pores, they breathe in the air, they shine in the light. I should not have thought that anyone would need to hear me enunciate on the subject. One look at me should be enough.

'You are very lucky to be married,' I said. 'Do not speak of this again.'

'But you have not met my husband yet,' she demurred.

'I do not need to meet your husband. What is the use of being a clairvoyant if you have to meet husbands? I know your husband already, as if I had met him. Go and have babies.'

She appeared quite delighted and, at last, retired, mumbling her thanks and smoothing down her frock. She left a strong, musky odour in the room which I was forced to open the window to remove, it was a clement night. I have found on some occasions it can induce a migraine.

The same pattern was to a greater or lesser extent repeated by all my successive clients. The men, of course, were less willing to be impressed, but they in turn were won by my evident acquaintance with their tendencies, my optimistic view of their capacities, and my general mastery of my trade.

The man Cone, husband of the melting beauty, seemed especially taken by the way I could pinpoint the subject of his collection and talk with some semblance of authority on the Nude in Magic and Ritual (thanks to a preparatory session the day before in Chelsea Library: one gets something back for one's Rates).

He appeared to be somewhat the worse for drink but quite affable. I daresay his wife drove him to it, in which case I had not done him a favour. He told me he did not know exactly why he had been asked to this particular dinner party but he said he found this was often the case.

As for the women, the fair young croupier, no doubt a colleague of Richmonde's concubine, gave me no problems at all apart from presenting rather more bosom than I would have done under the circumstances. I had serious fears for her décolletage as she craned over the table to see her Heart line while I prodded her mercurial finger under the lamplight.

Even the moustachioed Madame gave me a grudging endorsement to my skills – a Pisces with a brisk manner (which could be taken by the superficial as a sign of scepticism) and startled eyes. She was the only one in whose hand I discerned signs of imminent misfortune: when I inspected her life line there was a unmistakable what we call 'star', meaning death or accident to someone close. It is mostly rubbish. There were no 'stars' when Isobel was taken.

I did not mention this 'star' to her for fear of disturbing the peace, she was a motherly soul who spoke execrable English, but contented myself with talk of her children and, her corpulent figure betokening her love of the table, listed the better restaurants in London which I had culled from a gourmet's compendium.

Finally there was only her husband left.

When he entered, it was evident – even if I had not already known it – that he was exceedingly rich. No wonder Richmonde had gone to these lengths. It was plain to me that he was a prize catch. In person, he was a small spare man with dark hair and a nautical beard. He had that patina of the skin and watchfulness of the eye that is the hallmark of the king of the muck-heap, but, at the same time, I must admit, to give him his due, there was still a certain puckishness, a redeeming irresponsibility.

I nerved myself for the challenge. I was now in the firing line, a small thing perhaps for one who has heard CTs approaching along the game-tracks of the Tai, but taxing nonetheless. I wondered what sort of nutter he might prove to be.

It turned out, however, that he was not a nutter at all. His was not the anxious obsession with the occult that characterized the latter days of the Emperors Tiberius, Galba, Otho and Adolf Hitler. For him it was a game. Since nothing could reasonably be expected to go wrong with his material circumstances, it amused him to tinker with the Unknown. It was the only challenge left. It was clear at once that he would have preferred a full-blooded seance, but mercifully that was not included in my brief.

Ectoplasm, Madame Palmyra always used to say, can go either way, so I obliged as best I could with the means at my disposal. I gave him the cards, I did the numbers (he was a lucky ten), I debated his horoscope. He was a Cancer with Taurus rising, and an interesting cluster of Venus, Mercury and Neptune rising in ascendant. I was not too happy, I told him, with the Pluto afflicted in the 8th House, or his Uranus in opposition to his Moon, but then we cannot have everything.

I wrung the crystal ball as dry as a handkerchief.

I told him everything I knew and nothing that he did not. He was indeed an expert. Even if I had wished, I could not have made him feel insecure about his future. He knew it, literally, like the palm of his hand.

Finally, I stopped. I had no more to give.

He looked at me with amusement and interest, and asked me some questions about Ghent to which I gave increasingly evasive replies, the Library being short of stock in the Travel section at the time. Why had I not chosen Bruges?

'Dites moi,' he said, 'dites moi, Monsieur Frederick, you are good but you are not profound, and you are not a research graduate of Ghent or indeed of anywhere. Tell me, and I promise you I shall say nothing of this to our host and his charming lady . . . this is some kind of escapade, is it not? You see, in Magic, the true adept has a motto: "Nothing is as it seems." This whole party has been stage-managed, and you are part of the effect. He has asked you to say something to me but you have not done so. You may be sorry if you do not tell me – instantly.'

Suddenly I could see the menace in the man. Beneath the almost waggish manner there lurked a Mephistopheles.

I made shift to preserve my position under what was clearly superior fire. 'Keep your hair on,' I said. 'I was going to tell you anyway. He wanted me to make you feel insecure.'

The man suddenly relaxed and roared with laughter. I smiled politically. A laugh is not unlike a drink, it is unsocial not to join in the round.

'Ah. I understand. Thank you for your candour,' he gasped finally. 'If you ever wish to see some real magic you must call at my house. Good night, Monsieur Frederick.'

And with that he was gone. Frail vessels that the stars may be, on this occasion they had conveyed him perfectly. That Mercury and Venus in conjunction pointed to a rare combination of intelligence and acumen which I could never have hoped to bamboozle. I was glad not to have put his back up – he would be a dangerous opponent.

It was now time to extricate myself from my advanced position and, calling softly for the little Filipino, I collected my cheque, picked up my valise, and walked out into the night. The evening had not been without its rigours, but I could genuinely report that the audacity of the plan had been matched only by the artistry and fortitude of the execution.

As I shoe-horned the Traveller from its niche between the two leviathans, something seemed to cut off the light of the moon, I assumed it was merely an illusion, but when I turned I saw glaring eyes, cruel fangs, and spittle. For a moment, in my surprise, I imagined it might be something conjured by the man Selvan to teach me a lesson – the evening had been full of turn-ups – but as I stared in consternation, I recognized the lineaments of the dog Tory. Given the choice, I would have preferred an elemental.

I drove away at speed, his claws doing appreciable damage to my paintwork.

19

That Henri Selvan did not take up Tony's suggestion of a personal surveillance deal with Craxton & Kuhne was a considerable blow to Tony's expectations. He had regarded the thing as practically in the bag, and he was consequently resentful and alarmed.

'That guy,' he complained to his friend Max who was in the office for the morning before flying back East, 'he eats my dinner, he drinks my wine, he enjoys the show, but he doesn't come up with the goods. I thought you said he was a prime target.'

Max, who had spent an energetic night with Susie, could not throw much light on that or indeed any subject. He asked for a cup of coffee, swung his backhand thoughtfully, and wondered whether he had a rupture.

'I told you, Selvan's funded the Falangists. He's a prime target all right, but he doesn't seem to scare easy. He came down and said that guy you got, Fredericks or something, told him he had the best future of anyone he'd ever seen,' he offered.

'I thought we told that goddam little shit to put the fear of God into him. Laura?'

He pressed the intercom switch. There was a rustling of leaves. 'Yes, Mr Richmonde?'

'Put that goddam fern down and listen.'

'I'm listening, Mr Richmonde.'

'You are rustling.'

'I'm listening, Mr Richmonde.'

'If I say you are rustling, you are rustling. Like if you don't stop rustling, I'll rustle up a new secretary.'

'I have stopped rustling, I am now listening.'

'Did you try the agency Plain Folks?'

'Yes, Mr Richmonde.'

'And? C'mon c'mon.'

'They say they are sorry but they're unable to contact the man Frederick at the moment.'

'For chrissake, it's like everything else in this goddam country. In New York clairvoyants work twelve hours a day.' He had no evidence for this assertion, but it made him feel better. A further thought struck him. 'Can you contact Bidwell?'

'Mr Bidwell is out on a job at the moment.'

'He's always out on a job.'

'That's just as well, isn't it?' cut in Max. 'You don't want operatives hanging around. Remember Old Kuhne? "An operative in the office is an outfit out of pocket"?'

'Yeah, but I never know what he's doing.'

'That's security for you.'

'I'm meant to know what's going on around here.'

'Only in your department. Get that right, maybe you'll know everything. You ever had a hernia?'

'Have you finished now, Mr Richmonde?'

'Can you get me Mr Bracewell-Smith?'

'He said he was out beavering.'

'He better be right he is.'

'Would that be all, Mr Richmonde? I have some typing.'

'Yeah yeah, carry on, Laura.'

There was an admonitory click. The two men pondered their problems.

'What are you going to do about Selvan?' said Max, his problem being the more tractable (probably, he thought, merely varicocele, painful but unimpairing). 'It'd be a shame to let him get away.'

'Leave it with me, Max, huh? I'll be in touch. Thanks for the lead anyway.'

But when Max had gone, cradling his strained part with

hand in pocket, Tony continued to sit at his desk, scowling at the intercom, wishing the solution were as simple as he had airily made out. What he was now contemplating, he must do alone, darkly. No one must know of its planning nor have the opportunity for even a whisker of suspicion that he had been acting unprofessionally.

Unlocking a drawer, he took out a folder which contained a copy of a list of names and telephone numbers that he had extracted from Bidwell's desk one night when the Chief Operative was out supervising the installation of an in-store video monitor system, names and numbers that no doubt Scotland Yard would give its eye-teeth to get hold of, but which the surveillance operative would guard as his birthright, for without the Trots, criminals and terrorists who mainly comprised the list – along with one or two struck-off doctors, an illicit abortions clinic and a couple of greedy policemen – there would be no need of the surveillance industry at all. The goose might be unsavoury and aggressive but it was laying a golden egg. Cynical observers of the scene had also been known to wonder whether, without the surveillance industry, there might not be very much less terror.

Tony, of course, was very much on the outside of all the real action. As with the generals of the First World War, for the marketing man the battle is always in the distance, not in the carpeted office but far off on remote check-out counters amid the rattle of tills and the scream of dying brands. His is the long-term, the panoramic view. He exercises helicopter vision, ignoring the local cost of the engagement and pressing onward to the strategy ahead. There is no immediate pain. It is a world of figures and paper.

Thus, in lifting his outside telephone and calling Mr B. Umfreville of Brook Green, Tony (while aware that there was a certain risk and audacity in his plan) was in his own terms doing no more than calling in a specialist, just as he might use his advertising agency, to help him win an important store account.

Mr Umfreville was a mercenary, dormant at the moment following a particularly delicate series of negotiations between the London and Dublin governments that his clients were anxious to have concluded before launching into the next phase of mainland activity, and growing so bored in his bedsitting room that he was almost thinking of taking a job. So when the call came from the American, quoting his prearranged call-sign and suggesting a meeting, he was more than ordinarily accommodating.

'Certainly,' he said. 'Let us meet at my club.'

And he gave Tony an address.

The club turned out to be a dark back-room in a West Kensington lodging house smelling of oilcloth, Guinness and surprisingly chilli con carne – a Salvadorean who had recently come over to learn the latest techniques in electronic firing-devices had finally jibbed at Irish stew and had won many converts with the dish. Even now, though he had returned home, the fragrance lingered on.

The room contained, apart from an aspidistra that even the devoted care of a Laura could never coax back to life, three of the largest and knobbliest-looking men that Tony could ever recall having laid eyes on. They looked like enormous undertakers. One of them was black. He had never heard of a black Irishman.

At this stage, he was aware of having made a mild error in interview psychology. His tutor at Sales College had always stressed the advantages to be derived from physical dominance, even suggesting, though Tony was a good 5ft 11, that a pair of elevator shoes might add to his sales technique. He wished he had followed his advice and brought them with him now. Or else gone visiting the smaller-boned Iranians. However, he comforted himself, at least these people talked his language.

'Now then,' said Mr Umfreville, after he had introduced his colleagues Mr Toop and Mr Fitzgibbon, 'shall we go into conference? Mrs Twomey,' he suddenly opened the door and yelled.

'Yeh?' a distant voice proclaimed.

'I am in conference.'

'What the fuck do yer want me to do about it?'

Mr Umfreville shut the door again.

'A sterling woman,' he said. 'You could trust her with the Crown Jewels. Now then. Mr Richmonde is a friend of Mr Bidwell, boys, isn't that right, Mr Richmonde? A fine man, Mr Bidwell, we have always had the most cordial relations with him. I wish there were more about like him – not like some of the people we have to deal with, isn't that right, boys?'

Mr Toop and Mr Fitzgibbon rumbled their assent. It was like the shifting of furniture in an upstairs depository.

'Well uh I'm glad to know it, Mr Umfreville, but on this occasion I'm kind of making it a condition that Mr Bidwell does not get to hear of any agreement we might reach. I wish to give him a pleasant surprise.'

'That is perfectly all right with us, I assure you, Mr Richmonde. Discretion is the name of our game. The very fact that we are sitting comfortably together in the heart of London having this little chat must be a tribute to our ability to provide a confidential service. Would you like some tea? Mrs Twomey's rock-cakes would melt the heart of an Ulsterman. Mrs Twomey,' he shouted.

'What is it?'

'Tea and rock-cakes, if you would be so kind.'

'Get it yourself.'

'She loves having visitors,' he said, returning to his seat. 'You'll see, the rock-cakes will quite unman you.'

And indeed in they came, hardly two minutes later, with a very large brown teapot and four chipped mugs, carried on a tray by a tiny woman almost totally concealed by a head scarf, from which protruded a pair of thin lips and a cigarette.

'Hope it chokes yer,' she said as she retreated, the cigarette wagging in confirmatory semaphore.

'Shall I be mother?' Mr Umfreville said, his large hands obscuring the enormous pot. 'A rock-cake, Mr Richmonde?'

'I uh no thank you.'

'You are missing Paradise. You will forgive me if I indulge? Boys?'

The three men tucked into rock-cakes as if their lives depended on it.

Tony grew more and more impatient but did not like to say anything. If rock-cakes made them tractable, let them eat rock-cakes.

Finally, the man Umfreville wiped his lips. He enjoyed the rock-cake ploy. It always made them restless.

'My word,' he said, 'that was good. I swear she gets better all the time. We only allow ourselves rock-cakes when we are in conference. It makes us the more assiduous in our quest for new business. Now, Mr Richmonde, let us get down to the details of your esteemed order. We have a structured service at inclusive rates ex VAT which is very popular, or would you be more interested in one of our à la carte specialities? I think you will enjoy knowing us. We have recently had the services of a management consultant. Our customer relations are now second to none. Mr Fitzgibbon is our Race Relations Officer, so you can be quite at ease whatever your request.'

Tony outlined his requirements standing very slightly on tiptoe.

20

The May weather proving mild, it had occurred to the man Richmonde and his lady fair that they might take a picnic. I had noticed recently that he was looking increasingly preoccupied and I daresay he thought that a little jaunt into the country, leaving the office for the day, would be just what he needed to pick himself up. It just shows how wrong you can be.

From my vantage point at the back of the Traveller, where I was pretending to put cladding on the baffle plates, I saw them loading rugs and a wicker basket into the boot of the Cadillac, and chatting animatedly as they did so.

A light breeze wafted puffballs of cloud across the vault. God, or someone rather more benign, was in his heaven that day, make no mistake.

I heard the girl speak of Marlow.

At first I imagined that she was talking of the Father of our Stage, and craned eagerly to hear what her opinion might be of the quarrelsome dramaturge, but alas it was not to be (and I confess I had not really expected it, but I will have my little joke), no, she meant the resort on the Thames about eight miles down river from our old friend Henley.

I was feeling buoyant that day. Whether it was the sun that uplifts and nourishes all things, or the growing sense I was experiencing of a successful enterprise, I do not know, but I had not been so cheered since the days when my late lamented trod the world beside me.

'Isn't that a little near Cowden for comfort though?' asked the girl, reading my thoughts, I had edged round quite close now, adjusting my front number plate the better to hear them.

'Joanie hates driving and Margaret says it's gas-guzzling, even the little Fiat,' said Richmonde. 'Anyway, Henley's right at their outside edge.'

'Fine,' said she, 'Marlow it is, there's a boat-house on the left just after the bridge.'

She had been around, I will say that for her.

'Great,' said the American. 'Let's go find it.'

Alas for them, Richmonde and his fair Chloe had played right into my hands. As the massive black hulk moved off, it was but a moment's work for me to stride to the two telephone boxes which I had already had cause to mention. One I found still out of order, the other had collected details of a brace of new temptresses, Michele and Liz, and it was to this booth that I turned, dialling the number that I had previously noted in my little black book.

'Mrs Richmonde?' I breathed.

'Yeah? Who is this?'

Oh mischief, mischief, the spirit of misrule was being given its head.

'That need not concern you now. Listen carefully.'

I heard a sharp intake of breath. I truly believe she thought I was going to blackmail her. As if I would stoop.

'What d'you want? Who are you?'

'Proceed to the first boat-house on the left after Marlow Bridge as you come from London, or alternatively the one on the right just *before* the bridge as you come from Marlow. You will see something to your advantage.'

'You want money?'

'I want you to go to Marlow Bridge. I am a friend. This is not blackmail. I wouldn't soil my hands.'

'Say, wait a minute.'

'Goodbye, Mrs Richmonde.'

I felt my gaiety momentarily checked as I thought of her

habits as disclosed through the French windows: French habits I daresay, not what we need over here, it would be better if she left.

I think, looking back on it, that day marked the beginning of the end for Tony Richmonde with an e.

It is strange, is it not, but I have noticed it to be the case that those couples who are the least harmonious or constant in the nuptial state are sometimes those most offended by their partners' revealed misdemeanours. So it was with Mrs Richmonde. Working the old Traveller into a regular lather to catch up with the Cadillac, I sped along to observe the woman's discovery of her husband's dalliance, and I was not disappointed, arriving in the nick of time just as the American's car swung into the carpark. I tucked the Traveller discreetly at the back, and followed at a distance. The little plot worked as sweetly as a comedy.

The American, of course, did not see them, he was too busy talking, and the girl would not know who they were anyway, but with eyes trained to spot the slightest movement in bamboo or wait-a-bit thorn, I noted them at a glance. There they were, she and her unnatural friend, under the shadow of a kiosk, watching the arrivals park their cars and make their way towards the serried craft bobbing at the landing stage.

They did not, as I half expected, create an instant awkwardness, but the trained eye could discern the intensity of their interest. They craned, they peered, and I sensed that there was indeed some discussion as to whether the guilty pair should be accosted. The woman Margaret, in spite of her enthusiasm for peace and love, seeming to be the more in favour of instant recrimination, especially when Richmonde and his paramour exchanged an embrace as he handed her into the elegant slant-backed cruiser he had hired, and I thought for a moment that the two women would indeed rush forward like avenging harpies.

But no, the older female restrained her and, after many a

glance upriver where the oblivious lovers were carving a swathe through a regatta of tiny blue and yellow sails, they withdrew to their car. Here they sat and spoke heatedly for some minutes, looking around suspiciously the while (no doubt for a breathy-voiced poison telephoner), until finally the tumbling-haired ecologist drove them away for a cup of herb tea and unnatural practices in the hills.

Later on, perhaps I would follow and make one or two dispositions that would exacerbate a dissatisfaction with living in this sceptred isle that I had already noted in their general manner. I am a dab hand with a dead crow, an alarming sight on your doorstep first thing in the morning, and I know the consternation specific noises can induce in fit young soldiers and others who dwell under the lee of the forest. In certain woodland areas of England, as well as on the silver screen, there is still a considerable tradition of lycanthropy.

Yes, I could not help feeling that things were going my way, and when I returned to base, having passed by my poste restante to pick up any mail, I found – along with an invitation to trade in my electric cooker, and another to attend a series of singles dinner parties in Surrey addressed to a Mr Poznik – a letter asking me to report to Livonia Studios on the morrow to work as an Assistant in their extensive Library Department.

My pincer movement was developing in a way that Von Rundstedt would have given his right arm for.

21

When Tony received notice from his wife that she had discovered his affair, his first instinct was irritation at being found out, his second, one of relief. The cat was out of the bag. He would not have to keep making those embarrassing pilgrimages down to the cottage – what the hell, she must have suspected something anyway.

But when he thought about it a bit more, he realized that the timing was bad. The presentation to the video producers safely under his belt, the little matter of the Lebanese millionaire successfully tied up, all this would add muscle in his dealings with Old Kuhne, who would otherwise not be too pleased to note that his daughter was returning home minus his guarantee of domestic quiet. To throw sand in his face at this juncture would be at best pointless and at worse lethal. (He was well aware that Kuhne's regard for his daughter was a mixture of parental guilt at not wanting her around and a very natural desire to see her at the far end of the Gulf Stream, or further. The warring elements produced an effect in him as unstable as water and nitroglycerine.)

So it was with some concern that, after the first few sentences of outraged bawl-out, he heard her telling him on the telephone that she was returning to the States with Margaret. He would not like to be answerable for the consequences if her father found out that he had allowed her to leave with a lesbian (he realized that the affair had progressed from being just pals to something rather more contemporary).

'Oh,' he said. 'Isn't that taking things a little too far, dear?'

The telephone seemed to bubble in his hand.

'A little too far,' snorted Joanie. 'I would say it wasn't taking things far enough. I'd say I'd take it all the way to the Divorce Court.'

'Well now, take it easy there uh Joanie. I was only going on the river with a friend. It was a planning session. I need to get away from the office.'

'Planning? You reeked of sex.'

'Now hold on a minute there . . .'

'You hold on a minute. I will draw a veil over your filthy behaviour for the moment. Whether or not you were screwing that woman, are you saying you want me to stay?'

'Well uh yeah, of course . . . of course, I want you to stay.'

The words almost stuck in Tony's craw but survival came first.

'Say I want you to stay.'

Joanie, in spite of everything, still had a possessive instinct to moor her water-boatman husband.

'C'mon, Joanie.'

This was asking too much.

'If you want me to stay, you've got to want to stay with me. Not just weekends . . . every day of the week,' she insisted.

'Now you know you don't like London.'

'Who said anything about London? You've got to stay right here in Cowden where I can keep an eye on you. If you want to go to London, you've got to commute.'

'In Cowden . . . with you and Margaret?'

He could hardly keep his voice in the bass register.

'Margaret thinks you're kind of cute. Give up meat, she says, and you'd be adorable.'

A terrible vision of a troilistic ménage with Joanie and Margaret swam across his mind, causing him almost to swoon. They would put his balls in a noose and drive him like a pony to their pleasure. It was not to be endured.

'I am not married to Margaret. You are not married to Margaret,' he ventured.

'You are quibbling, Tony. Margaret is our very very good friend. Margaret and I believe the cottage is under some kind of threat. We had a peculiar telephone call. We need surveillance. You are in the business. Come and surveille.'

'I am Marketing Director, with special responsibility for new product development. I am not an operative.'

'Bring Bidwell down.'

'Bidwell's kind of tied up.'

'Look, Tony, get off your ass, will you. There was a dead crow in the Frigidaire.'

'A what?'

'You heard.'

'That's funny. I had a grass-snake in my laundry box.'

'That's nothing.'

'Like hell that's nothing.'

'And this morning we had something like a bowel right there on the patio.'

'I can't tell Bidwell that. He's uh, let me see, master-minding a security system for one of Britain's largest computer-dating operations. I cannot go to him and say my wife is being threatened by a bowel.'

He did not know exactly that that was what Bidwell was doing – come to think of it, he never knew what Bidwell was doing – but it sounded good.

'There was this howling in the wood last night.'

'Now uh look, Joanie, aren't you and Margaret letting this thing get on top of you?'

Like hell they were.

'I tell you it was like *Curse of the Werewolf*, know what I mean?'

'Did you have a look?'

'No way was Margaret going to let me go into that wood in the dark. No way. I told her, this place has always had such a good Karma. It was the first thing she said when she arrived. Good Karma. But now she says no way.'

Tony put on his sincere voice.

'I tell you what. I won't see the girl any more. It was just sex that was all. It's over now, I promise. And I'll come down first thing Saturday, OK?'

'Well.'

'And I won't keep saying "steak" and "burger" in front of Margaret.'

'OK. But if I hear you've been messing around with anyone again, that's it. Finito. Understand?'

'Sure. Sure.'

'Margaret says I ought to leave you anyway.'

Margaret could go screw herself he thought, but forbore to say so. Instead, he slammed the telephone down with unnecessary passion and sagged into the recesses of his captain's chair. It was the effect a conversation with Joanie always had on him when his hands were tied.

Courage, he told himself, only a week to go and the pickings of the video world would drop into his lap like harvest-time. On the other front, the Irishmen had also promised results within the week. With these two under his belt he would have both immediate funds and long-term benefits securely tied up, and Margaret and Joanie could go jump on the Jumbo.

He picked up his telephone.

'Hugo?'

''Ullo, squire.'

'How's the presentation coming along?'

'Great, squire. There's just one thing . . .'

'I don't want to louse this one up.'

'Right, squire. Like that's what I was trying to say.'

'What's that?'

'We're loused up. We've been pipped.'

'We what?'

'Somebody else has got there first. One of the big boys,

a consortium led by a bloke from one of those TV companies that lost their franchise. He's opening his doors Tuesday.'

Tony's heart dropped like a kestrel on a clockwork mouse.

'That doesn't mean we can't open up too.'

'He's got the limelight, squire, and the name in the business. The market's not big enough for two operations yet.'

'Do we have a fallback situation?'

'Well, squire, I *did* have another idea.'

'It better be good, Hugo, or the shit's going to granulate.'

'It's on the same kind of lines, squire. Easy to set up. More in the company's line of country too.'

'Well, don't hang about. C'mon, c'mon, shoot, Hugo. Spell it out.'

'It's very simple, squire. You know those dummy monitors you sell, the ones in stores to make people think they're being watched, but it's just a recording? Fit 'em with a cassette machine and bingo.'

'Bingo?'

Tony knew the British had a peculiar affection for the game.

'I don't mean Bingo, I mean there you are.'

'Where am I? You are talking obscurely, Hugo.'

'You have a new advertising medium. Actually in-store advertising at the point of purchase. Isn't that what we've all been looking for?'

Tony had to admit it did sound like a good idea. A few more minutes and he might even think it was his own.

'What about the monitors, Hugo? Is it technically on-lineable?'

'I've looked into that, squire. It's dead easy. At intervals in each recording, we simply insert Natural Breaks.'

'I have to admit it sounds possible, Hugo. Possible,

possible. But what about our timing? We'll have to put back all our planning for months.'

'Not exactly, squire. We can use many of the charts and much of the research we had in line for the other one. Purchasing habits, leisure interests and so forth. The only difference is the people we need to pull in. This time, it's advertising agencies and media brokers as well as the big manufacturers of consumables. But we can line them up soon enough. Give me a month and I think we can get it all together. I'm collecting in-store cassettes already and sending them over to Livonia to have sample commercials inserted. No, this idea's a big one, squire, even bigger than the last.'

And Tony, reflecting about it, had to agree. The ride might be bumpy, the arrival time might be postponed, but through the clouds he thought he could still discern the glint of gold.

A nasty jolt, though. He just hoped those Irishmen got their asses in gear.

22

He had telephoned in person after the dinner party to thank her for her hospitality and compliment her on her cooking. He went on to say that he recognized her interest in culinary matters, and that he would be most grateful if she were to accompany him to an English restaurant in which he was thinking of making a small investment; he wished to involve himself commercially in his new place of residence.

'London,' he said, 'is full of every nation's cuisine except its own. And yet I have eaten superlatively well in certain English country houses and hotels. If there is an area of potential for the restaurateur in London, it must be for the native product.' He confessed, however, to an inadequate understanding of English food and needed the advice of a practitioner.

She was glad that she had given him roast Southdown lamb and summer pudding, both dishes that the academy in Kensington had particularly impressed upon its alumni.

Although she had violently conflicting emotions about the man, it was too flattering to refuse. There was something fascinating about him, that repelled and at the same time attracted. Clever of him to put their meeting on a business basis, she thought.

'That's what I call style,' she said to Cheryl when she met her later for coffee, though she didn't tell her one important detail.

'He wants to get inside your knickers, dear,' said Cheryl. 'Natural enough, I daresay, but commonplace in spite of his winsome ways.'

'I know,' said Chloe, not unhappily. 'He could afford anybody and he wants me.'

'Honestly dear, sometimes I despair of you. You've got no morals.'

'No morals is the same as innocence, though, isn't it? Like Nature.'

'I suppose you could say that, but there's a flaw in it somewhere. I shall ask Father Jeremy.'

'Father who?'

'The Gays' Vicar. He's our new Visitor at the Club. Drinks Tequila Sunrises and looks after our spiritual interests. Talks to the girls about the modernist movement in the Church. They like to keep abreast of ecumenicalism.'

'If not two,' said Chloe.

They both had a good laugh.

The food at the restaurant (it was called Cobbett's and had a woodcut of the stalwart essayist trampling resolutely across the top of the menu) was indifferent, but Selvan put himself out to be delightful. He chose an excellent Corton Charlemagne, made easy conversation, asked her about herself but not too much, and almost made her forget that Roy might well be lurking outside.

At the end of the meal, Selvan suggested a second lunch-date the following week to make up for the poor quality of the first, and duly took her to the Ritz, which she thought had to have the prettiest dining-room in London.

He told her he wanted to take her into his confidence, and would she promise not to repeat what he was going to say to anyone, not even to Tony – especially not to Tony? It seemed like something of a betrayal but she agreed.

He told her that he needed personal security and, rather than hire an outfit, he was thinking of buying one. Something not too big – of the size, say, of Craxton & Kuhne.

'But that's Tony's company.'

'Exactly.'

'And?'

'I will tell you later. I want your opinion on various matters. You have a most perspicacious way of looking at the world. You have beautiful eyes but they have seen a great deal. Come,' he said, delicately dabbing at his mouth, 'I have some very remarkable champagne. Let us go and drink it.'

'No, you don't,' she said.

He produced a small revolver from his briefcase.

'See,' he said, 'it is loaded, it is for you. If I harm you, you can shoot me.'

It was melodramatic but persuasive. There was no doubt he was enormously rich.

His Arab chauffeur drove them to a door beside an undistinguished chemist's shop in Pimlico. They dismounted, and Selvan led her up a spiral stair to a circular room in a pinnacle of the building overlooking the river. A tray with a bottle of Dom Ruinart '64 and two fine-stemmed antique glasses sat on a low table beside a vast sofa.

He poured, sipped, nodded approval, and she moistened her lips in the honey-pale bubbliness. It tasted of all the very best things she had missed. She kept her handbag with the revolver near her all the time, though.

'Tell me,' he said, 'you are a little worried about something. You look around as we drive here. I have told you my secret. Tell me yours.'

There seemed no point in reticence. He appeared to possess an endless fund of knowledge anyway. He probably knew already.

'My husband who I left six years ago is following me.'

There was no point in being exact about how many years it had really been.

'Following you? Does he do anything?'

'Well, he didn't used to. But he's starting to do things to Tony.'

'Things?'

'Like putting green in his milk-bottles.'

Selvan laughed.

'It doesn't sound too dangerous.'

'It worries me.'

'You wish to have him stopped.'

'I don't want him hurt or arrested or anything. I just want him to leave off.'

'Describe him to me.'

Chloe gave a closely-observed portrait.

'I wonder,' Selvan said, 'yes . . . I think I see a way. Of course, he might just be working for someone. Enfin . . . a little diversion might be arranged. Games are the only luxury of the rich.'

'But . . .'

'Leave it to me. And now, my dearest, permit me to say how much I am going to enjoy making love to you.'

But Chloe shook her head.

'It isn't very nice for Tony.'

'On the contrary, my dear, it is much too nice for Tony.'

But Chloe was adamant, even though she couldn't suppress a feeling of excitement, and he knew it.

Selvan was not a man used to being refused, and found the experience fascinating.

'B[illegible]rely . . .'

'No.'

'Never? You must give me some hope.'

'Never until I say so.'

He was beside himself.

Even so, he didn't go back on his promise to do something about Roy.

23

The wallpaper magnate had taken up residence in a large white house with something reminiscent of the wedding cake about its exterior decorations in the oblong south of the Brompton Road known as The Boltons.

It was hither that I bent my steps at 23.00 hours after my third week at Livonia Studios, not a taxing job, but my word how the night school training was paying off. It was June 24th, Old Midsummer Night, Puck's Night no less.

He had offered me a magical entertainment if I so desired, and the invitation had duly arrived at my poste restante. No doubt he had been impressed by my coolness under fire and wished to find out more about me, perhaps even to employ my services in an advisory capacity – not that I was to be bought, but it might be instructive to see what he had up his sleeve.

As I strolled through the tree-hung streets north of the Fulham Road, I reflected on the peculiar spirals of Fate, a favourite contemplation of mine, that should have led me, a humble retailer-of-hardware and plumbers'-merchant's son, to rub shoulders with the cream of inter-continental society. It is but rarely I allow myself to come out.

The night was very warm, but at the same time fresh, like silk on a young girl's body I dare say, and the scent of jasmine and night-scented stock lay heavy on the air. The whole of London SW10 seemed like some enormous courtesan's boudoir, not that I have first-hand experience of such places, though I have followed young hostesses in an observational capacity. You would not give them the time of day if you knew what some of them get up to.

The languorous sweetness of the night, reminding me of

other distant evenings in palm-fringed Port Swettenham, appeared to have filled the very people on the streets with its own magic, so that diners, as they paused before the restaurants of Park Walk; irresolute topers, drawn now to the wine bar opposite the Hospital, now to the Goat in Boots (aware that a craving for Real Ale would involve them in a longer trudge to the Anglesey, as would indeed a thirst for the intellectual delights of the Queen's Elm); late devotees of the silver screen, scanning the lurid posters outside the ABC; late shoppers at the supermarket; teenagers studying jeans and revolution at the all-night washeteria; all seemed to quicken and stir and sigh like leaves before a breeze, puffed for an instant by the possibility of things.

Arriving at the large house in The Boltons, more a small palace really, I opened the gate, crunched over expensive gravel, polished by hand I dare say, mounted a flight of steps and pressed the bell, noting the predictable array of anti-burglar devices. You could not let a house in The Boltons without them.

A metallic voice emanated from the grille beside the bell.

'Who is it?'

'Mr Frederick for Mr Selvan.'

'Are you sure?'

'Of course I am sure.'

I do not make mistakes about such things.

'You appear to be a Greek Orthodox priest.'

'Yes.'

'Are you a Greek Orthodox priest?'

'No.'

'Then . . .'

At this point the door opened and Mr Selvan himself appeared.

'I apologize for my man's sluggish understanding. Your costume is a capital notion.'

I must confess I had thought so too, call it a midsummer madness, until the proprietor of the Wine and Kebab spotted me as I passed. I had had to put on quite a turn of speed.

'Things are not what they seem, eh, mon ami? The essence of thaumaturgy, we agree.'

The more I saw of him, the more I was impressed by the man, a confidence of manner, a brio of spirit that reminded me more than a little of my old Platoon Commander. A large blue Persian cat appeared to share my view, rubbing itself between his legs as if there were no tomorrow.

'I fear Attis is somewhat partial,' he observed of the animal.

'Perhaps he knows which side his paws are buttered,' I countered, continuing: 'I hope I am not previous.'

'Not at all. The hour is excellent. Come into the study. Do not mind the cat, he is my wife's but I dote on him. My wife is staying with relatives. We shall have the place to ourselves.'

Selvan escorted me towards a chamber situated at the back of the house. We passed evidence on the way, packing-cases and such, that his advent was but recent. I was the more honoured that he should have found the time to divert me in this way.

Turning to the right at the end of the long hallway, he showed me into a small room whose window looked out across an extensive garden with a single weeping beech, silver feathery in the light of the moon.

'It is full,' my host vouchsafed. 'Not since the time of Eliphas Levi have we had a full moon on Midsummer Night.'

He could, of course, have been pulling my leg.

'Fancy,' I said, noncommittally. 'A fortunate concurrence.'

I had hardly time to sit down before Selvan was hard at

it drawing cabbalistic signs on a large board and reading dog-latin from a grimoire that lay before him on the table. The cat Attis seemed beside himself.

'Now I cleanse the chamber,' Selvan announced, throwing a handful of incense on an elaborate tommy's cooker affair which stood on a wide bowl in the centre of things. 'I have invoked the protection of Asdiel, Uriel and Gabriel. Now let us see what we draw from the abyss.'

'Hold on a moment, please,' I said coolly. 'I am not at all certain that this is my cup of tea. I have heard this kind of dabbling can be ill-advised.'

'Dabbling,' laughed Selvan, and I could see his beard wagging at me through the incense-laden gloom like a homunculus. 'Come, my friend, you have dabbled on the fringes of the Art with your cards and your low magic. This is merely raising the curtain a little further. Besides, I know what I am doing. Courage, mon ami, do not your SAS have the motto Who Dares Wins?'

He had struck the right note with his reference to the military. The Royal West London Regiment may not have pranced about liberating hostages in front of the TV cameras, but in 1954 they were a fine body of men, especially those seconded for special duties.

'I am not afraid,' I said. 'I have seen service in the East. I have visited the Batu Caves and have heard the babaling that keeps the evil spirits from the ladang. But it is military practice not to court needless risk. I have no wish to brush with an elemental.'

'You will be safe,' he replied, 'so long as you follow my instructions precisely and do not leave the table. I have put a cordon sanitaire around it.'

With that he started his latin again, and threw more incense on the guttering flame. The cat Attis, I noted, had settled himself on the table beside his master, and stared at the cooker with unblinking eye, reminding me of the sacred temple cats at Batu.

I assured myself that the man was playing a game, that it is the sport of the wealthy to mastermind a prank. Amused by the little deception I had tried to perpetrate on him, he was clearly determined to teach me a lesson with effects and background verisimilitudes more sophisticated than anything in the catalogue of Madame Palmyra. But I had to admit he was doing a good job of it, even down to lowering the temperature, I reflected, as I caught myself giving an involuntary shiver, though no doubt that could have been the air-conditioning.

Vapour, I noticed, now started to swirl about the table – very clever, but in the army we knew all about smoke.

Then suddenly all my defences were shattered at a blow.

'Barnie.'

It was her voice. The voice I had craved to hear again, that Madame Palmyra, try though the good soul might, could never satisfactorily reproduce.

'Barnie.'

They are her accents, though little more than a whimper. I gazed distractedly at Selvan but his eyes were as entranced as the cat's. I forced my lips into a reply.

'Isobel?'

I spoke the name almost with a groan.

'Barnie. It's cold. I'm so cold, Barnie.'

I must confess that those who knew me in the Ulu would have been hard put to it to recognize their old Corporal at this stage. I wept like a child.

'Isobel, my dearest, where are you? I must see you. Tell me, dearest, it's been so long.'

The words came tumbling out without order or thought.

'It's lonely here, Barnie. Tell me about yourself. What are you doing? Why are you following . . . that man? Who are you working for?'

I opened my mouth to reply, and then shut it again. My Isobel would never have asked questions like those: she had not the faintest interest in that kind of thing. Also I suddenly remembered that the Batu cats were drugged, it was all part of the juju, and no doubt Attis had been treated in similar manner, hence his earlier excitement and subsequent lethargy.

The man might not be a magician but he was certainly a devil. It was playing with the most sacred springs of a man's emotions. What, I asked myself, could possibly be his purpose? Certain it was that he was far cleverer than I had bargained for, and that he had penetrated the cloak of secrecy which for so many years had been my most cherished possession with no more trouble than if it had been an open seam in my archimandrite's robe.

I was torn between a natural urge to remonstrate and the old fieldcraft instinct to adopt the shadows. If he knew I had tumbled to his ruse, he could become more dangerous still – he was a man of limitless resource.

But even as I weighed the two courses in the balance and pondered how to make reply, my eye was caught, through the irregular wafts of vapour, by a familiar movement in the garden.

When you see the glint of a rifle barrel parting the fronds of a creeper, be it jungle water-vine or English garden honeysuckle, your immediate instinct is to hit the floor with all the dispatch at your command. This is what I now did, taking with me, an act of considerable charity I thought under the circumstances, my host and sometime magician. The only member of the party to show superb indifference and coolness under fire was the cat Attis, who continued to sit entranced by the embers of the lamp.

At the instant I bundled Selvan to the floor, the glass of the window shattered, and a popping noise indicated to my practised ear that a silenced small-arm had been discharged among the expensive flora without.

Plainly the bullet was meant for one of the persons in

the room, and – since I reasoned that no one could have wished to visit destruction upon an unknown and indeed un-ordered Orthodox priest – the intended recipient must have been Selvan himself. However, judging by the demonic yell which the cat unleashed, the weapon appeared to have found its mark upon the person of poor Attis. The animal leapt a foot into the air and, on recovering terra firma, commenced to lick its posterior with a pitiful assiduity.

'The devils,' hissed Selvan from the floor. 'They have clipped Attis.'

I could not help but notice, as we lay there, that a wire ending in a small speaker had been fitted to the underside of the table, thus confirming my earlier supposition that trickery was afoot.

Selvan crawled to the curtains, pulled them shut, and by the light of the guttering flame located a small table lamp. He switched it on and we inspected the animal. The creature, named after the luckless God who died and rose again if we are to accept the fertility myths of Asia Minor, mourned over by the Mother herself, had been neatly doctored by the bullet which, passing on, had lodged in a corner cupboard at the far end of the chamber. I have often asserted that names have a curious power to affect one's destiny and here was a prime, if somewhat messy, exemplar.

While Selvan comforted the animal, I cautiously peeped out of the window. There appeared to be a considerable amount of activity. Flashes of light appeared and faded like summer lightning, and there came to my ears a noise of grunting and scrabbling, punctuated by further popping which sounded to my practised ears like a silenced No 5 rifle with flash eliminator.

'They will pay, I promise you,' sibilated Selvan. 'And you . . . if you are part of this . . . I have a mind to destroy you.'

'I would hardly have saved your life,' I replied stiffly, 'if I had anticipated that brand of gratitude.'

The justice of my remark appeared to assuage him, for he forgot me temporarily, calling for hot water, bandages and disinfectant, and ordering the manservant to telephone the vet. Finally he turned back to me.

'You are involved somehow in this matter,' he said, 'although you are not, I think, responsible for this particular outrage. I apologize for my anger. I shall let you go now, but do not forget that my eye is upon you. Those who know me will tell you that I am a dangerous enemy. I will find out the source of this attack and take appropriate action. Where I come from, Mr Frederick, we simply snuff out those who wish us ill. From what I have heard, London is no longer a sanctuary from a violent world. The British bobby is taking to arms. Factions seethe. Crime masquerades as politics. Politics pirouette on the fringes of terrorism. Beneath the veneer of normality, even the respectability so religiously preserved, the insects are busy in the woodwork. No one is safe any longer. I will not ask you what you are up to. You are an unusual person. I am intrigued by your mastery of the past and the tight grip you have on the present. You would make an excellent terrorist. Let me know if you wish employment. What next, mon ami? I will allow you to go now. I have no quarrel with you. It is the others who will feel the warmth of my displeasure. Good-night, Mr Frederick.'

I returned his good-night civilly enough, betraying nothing of my feelings, and made my way across the luscious gravel conscious that for the first time in many months, my guard had been allowed to slip – not for long, but a chink had been opened. To have brought Isobel back . . . the one thing that could have weakened my resolve and sapped my purpose.

How could he possibly have known she called me

Barnie? You would need to be a fly on the kitchen wall to know that.

I walked smartly away down the pavement past the curving row of wedding-cake architecture, and then doubled briskly back up the other side of the gardens, taking up a concealed position in the shadows of the shrubbery near St Mary's, scene of so many society splicings, it is still two nations, and observed Selvan's mansion, noting the arrival and departure of the vet, activity in the pathway of the house next door, and at least one fellow denizen of the shrubbery who did not notice me. I had reason to bless my black gown and whiskers, prophetically, if puckishly, donned.

After almost an hour, a mini cab drew up outside Selvan's front gate and the slight figure of a woman emerged from the house, climbed into the back, and was wafted swiftly away into the night. So, I thought, you are the voice of my dear departed. I consider it suitable that your getaway car should be an ageing Minx.

With this thought, I started to laugh, silently, painfully, under the great claw of a rhododendron that shaded me from the indifferent blond gaze of the moon.

24

The Irishman Umfreville was more sorrowful than reproachful.

'I should hate to think badly of an American – I wish you could see the latest trembler fuses fresh in from our friends in Boston, a sight for sore eyes – but I somehow have the impression you haven't been playing completely straight with us. Somebody was expecting us last night. We were given quite a reception. Now I am normally a sociable sort of person, Mr Richmonde. All the boys are. Mrs Twomey, if you got to know her better, also likes a reception. Her cheese-straws are out of this world. But last night the party was somewhat over-boisterous. Indeed, the boys and I had to retire at some personal inconvenience just as we were serving up your order. What I am trying to say, Mr Richmonde, and do forgive me if I seem to prattle on, is that it looks as if you were trying to set us up. There were guards already there. There was a trained operative in the room with him, presumably your man, no doubt your way of emphasizing the advantages of your service to a valued customer, but it made us look awful fools.'

Tony swallowed.

'Now see here uh Umfreville, I know nothing of all this . . .'

'Come, come, Mr Richmonde, you will have your joke. No, it's a very small world, our business. If the word gets around that we have had a client go bad on us, it's terrible for the trade, and that's the truth of it. That is why the boys and I will have to take it up with you. I have run out of 10ps. Would you have any objection if I were to reverse the charges?'

'No, no, go right ahead.'

And he did, running up, Tony estimated, around £5 worth of telephone charges, but he still did not seem to be satisfied with his explanations. Tony finally decided that the moment had come for engaging candour.

'Now see here uh . . .' said Tony.

'You can call me Bryan,' said Umfreville, scenting money.

'See here, Brian.'

'Bryan with a y, one cannot be too careful.'

'Now see here, uh, Bry, I'm going to be straight with you. I loused it up. Not on purpose. But I loused it somehow.'

'That you did, Mr Richmonde, though I appreciate your saying so.'

'Well, I'm going to make it up to you. I'm going to give you a double fee as danger money, and I'd like to put you boys on a regular retainer just as soon as I get this place straightened out.'

'That is indeed most gentlemanly of you, Mr Richmonde. I will discuss the implications of a consultancy arrangement with my fellow directors. Meanwhile perhaps I might run over the arrangement as I see it. A down payment of cash within the week or the equivalent in Armalite rifles, or better still, enriched plutonium if you can lay your hands on the stuff, it's like gold-dust. Just as important, no word must reach our colleagues in the business. I must insist on that. We have our reputation to consider. Reputation, reputation, Mr Richmonde, you know what the poet says.'

Tony didn't, but he felt he could catch the drift, and he found himself sweating as he looked at the telephone. Where had he gone wrong? He had never known a sampling operation backfire like this. And who had arranged a security back-up for Selvan?

'Let us know if there is anything further you require

And please let us have our questionnaire back with your comments and suggestions. We strive all the time to polish our service. Have a good day now.'

Tony's whole world seemed to be falling apart. He pressed the intercom curtly.

'Bidwell.'

'No.'

'What d'you mean no?'

'I am not Mr Bidwell.'

'For chrissake, Laura . . .'

'Go quietly amid the noise and haste.'

She was beginning to sound like Joanie. What had got into women these days?

'Why don't you . . .'

'Ah, Mr Bidwell's just come in. You wished him, Mr Richmonde?'

'Yes, Laura. I wished him very much. Send him in, please.'

Over the intercom he heard her very loudly starting to spray her Cheese Plant. The door opened and Bidwell appeared, courteous and remote as ever.

'Mr Bidwell.'

'Yes, Mr Richmonde?'

'I want you to . . .'

Tony checked himself. He could not give orders to the man yet. He was still technically Tony's superior.

'I would be grateful if you could find out about this man's security arrangements.'

Tony scribbled Selvan's name and address on a pad and handed it to the Chief Operative, who perused it gravely.

'He is Lebanese,' said Tony, filling the silence.

'So I understand.'

'You know him?'

'Indeed I do. He asked for a security system.'

'Asked? Asked who?'

'Why, me, of course. He was given my name by a

personal contact in Beirut. He asked me to put up a full tailor-made recommendation, and to arrange immediate off-the-peg security with effect from last week. Just as well, as it happened. We were able to foil an attempt on his life. Unfortunately the bandits got away.'

'He asked *you*?'

'Of course. He was recommended by C & K International.'

Tony ground his teeth. His pitch had been queered by his own people.

'Why did you not tell me? You knew I had Max here.'

'You did not ask. It is your business to find new business. It is mine to service our clients' needs.'

Tony stifled with difficulty the bile that seemed to be surging in his stomach like Old Faithful on a particularly gusty day. He could hardly tell his colleague that he had embarked upon an operational activity without consultation. At the same time, he could not possibly claim the commission on the business. As for the Irishman, if he now got wind of what had actually transpired or if the story of the sheer scale of the blunder got out, he would come down on him like a ton of bricks. A ton of Micks, he thought, wondering whether he could laugh himself out of this thing. But that again, like so many of his ventures at the moment, seemed to lack the winner's touch.

Another thought struck him, concerning winners.

'Livonia Studios.'

'The video people round the corner?'

'We have a great deal of confidential material going through there. I want, I mean would like, the place checked out.'

'We have checked it out.'

'Fine. Great. And Bidwell . . .'

'Yes?'

Tony searched in the increasing mother-hubbardn

of his mind for something that would suggest togetherness and authority.

'Uh. Take it easy, huh?'

'In our business, Mr Richmonde, that is one thing we can never afford to do.'

25

A member of a platoon in A Company disappeared one night while out on patrol, a big fellow, represented the Regiment in the Command Boxing Championships as a heavyweight, though succumbing in the end to a giant Gunner who butted. He simply disappeared that night, no one could account for it, out in the secondary jungle beyond Segamet.

I would make no special point about it. It did happen from time to time, a straying sentry, a crafty Woodbine alone with your trousers down or simply having a slash, a separation from the main body of men if you were back-marker, and you could find yourself with your throat cut, a dart tinctured with Ipoh poison in your back discharged by a disaffected aboriginal (the CTs used to work on them), or merely wandering for days in the trackless scrub until you went mad or died of snake bite or Wilde's Disease, contracted through drinking river water where rats had been pissing. Did you ever see a survey map of those parts? Nothing but streams, rivers, hills and jungle. It would make your average suburban wet his trousers just to look at it. Well, it did so happen that my patrol was passing through that area a couple of weeks later – we had word that Chin Pang himself was on the move – and rounding a fallen rambutan, in lead position, I was hard put to it to suppress a cry of disgust as I almost trod on what seemed at first to be a huge bright softly-heaving bolster glimmering diagonally in the slats of the sun.

I raised my hand in the regulation gesture of Halt! and Mr Parsons hurried up to examine the object. It turned out to be Private Sharland, the missing soldier, once bold and young in the full bloom and vigour of youth, though somewhat coarse-tongued, now overrun by the variegated and manifold insect life of the Malayan rain-forest.

You could hear them now – we observed silence at all times on patrol – buzzing and clicking and whirring there right at our feet. The colours were really quite beautiful. It was impossible to tell how he had died: even in that short space of time the corpse had become bloated beyond our analysis. We could only surmise that the body belonged to 35217614 Pte Sharland, E, by its size and regulation jungle issue denims, and this was confirmed on closer inspection, the smell was enough to wake the dead, by the identity disc around its neck. We buried him where he lay and continued the patrol.

I only make the point which I trust is not over-gruesome, because somehow that image from those far-off days had recently been coming back to me with increasing frequency. The bright garish insects clustering and burrowing over the once-proud body. And more and more, as I looked round London, I seemed to hear again the scuttle of legs, the clamorous whirring of bright wings, the clack of jaws tearing at the decaying fabric of a fallen country.

Nobody, I reflected (and I could not excuse myself from the charge), seems to do anything any more, it is all tinsel and no substance, all gloss and no text, all chips and no fish.

This view, at any rate, was confirmed after my first week at Livonia Studios, where most of the traffic was adverts, documentaries and promotional films for pop groups. Everyone involved in the projects was highly paid, lived well, drove smart cars, but when you came down to it, what on earth were they all doing? If half the talent and energy were spent on actually making better products as opposed to selling tired old ones, the country would not be in its present pass.

The lines of Cardinal Newman's great hymn, so thoughtlessly chanted in those distant days at St Theodoric's, came back to me often now in my cubbyhole behind the film racks.

> 'I loved the garish day and, 'spite of fears,
> Pride ruled my will . . .'

Not that anyone seemed to be experiencing any fears. It never occurred to them that they were living off dead flesh. The very arrays of screens and lenses reminded me of insect eyes, and everywhere there was a whirring of busy tapes.

I was often left alone in the basement (I had won my spurs as a warehouseman by helping them over the weekend with a rush job to transfer a consignment of Continental films), and it was not long before I familiarized myself with the racks where Craxton & Kuhne work was allocated pending Process Control. I was even able to have a crack at the transfer machines. The hirsute ex-Malaya Director had held a birthday party for the staff, and the equipment was left unguarded.

My night-school instructor had taught us on different equipment, but the principle was the same, and indeed it was not long before I became a dab hand at the telecine and would no doubt, given a few months, have landed a top job with an expense account, Porsche, glossy girlfriend and all the trimmings if that had been my wish, but my mind was fixed upon a higher enterprise.

The attack was developing on all fronts.

I have observed that sometimes, perhaps as a relief from the blonde perfections of his ladylove, the American would on occasion take out other women on nights when she was working. One in particular I remember I had cause to disapprove of, a brunette with the fastidiou manners of a Chairman's Secretary but in fact no bett than she ought to be, with a voice that always seemed to me to have an edge of complaint to it, too much whiny stress on the last syllable, it really got my goat.

'Toe-knee,' she would say to him, 'why do you never take me to the thea-terr?'

I decided to play a little prank on the lady, not very gentlemanly I admit, but there are some things that one simply has to do or, as the English Master at St Theodoric's used to say, one bursts; innocent days past recall, they do it all the time to visitors in Moscow.

I had noticed that on previous occasions, as far as could be seen, in the bar of the Brasserie, for instance, she had shown a fondness for vodka and tonic almost amounting to idolatry. One afternoon, then, when I had leave of absence from Livonia on account of my weekend's work, I ascertained from the diary in his flat (the porter seemed to be getting more vigilant, but I usually managed to effect an entry) that next day he was meeting his temptress there for a drink prior to dinner, and I changed the vodka in his bottle from the normal 65.5 proof to a special Polish variety at 120, hastily purchased from the hang-dog Glebe.

I envisaged that with three of these inside her, followed by the inevitable aperitif at the restaurant, pursued by wine and chased by liqueur, there could well be some kind of fireworks in store for the hapless couple before they reached his flat again, and so it proved. As they came out of Number 46, I could see from my vantage point over by the railings that my export-strength Wyborowa masquerading in the Smirnoff bottle had already started to take effect.

The girl, or woman I should say, was laughing immoderately. 'Whoah there,' he said as she nearly stumbled and clutched his arm with her thin hands white beneath a bead hawl over a white dress with matching accessories. She hoahed enough to get in his car and sat back hilariously as the monster surged towards Pont Street. I followed in the Traveller as best I might. I did not have to read his mind as to the appointed eating place, since I had read his diary – he was a methodical man about his pleasures.

He had selected a Caribbean restaurant popular at the time, noted for its particularly potent punches. No doubt Richmonde, being aware of the woman's enthusiasm, had chosen it for the purpose, but on this occasion he got rather more punch than he had bargained for. I dare say he would have liked them to pull their punches.

They spent two hours inside the restaurant, allowing me time to survey the broad spectrum of the clientele as it arrived, public relations men, television executives, art directors, solicitors, civil servants, and their assorted bints, moths of the evening, beating their fine wings in the spicy breezes. Was it for this that Private Sharland, E, ate his heart out in the jungle and died with a full stomach?

At eleven o'clock there was a slight commotion, and Richmonde emerged up the stairs, looking embarrassed, with the woman slewed slackly across his shoulder, assisted by a waiter. You doubtless remember how difficult it was to stuff a bolster of straw into an old overcoat to make a Guy for Fawkes Night without the bolster slipping out again?

Richmonde had similar difficulty getting the woman into the car.

'For chrissake,' he kept saying, worriedly glancing over his shoulder. 'The police will see us. I don't want to get myself breathalysed.'

'Hahahahahaha.'

At length, he half picked her up and threw her bodily through the door into the cavernous vinyl interior. This seemed to sober her for a moment.

'Toe-knee. Why didn't you let me finish my puh-unch? Let's go somewhere and have a little dri-ink.'

Toe-knee did not answer. I followed closely as he made

off down Berkeley Square. I had my Olympus Trip with flash attachment at the ready to take a compromising picture of them as they got out at Cadogan Square, but to my discomfiture he drove straight down Sloane Street and turned into the King's Road, making west for Fulham. Every now and then I detected a flash of gauzy white waving from the window. Sometimes I thought I could hear high-pitched singing, and once a shriek. He was taking her home.

He traversed the length of the King's Road, erstwhile garden of delights and now full of dwarfish grotesques wearing bicycle chains, and I nodded at my little home in Driffield Street as we coasted past the World's End, haven of sanity. From what I could see, the girl appeared now to be quiescent. We crossed Stamford Bridge, leaving Lots Road Power Station rearing up like Vulcan's Forge on our left and the old Balloon pub, site of the first hot air balloon launching in the British Isles, now empty and abandoned with its shutters rattling in the wind like so much else.

Entering the New King's Road with its serried wrought-iron ranks of costly little shops, I noticed that the woman seemed to have entered a manic phase again. From the way he leant over from time to time, it looked as if he were trying to pacify her but without success. Finally, as we passed Parsons Green, I spotted her arms flailing wildly as if to make an important point, and saw his indicator signalling a left turn. I stopped at the tip of the little residential avenue down which he had eased his monster, meaning to give him time to proceed a little, but noted that he was urgently pulling in beside a loaded skip.

At this instant, the woman sprang out like a crumpled Christmas Tree Fairy, crouched under the lee of the skip, spread her skirt around her, slightly raised it, and started to what I can only describe as urinate. She had been caught short.

Appalled though I was to see the depths to which the fair sex can stoop, I was at the same time naturally intrigued to see how this turn of events would impinge on Richmonde. I knew his face would be a picture.

First of all he got out of his car. Then he paused irresolute: he could hardly assist her with this most private of acts. Then, as one or two late-night revellers passing in the street started to gather, and even to wave and whoop – the woman could not have been more visible in her virgin white attire – he started forward again with a sort of covering gesture. The woman seemed inexhaustible.

I edged forward with my Olympus. Finally she began to get up, wobbled, took his hand to prevent herself toppling into her own puddle, and 'Hahahahahaha,' she was laughing again. It was at this instant that I took my picture – rather a winner though I say it myself – for afterwards when I exposed it in my little dark room, the scene told all. Her skirt had become somehow partly tucked up in her drawers, which helped, of course, but the really tell-tale part about it was his face. Guilt, shame, rage, fear and the ghost of a kind of sleek lust played about his features, immortalized forever in my negative.

It was one of my most successful patrols to date and congratulations were in order.

I naturally sent a dated copy of the colour print – no seedy black and white snaps for me – to his wife in Oxfordshire by first class post, marked Personal and signed 'A Friend'.

26

As Tony looked out from the lecturer's podium across the sea of faces in front of him – amazing for the time of year – he felt that all his efforts had been worthwhile. Some of the most expensive media executives in the UK, summoned at such short notice, were gathered here in his chosen venue (a small private cinema in Dean Street).

As the last latecomers settled into their seats, and Hugo busied himself filling the glasses, he allowed his mind to wander over his situation. There was no doubt about it, someone had been out to screw him. He had known it for weeks but somehow it was all too ridiculous. Who could possibly have it in for someone like himself? He had no enemies that he knew of apart from the Irishmen, and they were squared. Here he was, working with a surveillance outfit, and yet he personally was under attack, and sometimes such goddam pointless picayune little things you'd hardly notice if they didn't add up. And in London of all places! It would be funny if it weren't so irritating. He would just have to be more careful, keep his eyes open, and when he had settled the more pressing matters in hand he would get down to it and flush the bastard out.

One of the more pressing matters was Joanie. Someone, no doubt the same guy who had snapped him the other night, all right maybe not so picayune, had sent Joanie a picture of the appalling scene in Fulham, and Joanie – deaf to his ingenious excuses, and admittedly they had to be ingenious – the squatting figure would have taxed the explanatory powers of a Presidential candidate –had returned to the States two days later with Margaret, cabling him from Atlantic City: 'WILL NEVER

RETURN. DIVORCE PROCEEDINGS FILED. DADDY ENRAGED. STOP YOGHURT.'

It did not augur well for his future with Craxton & Kuhne.

On the other hand, Joanie had actually gone. That had to be counted as an asset.

He had told a carefully edited version of the story to Chloe, who was amused but not over-sympathetic. 'Who cares about her?' she had said. 'You're going to be rich anyway, aren't you? Then you'll be marriable again.' He hadn't been totally happy with her order of priorities there, but he could hardly quarrel with it.

And anyway, surveying the prosperous audience sitting out there, he felt that the day when he could put all his financial troubles behind him was very close indeed. Preliminary interest among the retailers had been high so long as the advertisers could be found. And here they, or their representatives, were.

It almost made the mouth water to look at them. And no doubt, he thought, they would be drooling quite a bit themselves, for a new in-store media opportunity in an age when all the TV rates were being thrown into the melting-pot with the advent of satellite television was a sure-as-hell opportunity to persuade their clients to spend more on advertising. That was why they had all been prepared to attend at such short notice.

The preparations had gone without a hitch. The video equipment had been delivered in time, and checked and re-checked. Drinks had been served by pretty girls in miniskirts, provided by a friend of Chloe's who ran a Promotions Agency. ('Quite like the old days,' murmured one veteran of the Sixties to his neighbour, goggling at a piste of white-tighted thigh.) Talk had been slow at first but became lively and involved.

True, there had been a last-minute panic involving a tape they had been waiting for, a vital composite of recent commercials one of which, acutely relevant to the presentation, had only just appeared on television two nights ago causing a last-minute adjustment to the reel, but that had come in, been checked, found to be badly graded, sent out again, and finally been safely re-delivered. Everything that could possibly go wrong looked to be eliminated. Even Hugo was going easy on the cockney accent.

The lights went down.

In spite of his other problems, Tony felt the natural elation of the marketing man in full ritual dance before a financial mating, and he gave a bravura presentation.

First came the charts.

There were charts to show things that everyone knew perfectly well already but were there simply to show that the organizers had done their homework. The population of the British Isles; the purchasing pattern of the ABC1C2 socio-economic classes analysed on a demographic and then on an age basis; the size of the consumer market by categories of outlet. But there were others more specialized: the incidence of shop-lifting over the last fifteen years, anatomized on a regional, age and social basis; the projected growth of in-store security monitors over the years 1980-1990. (This brought attentive whispers.)

There was a more imaginative section dealing with developments in parallel marketing areas; the growth of shopping-precinct poster sites; the development and shortcomings of in-store radio; the shopping-situation implications of the Do-It-Yourself and Leisure explosion even in a recession paradigm. There were charts that needed still more charts to explain them. Hugo had done his homework and, prompted by Tony's insistence on a display of overview, had produced a format that demonstrated a grasp of the broad sweep as well as the immediate tactical opportunity.

Tony, as he outlined his proposals, felt an irresistible fervour emanating from his oratory. Never had he appeared so cogent, so plausible, he could almost feel his audience fumbling for its chequebook, and as he entered upon the final run-up, he was already reckoning what the fruits of such a successful launch might be.

He could leave Craxton & Kuhne (not a moment too soon). He could sit like a money spider in the middle of a vast web of advertising revenue. He could afford the loss of Joanie. He could settle his debts, marry Chloe, pay off the Irishman, fix the asshole that was following him around, and probably ditch Hugo into the bargain.

'And so, gentlemen,' he cried, entering upon his peroration, 'it looks like we've got the mix exactly right. We have seen the growth dynamic for point-of-purchase advertising on *chart*, but I now ask you to instinctualize. Does it feel good? Does it smell good? I do not think I need you to answer that, gentlemen. I read it on your faces . . . It has to be the way things are going. But . . . and this is the sixty-four thousand dollar question, the uh philosopher's stone which many have sought but none has satisfactorily resolved . . . How do we make it happen? You are very intelligent people. You have perhaps thought about it, dreamed about it . . . but the answer is, like all great leaps forward, amazingly, luminously simple. It has been right here all the time, staring us in the face. It has been like penicillin – unnoticed, undervalued, part of the scenery of life, and we simply have not harnessed the power for good implicit in it. Gentlemen, I give you the security monitor.'

There was a gasp, and a little spontaneous applause.

Tony reached over and whipped a drape off a television screen suspended monitor-like from the wall.

More applause.

'And now, gentlemen,' he said, 'I am going to play you a short excerpt from an ordinary security programme. It could be anywhere. Just pretend to yourselves that you're looking around your favourite store, thinking of buying could-be-anything, strolling along, looking around, monitor unobtrusively doing its vital work up above . . . and here goes . . . welcome, gentlemen, to Monadvision . . .'

Tony nodded to Hugo, who switched on the equipment, and a black and white vista of endless shelves groaning with supermarket products presented itself to the audience, who all tried to recognize which chain the store belonged to. Tony had foreseen this, audience participation time was built into the module, and the executives bantered happily for a while before settling down again to watch the film.

In the store, people milled around in desultory manner, picking up items, turning over merchandise, sometimes vacuously stuffing goods into trolleys. A black and white monitor, identical to the one in the presentation room, could be seen discreetly overhead.

'Nothing much going on, gentlemen, you observe, an ordinary day in an ordinary store, the pattern in a thousand places up and down the country. Now, on the same day, in the same place, we run a brief burst of commercials . . .'

Hugo pressed another button.

The scene had changed in one small detail. It was in colour. And the shoppers were looking up at the monitor which was also now screening in colour, and officiously chiming. The chiming ceased. Six thirty-second commercials for consumer products of the kind being purchased below were shown, and the monitor reverted once more to silent watchfulness after a sign-off electronic carillon.

There was discernibly a difference in the shoppers. Not too much, that would be straining credulity, but they were undeniably more activated. There were close-ups of hands reaching out, housewives were poised like pigeons over freezer cabinets, indeed one matron was actually seen trying to secrete a tin of tuna fish up the elastic of her long dirtyish bloomers.

'You see, gentlemen,' said Tony, 'the power of persuasion, in the right place, at the right time, at the point of sale.'

'Yes, but wait a minute.' One of the executives put up a hand. 'That housewife was actually so encouraged she started shoplifting.'

How had the goddam sequence got in? thought Tony. He had specifically ordered at an earlier run-through that it should be left out. It had seemed, at the time, over the top.

'You're right, sir, I'm glad you spotted that. We kept that in to make a special point. Before the Monadvision test, there was hardly any pilfering in the store due to an exceptionally low rate of purchase. Low sales. High security. Better to have high sales and the risk of a little shoplifting, don't you think? You can't make an omelette without breaking eggs. Besides the retailer has the option of our Live Monitor version which actually switches from Record to Play automatically.'

'Yes, but . . .'

'Questions later, please, gentlemen. I'm sure you will all have plenty you want to ask, but I would first like to show you something else.'

Tony signalled to Hugo, who winked perkily back. He would bawl him out later for not checking the tape again but the moment had come for the pièce de résistance. After this they would be eating out of his hand.

'Gentlemen,' he announced, 'the commercials you just saw were ordinary television ads, lifted without any doctoring for the new media. This can of course be done very effectively. But to maximize the benefits of in-store advertising, we would recommend a more specifically in-store message. So we have made three commercials, scripted and taped them just for this presentation, to show you just what I mean. Not one of them cost more than £1,000 to make. In these days of £100,000 commercials you will appreciate the saving achieved. Incidentally, there are at present no Union or IBA regulations governing the showing of point-of-sale commercials, so that has to stop the time-consuming script vetting and expensive over-manning syndromes that plague the production of ordinary commercials.'

There was now another pause, deliberately engineered so that the executives could discuss among themselves a favourite topic, the folly and pernicketiness of the IBA and its sibling the ITCA (Independent Television Contractors Authority).

'Always puts people in a good mood,' said Hugo. 'Everyone has his story about the ITCA.'

'We had this script,' the Media Director from Pratt, Webster and Vipan said, 'it was for a car tyre commercial. It showed this tyre dealer bloke, at the end of the day, shutting up shop for the night. He gets in his bargain notices, gathers up his display racks, hangs up his white coat, puts out the cat, locks up and walks over to his car. We see he's driving on our tyres. Point made. Voice over says: "At the end of the day, more tyre dealers (who have a choice of them all) drive our tyres than any others." Simple. ITCA says: "You can't show the cat being put out. It's cruel to cats."'

There was a burst of ribald laughter in which Tony joined in. Not for too long, though. He had them now.

He rapped with quiet authority on his desk. All eyes turned on him.

'Now, gentlemen, I want you to watch very very carefully. First look at these commercials. Then see the effect on shelf take-off in the store. Oh, and one other thing. The ordinary shoppers you see in the sequence had no idea that they were being recorded. Thank you.'

Hugo hit the Play button, and Tony stood back nonchalantly. This was going to be the clincher. He had rehearsed the shoppers in the studio until their varicose veins throbbed.

The statutory splutter of lines and dots hissed about the screen for a second or two, and then the commercials began. Tony turned away from the screen confidently, and inspected the serried faces, ready for the inevitable gasps of admiration and the murmured British enthusiasms for which he was well prepared.

The Brits, he had to admit, were looking at the commercial with quite exceptional attention. Bully for them, and indeed for him.

But, as he eyed them, he saw their faces begin to express confused emotions: astonishment, yes, but of an uneasy kind; fascination, indeed, but the sort with which a rabbit regards an oncoming vehicle. He turned back and looked at the screen once more, aware that the noises coming from it did not immediately coincide with his recollections of the film he had so painstakingly selected, and, in spite of himself, experienced a little wriggle of unease in his stomach.

If the sound effects had indicated a departure from the plan, the visual side of things more than confirmed it. The wriggle in his stomach deepened and lengthened.

The commercial, if you could call it a commercial, and frankly he was beginning to feel he couldn't, showed a refectory table groaning with provender. Capons, geese, turkeys, a glazed sucking pig, a boar's head, massive game pies, hams, savoury puddings, galantines, a vast triton of a salmon around which little pink prawns gambolled in aspic, creamy fools, gateaux and syllabubs, profiterole mountains, îles flottantes, bulging bowls of exotic fruits, all these displayed themselves to the camera which tracked lovingly across them, not omitting to include magnums of Château Margaux and Pommard, jeroboams of champagne, and refulgent decanters of port and cognac, which served as punctuations to the feast.

Right on cue, the camera pulled back, revealing the various participants in the occasion – a chef, a cardinal, a ballet-dancer, a gaunt philosopher, a world-weary rake, a grande dame, a night-club bouncer, a society beauty, a bloated banker – an incongruous party by no means accurately reflecting Tony's stated target market – some lolling, temporarily replete, others still busily gobbling away at the spread. Every detail of their condition and deportment now began to be relayed on screen. Initially, Tony had received the general impression that they seemed to be overdoing things but, as he watched, too shaken for action, glued to the peculiarly patterned art nouveau carpet so beloved of small viewing theatre proprietors, judicious cutting now revealed that the guests at this particular clambake had regressed several light years beyond the bounds of even nursery standards of decorum.

The ballet dancer seemed to be letting the banker eat something that looked like Noodles Carbonara out of the recesses of her tutu. The chef was proposing a Solognote fish mousse shaped in perfect resemblance of the female buttocks to the grande dame whose clinging black dress, one now observed, was, in fact, bitter chocolate which was being licked away assiduously by the strong man. The world-weary rake, who had just finished sucking at the spigot of a conveniently placed pipe of port, clambered up and puked in the baronial fireplace.

Surfeit in its vilest manifestations belched and farted and spewed across the screen. Huge mouths in close-up gobbled pâté, eyes bubbled, lava-like streams of vomit slowly encrusted on shirt-fronts, excreta hissed and writhed from overloaded plumbing.

Appalled though he was, Tony was able to register that there was a quality about the spectacle which reminded him of something he had seen some place before. Certainly this was not the film he had carefully checked the previous day, but what in God's name was it? Yes . . . yes

. . . it was coming back. He was watching excerpts, ingeniously edited he had to admit, from the film 'La Grande Bouffe 2' which he had seen in New York when he was screwing a librarian who took him to such things. He had not cared for it then, and he did not care for it now.

The assembled executives, like Tony, appeared to be rooted by surprise. There had been, and still were, whimpers of incredulity, but there was no immediate action. And even as, at last, they gathered themselves for comment, the ghastly sequence passed as swiftly as it had appeared, and the camera once more panned down to show the reaction of the shoppers in the store.

This time it relayed pandemonium. Housewives were snatching goods from their trolleys and hurling them back on to the shelves. A middle-aged respectably-dressed man who might have been a stall-holder at an antique hypermarket was taking cheese cubes out of his mouth and transferring them on to a tray at a German Week sampling stand. The shoplifter they had noted before was actually extracting chops, kidneys and steakettes from her bloomers and cramming them back into the freezer as if her life depended on it.

This last, for the Media Directors, was finally too much. The spell was broken. They made, as a man, for the door.

'Wait,' shouted Tony desperately. 'Come back, I can explain.'

'I've seldom been so insulted in my life,' said the Media Director of Rickett & Transome, a company that had recently been taken over by a Japanese consortium.

'An elaborate, ingenious, but in the end utterly pointless practical joke,' agreed the man from Pratt, Webster, 'the sequence with the shoplifter was in the worst possible taste.'

'For a moment, though,' said the Media Director of Westrupp's, 'I really thought they had something there.

Maybe we should talk to that intelligent looking man at the back, what was his name, Bracewell-Smith?'

'I enjoy a good joke as much as the next man,' began a short fellow with slide-rule eyes.

But the next man was a large international agency man in a temper who wouldn't know a joke if it made comical faces at him and lay in the aisles with its legs in the air.

'There can be no point,' he stormed. 'There's no possible profit for him or for anybody else. He's wasted his money and our time.'

'One does not joke about retailing,' said another dignitary, more puzzled than outraged. 'It is like speaking disrespectfully of the bloodstream.'

Tony flapped his arms some more, but it had the scarecrow effect of hastening them on their way.

'Wait, gentlemen, I can explain. There has been some terrible mistake. There is lunch laid on at Scarab's.'

But nobody seemed to want to lunch or listen.

Tony looked round the deserted theatre torn between rage and fear.

'Hugo. HUGO. Shit. Oh, shit.'

There was no sign of his cocksure assistant. Indeed, Hugo had left in deep conversation with the man from Westrupp's.

Suddenly, for the first time in his life (making an exception of the moment of nativity), Tony felt disturbingly alone. There could be only one explanation of the fiasco that had just overwhelmed him. That last-minute delivery had involved a switched cassette. Someone had edited in sequences from that French film and run out-takes of the supermarket scene backwards. Someone with a knowledge of, and access to, video equipment . . .

When taken into context with all the other considerations that had been going through his mind before he started the presentation, the inference was as plain as the nose on a surveillance operative's face. Somebody with almost supernatural powers of patience, intuition, contrivance, and most of all malevolence was gunning for him. It wasn't a minor or even a medium irritation at all. The man, whoever it was, meant business.

The consideration frightened him, supplanting his first alarm at where now he was going to find the money for the Irishmen – he could have borrowed thousands on the strength of a successful presentation with promises of orders, but this unknown assailant, this shadowy marksman, now had to be his top priority.

Whoever it was, he thought, it could be somebody he knew. Hugo? Bidwell? (He had after all said the studio was clean.) Selvan? Old Kuhne himself? Or one of the other surveillance companies? The Micks? The list of possible candidates seemed, now the veneer of security was being stripped away, suddenly endless.

One thing was for sure. He was going to get out of town for a while. The Irishmen could not be paid immediately. Selvan was after his blood. And had he not noticed a message from Laura on his desk before he left urgently requesting him to call Atlantic City?

He telephoned Chloe from a callbox.

'How about coming down to the cottage for a break, honey?' he asked, half expecting, since everything else had gone bad, that she would refuse.

'What's wrong?' she asked.

How could he explain to her? The company apartment, the office with the captain's chair, the dreams of empire, these things were now out of court until further notice if not longer.

'Oh, I dunno,' he said.

'Didn't the presentation work out?'

'It worked out fine,' he said. 'That's my trouble, postcoital blues.'

He couldn't tell her yet.

'Oh good,' she said, 'clever Ant. I'll get out the champagne.'

She was always ready for champagne.

She then surprised him by saying that, yes, she would come down to the cottage, although she, for her part, was not totally open with him either. What she didn't tell him about was the plague of cockroaches in Prosser Street. It wouldn't have mattered too much, though she hated the creatures, but there was some sort of hold-up with the Pest Officer over a man who, it seemed, had been masquerading as an official exterminator without a Local Government and Municipal Workers' Union ticket. Until this was thoroughly gone into at every level (an investigation was being conducted through the proper channels as to whether the Council had or had not been employing non-Union staff on an ad hoc basis) there would be a regrettable though inevitable hold-up.

She thought she knew who the mysterious Pest Officer might have been. Meanwhile, her maisonette was uninhabitable. She did not like to admit to Tony that there was infestation in a place that, only recently, had been the scene of top-level entertaining, so she just said it would be lovely to go to the country for a day or two, the weather was too good to waste.

There was something else rather important on her mind. Maybe she would find the right moment down at Cowden.

So, with neither communicating their preoccupations to the other, they drove down that evening through cool woods under a turquoise sky to the flint-walled hideaway, where they extracted the Bollinger with more than usual haste. They both felt they needed a drink.

Tony suddenly remembered, with a sinking feeling, something that Joanie had said, and inspected the freezer immediately, sifting through great heaps of beanshoots and raw kelp, before he put the bottle in to chill.

There were no dead crows.

No doubt she had been kidding.

27

I have always enjoyed the drama of August in our native woodland. The exuberance of early summer has darkened to a swarthier green and the leaves lie thick and clotted along the bough, bending each twig with the weight of their maturity.

And yet, even now in summer's height, when the angular undress of winter is almost unimaginable, we see as in a Greek tragedy the first signs of decay heralding disintegration at the end. The sugars burning in the leaves, no longer capable of synthesis, glimmer here and there like turncoats.

Call me fanciful, but I have watched the woods closely at every season, and know the leaps and flows, the trickles and ebbs and starts of the tides that rule their economy.

Let me be more precise.

Cowden Woods lie exclusively on the upper and middle chalk. The steep slopes are mainly under beech, as noted, but ash, oak, elm and conifers are also found, looming above may and crab, guelder rose, pussy palm, spindle, holly, wayfaring tree and traveller's joy, with areas of scrub and wide grassy rides containing a rich chalk herb flora. The plant list includes Green Hellebore, Herb Paris, Columbine, Solomon's Seal with its carillon of flowers, Lady's Mantle, Adderstongue Fern and no fewer than seventeen species of Orchidaceae (among them Fly, Greater and Lesser Butterfly, Bee and Frog Orchids). Many interesting bryophytes and fungi also abound.

Breeding birds in these woods include kestrel, sparrow hawk, woodcock, woodpecker, willow tit and wood warbler, and there are fox, badger, stoat, weasel and fallow and muntjac deer, also adder, grass-snake (source of my laundry box inspiration), slow-worm, and common lizard. The insect fauna, now being fully explored for the first time, promises, I am told, to be as rich as the flora, and the moths include Maple Prominent, Scarce Footman, Clay Triple Lines, Large Twinspot Carpet, and Map-winged Swift.

Four new Home Counties snail records were established in one visit by a malacologist.

You see what sort of place this is.

These woods are, on the whole, lucky. They are healthy and well-tended, protected by the Conservancy at the westward end. Here and there we see sick trees that contradict the prevailing stream. The beech fungus nectria coccinea, so prevalent after the drought of '76, has made some few depredations, and we may observe too the gawky supplication of a dead elm at the edge of the forest. Man, the bigger pest, has been kept at bay. Half our native woodland has been destroyed at his hands since 1947 – we shall be pilloried by history – but here he has preserved and husbanded, the exception that proves the rule.

I had prepared my hide-out in advance at the intersection of a series of mounds and deep ditches of unknown origin, conceivably Neolithic, that run under the foliage a couple of hundred yards up the hill from the cottage. From here I could patrol down to a low trench on the fringe of the wood which actually overlooked the rear of the building, and could proceed under cover of the hedge I used on my first visit right down to the corner of the cottage itself. From here, also, I could retreat into the depths of the foliage, where old-man's-beard made a vast thatch, seemingly impenetrable as any wait-a-bit hedge but in fact lending itself to a line of retreat in any of three directions.

'Always safeguard your exit.' I could hear Mr Parsons as if it were yesterday.

* * *

The speed with which the American and his bit of fluff fled to the cottage after the operation of the switched video cassette took even me, I must admit, by surprise, though I could not help but find it gratifying.

I arrived soon after they had taken up residence, after a short interval for regrouping and issue of equipment back at base, and concealed the Traveller in a rutted lane half a mile away leading to a disused chalk quarry (I had taken the precaution of fitting the vehicle with false number-plates so as to be ready for any eventuality). From there, I made my way through the woods at twilight, in my denims and tropical boots, with all the kit and forage I needed packed in an extra-large bren-group hold-all which I was able to wheedle out of the QM long years past at Tampoi Barracks.

In terms of armament, I carried the good old .870 Wingmaster pumpgun so beloved in the Malaya Campaign, and which I was able to secure for certain operations (a rifle is not the optimum weapon in close vegetation and grenades are next to useless), but I also carried the Dyak headhunter's bow and little arrows that the Iban, Rauru, my friend and mentor, had given me for patrol duties in the dense uplands of Labis where silence was of the essence. It may surprise you to know that bows and arrows were still in use in the British Army as late as 1958, still are for all I know, but I assure you that this was the case.

It was not long after I had taken up my position, assembling my bivouac in the natural depression covered by dense foliage that I had earmarked previously, and taken my first reconnaissance, that I became aware of others entering the woods, somewhere to the east of where I lay. Whoever it was, their jungle-craft was lamentable. No doubt they thought they were observing silent discipline – there were no voices – but they sounded like a herd of the wild water buffalo you occasionally found wandering around the ridge-paths and whose dung, secured by a banana leaf, was so invaluable in cases of leg ulcers. The CTs would have eaten them for breakfast.

I edged closer to the source of the noise to try and assess their identity, rejoicing in the old jungle skills that seemed as natural to me as if it were yesterday. Conceivably it could be a couple of late sportsmen out after pigeons, though the light was getting bad, and most self-respecting pigeons would now be on the nest.

As I proceeded circumspectly forward, my movement through this kind of terrain a model for the young recruit, I became aware that the intruders' advance had ceased, and that they now appeared to be preparing some kind of base position on the ground. There were scufflings, and scrapings, and (worst crime of all in the jungle) the sounds of saplings being cut. I parted the fronds of a thicket, and peering into the clearing before me, was rewarded by a spectacle that was as unwelcome as it was incongruous.

Two large Irishmen (I took them to be Irish by the way one was handing round Sweet Afton cigarettes, a thing for which one would be court-martialled in the foothills of the Menlik) and, unaccountably, the swart sausage-maker of Prosser Street, Fitzgibbon, were clustered in a clearing beside a holly tree. At their feet were haversacks similar to, though not to be compared with, my own. And against the haversacks rested a couple of heavy shotguns whose barrels appeared to have been considerably foreshortened. Unless a pigeon had obligingly consented to pose for their convenience at no more than ten yards distance, the weapons in terms of that particular activity would have serious shortcomings, and even if the pigeon had been so charitably inclined, the guns would have obliterated it completely, rendering it unsuitable for supper. I thus concluded that that was not their game, and so it proved.

'Shall we go in for him now, Mr Umfreville?' asked one

of the burly Hibernians, breaking silence, rule number one.

'No, Mr Toop,' replied the one who by his stature and bearing might be taken as the leader, 'we will wait until the morning if you please. Gunfire at night is regarded with some suspicion in these parts.'

It was not that I was surprised by their appearance on the scene. I had been trained at Her Majesty's considerable expense to meet every eventuality with speed and precision. But their presence did encourage in me a moment of introspection. Having paused to ask myself what they were doing in the wood so late, a furlong from the castle gate, it led me on to review what I was doing there myself.

In Italy, if you remember, Mussolini always interferes – the nostrum for all military situations which had ever been our watchword in days of yore – information, intention, method and so on. I fell back on it once again.

The information seemed clear enough. The enemy was in the cottage flanked by bushy-topped trees.

My intention was to destroy his position.

My method would be to wait until he took a walk in the woods – or to lure him in through the use of devices, animal noises etc. – and then to play Puck with him, lead him a merry dance, exhaust his reserves of strength and self-control, make him promise anything, renounce his kickie-wickie, and then pounce when I had him at my mercy. Nothing too swift, there would be no satisfaction until I had taught him a lesson in woodcraft.

Administration I had already covered. I had supplies and ammunition to last as long as the campaign would take.

So far so good. But did I really want to wipe the man out, to administer as the Bard has it his quietus? Certainly he had got on my nerves, he was insufferable, he was a blight on the woodland, yes, but I had already taken him down many pegs. He was near bottom.

I sensed a fatal weakness dawning in me. The hunter

must be implacable, pitiless, and so I had been up till this moment, the milk of human kindness turned to Ipoh poison in my veins, but now? I had made the man ridiculous. It is hard to annihilate a clown.

I trembled. My tactics were superb, but my strategy was becoming cloudy. And then there were the Irishmen. I had seen them before, of course, nosing around Wardour Street outside his office, seeking information.

> 'Christian, dost thou see them, on the holy ground,
> How the hosts of Midian prowl and prowl around?'

They were after him too.

I suppose if you looked at it one way, you could say they were on the same side as myself, but I had no wish for assistance in my venture, therefore they had to be considered at best irritating neutrals and at worst a second enemy. Considering their origin, I felt that the latter category would be more fitting (I shall not touch on the Irish problem or I shall never be finished), but it still did not resolve the vexed question as to the fate of the man Richmonde.

At all events I decided, as I lurked beside the thicket, he should be hunted down and prised from his true love. If I spared him in the final moment of his ignominy, that would be my prerogative and his shame.

I thereupon resolved, since time was on my side, to conduct a recce round towards the other side of the cottage where the woods sloped up steeply over bank and tumulus to the summit – an eminence, I learned from my Ordnance Survey map, of some 800 feet. This rough terrain which included, I was pleased to note, a network of old marl pits and a thick copse of spiky hawthorn, would do nicely for the meanderings I had in mind for the luckless American, and would be at some remove from the attentions of the Irish.

It was as I was rounding a hump of hill, pockmarked by chalky hollows and screened with a low and thorny scrub, that I became aware of a second body of interlopers – another group of three men, this time dressed in the drab quasi-military denims that Security Guards sometimes affect in the field. They sported a rifle of the kind that is used to shoot tranquillizing darts into large wild animals, shotguns and, I noticed, a couple of useful-looking truncheons lying in their holsters among the impedimenta.

Whereas the Irish had been comparatively sparing in their conversation, this manky mob was positively garrulous, and would not have lasted five minutes in the hinterland.

'What's it going to be then, Mr Bidwell?' asked one loutish youth.

'A shooting accident, I think, Walter.'

Bidwell was an old subject of my scrutiny. For some reason I had never trusted him.

'What? A terminal?'

The youth was quite excited.

'Oh, I don't think that would be necessary, Walter. More like an impediment of some kind, I should say. Heel or knee, lad, heel or knee. Mr Kuhne said use our discretion, though he wasn't particular.'

'Can I give him a crack with this, then, Mr Bidwell?' said the lad, wielding a truncheon experimentally and bringing it down smack on a sapling.

'Certainly, lad, if you have a mind to. But go easy with it, eh? Cost sixty quid a time, those truncheons.'

Now I am not a violent man. What I have to do I will do because it has to be done. The enemies of my country I will spray with fifty rounds rapid as soon as look at them, enemies of myself I will pursue with the precision you would expect, but in any situation I do not like gloating lk of violence: it is little better than muslim, it brought up short. The wretched Richmonde now had two sets of enemies on his tail, three if you counted myself, and it began to dawn on me as an Englishman that the line-up was unfair. We in England have always prided ourselves on a sportsmanlike regard for the underdog however much of a dog he may be.

Who did they think they were, these people who now threatened the obnoxious but unfortunate Richmonde?

I had seen Bidwell before, of course, and knew he was in some way connected with the Craxton & Kuhne organization. He had even been into Livonia Studios for a cursory sniff-round and had looked at me, I thought at the time, perhaps over-quizzically, but he worked from another office. I had gathered that it involved security, but I had supposed that it was no more than a guard dog here and a camera there - there are a thousand such companies in London collecting takings from run-down washeterias. It now seemed that his activities had a more far-reaching significance.

Making up my mind with the lightning precision that is the sine qua non of the Acting Sergeant, a rank I enjoyed for three months at the end of my service, I stood up and stepped forward from my position behind the white umbels of a guelder rose. If I had been expecting surprise to be on my side (and I was) I would have been disappointed. My reception could almost have been rehearsed.

'Ah, Croucher,' said the man Bidwell.

It seemed he had done his homework. That is indeed my name.

A shotgun and a tranquillizing rifle swung perilously up and pointed at me.

'I was expecting you, Croucher.'

I did my best to appear nonchalant. The soldier is enjoined in numerous training manuals to remain resilie and combative in the face of superior enemy firepow but I could not help feeling something of a rooki having exposed my position so rashly.

'You felt I might drop in?' I enquired suavely, though inwardly ruminative.

'You see, Croucher, we have known of your interest in Mr Richmonde for some time.'

That I should have been outwitted by this motley crew! My face betrayed nothing.

'He asked us to investigate the studios and one or two other matters. We put a twenty-four hour watch on him, and you turned up. We did not tell him, of course. We wanted to see what you would do. As it turned out, you did our work for us. Please, sit down.'

I perched on a bank among a considerable outcrop of Self-heal. It seemed appropriate.

'You have been an enigma to us, Croucher. Indeed, at certain stages we thought you might be a special operative on a job. But at others you seemed guided by a purely personal and whimsical malice.'

The idea that I, tracker of trackers, friend of the Iban, should myself be tracked was almost too much to stomach. I supposed it had to happen sooner or later. None of us are perfect. Presumably it was he who had unearthed my past, pried into and (who knew?) bugged my house, relayed the findings to the devious Lebanese.

'I must congratulate you on your groundwork,' he continued. 'Your preparation is A1, as is your sense of invention. The astrological evening is my favourite, but the river rendezvous and the export-strength vodka affair also occasioned a spontaneous outburst of appreciation at this end, while the switched cassette was a masterstroke that even Klaus Fuchs would have applauded.'

'Thank you,' I said quietly, accepting praise where it as due.

And the way you managed to turn up at Selvan's house ight the intruders came, actually saving his life. That hat persuaded us you might be, unknown to us since some things are deliberately concealed, already in Mr Kuhne's employment.'

'I'm afraid I must guard my sources,' I said, reluctant to admit that on this occasion my presence had been purely coincidental.

'Quite. I understand. May I introduce Walter and Howard?'

I shook hands with the burly acolytes. I did not like the look of either of them. They would not last a week in the jungle, always stopping to salt off the leeches.

'And now,' said their master, 'whether or not you are employed by the Organization already, I suggest that I formally offer you a position with us. You have the makings of a Grade One operative and we can put you on a thousand pounds a week right away.'

I was tempted to teach him a lesson he would not forget – an operative forsooth, I who had come within spitting distance of Chin Pang himself and booby-trapped an entire kampong – but the snouts of the guns were ominously near and I had learned in a harder school to stifle irritation when faced with a tactical opportunity. This, of course, was what I had abandoned cover for.

'Very well,' I said, 'I will join forces with you. What is your mission?'

'To administer a structured penalty to Mr Richmonde for misdemeanour and disloyalty.'

'I thought he was your colleague.'

'He was indeed my colleague, and he could have been my superior. I who had built up the London end of Craxton & Kuhne to one of the top fifty security operations in the UK. I who had worked day and night. Recruit, train, mind, caretake, negotiate, activate, admonish, advertise, scrutinize, monitor, set up, pick up, stitch up, you name it, I did it, to be superseded by a smart-talkin pipsqueak using long words with his hand in the till. I sa to Mr Kuhne: "Is he all he's cracked up to be? Let m least put a tail on him." I'm glad to say Mr Kuhne saw my point, as does his new partner. I inaugurated surveillance procedures, and just as well, for the man has proved to be a liability. Apart from all his other double-dealing and disloyalties, to try and turn the stern gaze of the monitor into a kohl-eyed wheedling siren. Well, I needn't tell *you*, Croucher. It was the act of a madman, profaning the very mysteries of our art.'

How little do even the most watchful of us observe! We operate, every one of us, in small closed spheres of self-interest, but suddenly it seemed to me that one of my enclosing cloches had been removed, and I could see quite clearly (at least as far as the next enclosure which is a great deal clearer than usual) that we are all under observation. No one escapes. The concept, even as I sat there on the creeping carpet of purple Self-heal, affected me profoundly.

It made me reappraise my practices.

True, as a child I understood that the Almighty overlooked all my ways: even my tendency to pick my nose in the toilet was encompassed by his all-seeing eye. It was one of the sources of his power, his secret supervision, thou Lord monitorest me, and it was perhaps an inkling of that power that I had enjoyed in my own humble pursuits. But how aweful in the classical sense which our Scripture Teacher would drum into us, to realize that there was a temporal power with almost limitless capacities of supervision, that none of us however vigilant escapes the cold eye of scrutiny, wherever we go cameras record, bugs quiver, computers whirr. Of course, we can comfort ourselves with the notion that it is separate people recording our activities, a shop, a bank, the post office telephone, a credit-worthiness scan, but how are we to know hat it does not get back to some central intelligence, some wer that does not necessarily have our good at heart? Eye has a myriad lenses.

Occupied with these conjectures, I lost none of my customary alertness, and took in the details as Bidwell outlined his rudimentary plan to surprise the American in the cottage. It was clear to me as he spoke that Richmonde must be spirited into the trees, where I could better provide defensive cover.

'You may rely on me,' I said keenly to the creature Bidwell. 'I too have cause to dislike the man. No doubt you are considering an alternative plan of action? For instance to lure him into the woods where a shooting accident could perhaps be expedited?'

'I wasn't,' he replied, 'but I am now. Good thinking, Croucher. How d'you see it shaping?'

I outlined a plan which would allow me to put my evasive procedures into effect but which seemed in the face of it particularly credible. He embraced it as if it were his own, impressed with my Iban bow as much as anything.

I agreed to return before first light.

On a final recce before Lights Out, I became careless and almost fell across yet another occupant of the forest.

'No one owes me £1,600,' said a voice which I had cause to hold in some distaste, 'and gets away with it. You fool, Glebe. Did I not tell you no more credit? By God, if we don't wring it out of Richmonde, I'll dock it from your wages. Got the plan, numskull? You knock at the door looking as if you've been strained through a sheet and I shoulder past you with the bludgeon.'

It was the thread-veined ogre of the wine-vaults and his sad minion. Who could have put them on Richmonde's track tonight of all nights? Richmonde, it seemed, had the whole world pitted against him.

I strode briskly forward and explained to the impetuous vintner that there were others in the wood who wished no good to Richmonde and that a concerted attack might pay dividends, I being appointed to a supervisory coordinating capacity by the committee like a NATO general. This time I displayed my Wingmaster – it seemed more his line of country.

He agreed with my sitrep after some earnest conversation during which I was obliged to order a further three cases of Roederer to cut discussion short, and I then went in search of the Irishmen, whom I found drinking rum and eating rock-cakes.

'Ain't I seen you somewhere before?' said the man Fitzgibbon.

'You have indeed,' I replied, making a clean breast of it. 'I have been a silent witness of all your ways and if any harm comes to me a certain letter will be opened in the Kensington Town Hall, Hornton Street, cataloguing the enormities of your sausage factory.'

The Irishmen looked at each other and my armament and conceded that my plan did indeed hold attractions.

'You did not bring your dog into the wood?' I enquired acidly, stifling misgiving.

It was the one thing that could upset all my plans, the spirit of iniquity was in it.

'Hell, no, Tory he got sick with that poison you put down. Or maybe it was the by-election result. Anyways, he's back at home now. The roaches, they're bigger than ever.'

In an inequitable world, one hears things occasionally, that restore one's sense of fair play.

28

The cottage was not proving to be quite the rustic idyll that Tony had envisaged. Joanie had left the place looking like the *Marie Celeste* after a particularly rough night, and Chloe was restive. Though she liked the idea of the country, what she really meant was the terrace bar of a river pub, not experiences in the field.

'I always said,' she complained, after an encounter with a bullock, 'it's either smelly, mucky or dangerous, or all three. The animals are too big and everything keeps growing, especially nettles. There's always a drain blocked, or a sheep with fluke or you're being dive-bombed by a bee. As for the wood, it's all insects. I've never seen so many wasps. And if I see a hornet, I shall leave just like that.'

Tony crossed his fingers and unearthed a fly-spray. He had feared that she might want to go back, but he couldn't let her quit at the moment. He had to find the right moment to tell her that he had no money and no job and was probably in some personal danger but he loved her and why didn't they get married right away? He was conscious that the invitation lacked some incentive right now, but maybe if they gave it a little time she might fall for the simple life, you never knew.

Yet in his heart of hearts, a place he had not had much contact with before, he knew what her reaction would be, so his lovemaking became more desperate, more impassioned, while he got the curious impression that, like some kind of schooner in a gale, she was just riding him out – plenty of activity but little real movement.

She had always surprised him with her exuberance

bed. Her exterior was so demure, so contained, you wouldn't think such thoughts would enter her head, but now she seemed to want him to do things that no one had ever demanded of him before. There seemed no end to her ingenuity. Where had she learned such things? Did she enjoy them? Did *he* enjoy them? It all somehow smacked of the treats a condemned man gets before execution.

Curiously, it was in the minor rustic pursuits that he now began to find comfort. He had fled the wide meadows of Ohio in early youth, but now he discovered a sanity in the smell of new-mown grass which temporarily erased the images of trashcans, parking lots and dildoes which haunted his dreams. The comfortable English countryside seemed almost a guarantee of cleanness and security. Nothing ever went seriously wrong in South-East Oxfordshire.

Even so, he had kept a careful eye on the lane, mindful of the various threats that had been gathering like thunderclouds in London, so when the gentle knock on the kitchen door came on the third morning of their stay (it was before dawn, he couldn't sleep and had risen to make some coffee), he started so much that the beans he was pouring sprayed about the kitchen like shrapnel.

Luckily Chloe was still fast asleep in bed, cuddling the dog Gaby, seemingly untroubled by guilt or a sense of the ludicrous (their antics last night had been particularly elaborate). He didn't want her to notice his display of nerves at what quite possibly was a routine though early rural matter. Crunching over the tiled floor to the larder, he peered out through zinc-covered windows amid an odour of ancient leftovers.

There was a man in what he took to be his mid-forties wearing a faded camouflage jacket, denim trousers and a floppy jungle hat, standing at the back door in an attitude of almost aggressive furtiveness. Tony had the feeling that he had seen him somewhere before, but he couldn't quite place him. He didn't look like a hit-man, however, more like a keep-fit librarian, so Tony – after satisfying himself that the man was alone – returned to the kitchen, slid back the bolts and opened up.

Surprisingly the man entered with the brisk authority of one accustomed to searching premises (Tony got the impression of familiarity with a sub-machine-gun, although there was none discernible), and closed the door behind him.

'Now, uh, hold on there,' said Tony unconvincingly as the man strode across the room and yanked open the door leading to the hall and stairs, shutting it again when he had satisfied himself there was no one around. Maybe the guy could even be a cop, and then again maybe not. He might have the air of one who knew how to turn a house upside-down, but that didn't necessarily make him respectable.

'There is not a moment to lose,' said the man, crunching a blend of Kenya Peaberry and Mysore.

'Who is it, Ant?'

Chloe had an uncanny instinct for waking, he had found, when he wanted her to be asleep, though at all other times infuriatingly comatose. Mercifully, however, she did not come downstairs. That was another of her quirks: she was always cold, shivering infectiously at the slightest hint of a breeze.

'Uh . . .' Tony floundered, looking questioningly at his visitor.

The dog made one or two half-hearted yaps.

'A neighbour,' hissed the man. 'Follow me at the double.'

'Now hold it a moment, will you? I want to know what's going on.'

'There are at this moment eight men in the trees behind you who propose to lay violent hands upon you. If you wish to escape their attention, follow me. The girl must stay. She will not be harmed.'

Tony opened the door to the hall again and shouted up the stairs. There was something strangely convincing about Jungle Hat.

'It's a neighbour, honey. He uh needs my help for a while. Sick animal,' he added, knowing Chloe's feelings about such things, but making doubly sure she would not want to come.

'Do I have to get up?'

'Stay right there.'

'Bring up the radio, would you?'

She had taken to her bed in a way he considered almost unhealthy, liking nothing better than to stay there all morning. She would doze, read magazines, and tune in to the local radio station using the sound as a sort of aural quilting protecting her from any chilly draughts of thought. And yet, perversely, at other times bed seemed to be the only place she had any energy left.

Tony deposited the radio on the eiderdown and kissed the top of the sleepy golden head that did not turn to kiss him.

'Won't be long, honey,' he said, thinking of the golden places keeping warm inside. She seemed to have gone to sleep again, so he turned and hurried down the stairs. A thought had struck him. 'Hold it right there,' he said to Jungle Hat. 'I'm going to call the police.'

'I fear someone has cut the wire.'

Tony lifted the telephone and vainly jiggled the receiver.

'I'll take the car.'

'It wouldn't move.'

Tony believed him.

'OK, OK, I'll come with you. You sure she's going to be all right?'

'My life upon it.'

'I tell you, your life won't be worth a dime if anything happens to her.'

'Enough of expostulation. Follow me. And observe silence at all times.'

The man grasped Tony firmly by the arm, opened the back door, and ran him along the courtyard wall, down the hedge, and into the cover of the trees.

They had made their way up the hill for three or four hundred yards, with a remarkable stealth – his guide seemed to have a genius not only for avoiding the swishier branch and the cracklier footfall but for making Tony avoid them too – when all his faith in the man was abruptly destroyed.

He paused, looked about him, and gave a shrill whistle. Immediately there were sounds of distant trampling from various quarters of the woods which seemed to be slowly converging on their present position.

'Hey, uh, hold on there for chrissake,' whispered Tony. 'Whose side are you on?'

His mentor flapped his right arm with a downward motion.

'What's that supposed to mean?'

'Crawl,' the man hardly moved his lips.

'Crawl? Who's crawling? I'm not crawling for anyone. What is all this? You want me to get down there and eat dirt?'

If he was going to meet his fate, he would prefer to do it standing up with if possible a jest on his lips. He had not lived in England for nothing for the past six months.

'That is not dirt,' remonstrated his guide, apparently stung, 'that is rich humus.'

'You want me to eat rich humus? You should serve pitta bread.'

Tony, considering the precariousness of his situation, thought the joke showed considerable class, but Jungle Hat was unimpressed. 'Under that thicket,' he pointed, 'you will find a hide I have constructed. Crawl in and do not move until further notice.'

'I . . .'

But the man in the camouflage clothes had disappeared.

Tony lay down and wriggled forward into the foliage, the last fronds closing behind him as two pairs of Size Fourteen boots trampled a sapling a yard from where he had been standing.

Settling himself into the rich humus, it struck him that he had come a long way from the captain's chair, and from far back, like a voice in dreams, the voice of the schoolteacher in Bellington reached out to him, reading as was his custom, a text for the day drawn from Great Literature: 'He that is down need fear no fall, He that is low no pride', following up with a lecture on the medieval concept of the Wheel of Fortune, a lesson that Tony, contemplating the nose-cone breasts of Lucille Hartmann at the desk beside him, had not fully taken in at the time, but that was now, after so many years and triumphs, beginning to come home to him.

The only thing was, he felt, whoever had penned the lines had not been obliged to share his negative situation with a nest of earwigs or he would have included them in his status report.

29

Sometimes it was during the interval of a play, in a luxuriously-appointed roadmender's tent conveniently sited in Shaftesbury Avenue with women in fur coats milling outside and a grinning cripple squinnying through the slits.

Or on a forgotten coast, in a lost graveyard overrun by sea-grass and bobbly mauve sea-flowers, under a ruined wall where the sea moaned continually and the wind ruffled the tufts of hair along his back, like sea-grass, and the bones stirred among the shingle.

Or at a dinner-party, suddenly, spreadeagled across the shining table, disturbing the soup-tureen and rattling the glasses, with everyone pretending not to notice and carrying on talking about Ascot.

Or in the Summer Show at school, though Auntie nearly wouldn't let her do it and had to be talked into it by the Drama Mistress. 'Showing your legs to strangers' was what Auntie called dancing, and it was more than legs behind the curtain after everyone had gone, because suddenly he was there again, pulling her green insect's tights down and taking her just like that, on stage, when suddenly the curtain went up and everyone was there including Auntie in the front row, and she couldn't stop even though the man had turned into Uncle.

Or in the Black Hole where he and Maudie tied her with chiffon, and the bearded mouth was pink and wavy as a pool-anemone, and the hands fluttered and caressed pressing and stroking at the magic place that would ma[illegible] it happen like a man, it was all the rage.

Or in a storm, lit by flashes, beside a sun-dial, 't[illegible] so short, the art so long to learn', with laughter in the shadows and horned heads peeping from the maze.

Or in a wet-suit of the finest gossamer so he couldn't get in, only grab vainly at her through the material as she wriggled away slippery as a trout.

Or in a forest, unable to move, while the witch undressed her, showing her nakedness to the chained Beast who raged and whimpered in the background.

Or in the window of a sex shop, made to stand in a peekaboo bra, seamed stockings and spidery suspenders while he had to wait outside among the hobbledehoys who jeered and wah-hayed through the glass.

The dreams were shameful, delicious, she could have them to order but she wouldn't dream of letting him do it really, in real life; he liked things the hard way.

30

Some way out of Ipu, the battalion suffered its worst casualties of the hostilities. A young officer, Mr Bertish, had taken out a platoon from C Company still green from Training Camp. I was a Lance-Corporal with Number One squad, hardly sewn on my stripes, Mr Parsons had not yet rejoined the regiment from his Entertainment Course, so we were not the outfit we later became. We were to advance up river and mount an ambush for a CT patrol which had been reported in the vicinity.

Sure enough, the CTs were there all right.

They approached one evening along the track designated that ran between the river and the ridgepath where the deer came down for water, some five or six men, a large party. To the uninitiated, the scene would doubtless have been idyllic. Those tropical evenings, though brief, were of the greatest beauty, the jungle hanging it seemed in suspense, gratefully sucking in the cooler airs of nightfall.

Many were the times that I was to lie in similar circumstances, cradling my pumpgun, M1 carbine or as on this occasion sten, but this was the first time, and we were unusually keyed up. We were still putting on ointment to keep the bugs off at that stage, a vain precaution.

Then suddenly the long-awaited pressure on arm or leg which announced the advent of the enemy. This was the crucial moment. No sound or scent must reach the senses of the terrorist, who seemed at times to have the very instincts of the jungle creatures themselves. Even the gentlest release of a safety-catch could sound like a castanet in the primary hush; your trigger-finger would seem as big as a polony as it waited for the Platoon Commander's order.

Then came the first sight of the CTs themselves, a vision for which no amount of training at Kota Tinggi could fully prepare you, living men you were going to kill, little browny yellow chappies in coarse dun tunics, some of them looked like devils and some like girls (the two are not by any means mutually exclusive).

We could hardly believe that after so much preparation we actually had them in our sights. The seconds seemed as long as Religious Instruction as we waited.

'FIRE.'

The uproar of rifle and bren, the Christmas-crackery smell of the smoke from a dozen breech-blocks, the shrieks and flaps of the forest, the almost indecent haste with which the jungle drew a veil over the proceedings and fell back into darkness and silence, these were the scenes that were the meat and drink of the soldier in those far-off days of brief and bloody encounter when a packet of Weights cost 1/6 for twenty. There were no moanings of the wounded. Unless otherwise instructed, we shot to kill.

On this occasion, however, something went wrong.

Mr Bertish, who was a buckshee National Service Officer, failed to heed the words of the Training Manual with regard to ambush formation, and Sergeant Garraway, a man with troubles of his own, failed to remonstrate with him. I could, even then, see it all but it was hardly my place, and it was Silent Discipline.

The result was, of course, that without intending it (there was not a whiff of malice in the act) he shot up his own party whom he had placed opposite the Bren Group across the pathway.

Most of the CTs, it is true, were killed outright in the first burst, but it also caught Privates Callard, Levey and Smollett, and one of the CTs in the pandemonium managed to hurl a grenade into the group on the other side of the track, narrowly missing my good self and blowing Mr Bertish's radio operator's radio clean through the Sergeant's windpipe, putting an end to all domestic strife.

A bloody mess all round, a bad day for the Regiment, four soldiers killed including the Sergeant, and Mr Bertish sent back to England.

I only mention the incident to show that military activities in the low-visibility theatre of the forest can be fraught with pitfalls, and that even in the greenwoods of Merry England they are not for lumbering jackasses who think that an ability to monitor a shoplifter, transport bullion or place explosive charges under other people's cars is going to render them adroit enough to tangle with one who holds the purple ribbon of the Malay Medal.

I proceeded to run rings round them.

The Irishmen, alerted by my whistle, started to close in on the killing ground, and the Bidwell contingent, similarly briefed, came flanking up from the left. Further down the hill, a confused snorting and threshing heralded the advance of the infuriated wine merchant. Though I had taken the trouble to conceal Richmonde from all but the most practised eye, I thought it only right that the first stage of the engagement should take place practically over his head. I could not let him off scot-free.

Just at the moment when each party sighted the rustling of the other and discharged their first salvo into the innocent foliage, disturbing a rare White Admiral I was lucky enough to spot on the boughs of a guelder rose, I diverted their attention with one of my inimitable renditions of the Richmonde delivery.

'Say, you guys, can't we uh sit around and talk this thing through?'

Four pairs of barrels swung round and leaves fell like confetti around me as consecutive salvoes were discharged. There was much blundering and idle footwork as the various forces lumbered after me, at least one boot catching in ivy, sending its owner headlong to the woodland floor. The more the merrier, I thought, and calling and whistling, I led them on up the hill towards the treacherous marl pits.

It had rained heavily a couple of days before and, under a dense matting of last year's leaves, the pits were thick with oozy water. The matting at first held them up as they plunged towards my signals, but as they approached, from different angles and at different speeds, you could hear the crust breaking like crème caramel as it deposited the luckless warriors into the slime below – at which, throwing away their weapons, they struggled and cursed and clutched at their feet for all the world like bluebottles on a fly-paper or possibly, I had to laugh, on a spider's web. The Croucher in the shadows, it was like taking sweets from a baby.

I did not stay long to enjoy the spectacle. I had another duty to perform, though before departing I allowed myself a satisfying salvo with the Wingmaster over the heads of the entangled.

Avoiding the hide where I had left Richmonde, I made my way lightly down to the cottage and let myself in by the kitchen door.

And now a curious thing happened. All my training, my iron nerve, the discipline of a hundred sorties now seemed to fail me. My heart galloped like a bull buffalo up a forest ride, my breath came in sobs, I shook as if with sandfly fever. By a supreme effort of will I steadied myself and slowly mounted the stairs.

'Who is it? Tony, is that you?'

I pushed the door ajar. She lay propped up in bed, so soft and beautiful you would not credit it. She could not see me yet.

'Ant, what's all that noise out there? I couldn't sleep,' and then a note of suspicion and, yes, of fear: 'Who is this?'

I hate that use of the demonstrative, don't you? An academic habit affected by our transatlantic cousins.

'It is not who is this,' I said severely, 'it is who is that?'

I entered the room.

For a moment she made as if to get up, but then lay back as if she knew that further action would be bootless.

'Come, Isobel, dear,' I said, 'it is time to come home. I have prepared your room for you.'

31

Tony had lain very low in his dug-out while the pursuit raged at first almost overhead, and had still lain low as it circled and removed. You never knew who was up there with a shillelagh or worse.

He had heard guns discharge, cries of rage and pain with his name inextricably entwined about them, dashings and purposeful excursions, and it had worked powerfully upon his thoughts that all this activity had only one end in view. The infliction of damage, disability and quite possibly (as the circlers became more and more irate) parameters of terminality envisagable. It gave him cause to think.

What had happened to his life? Where (if anywhere) was he going? What and how was he to do?

He remembered, at Sales College, they had called him The Mouth. He had taken it as a compliment at the time, and had worn the name with satisfaction afterwards. He knew he was a mouth. He liked being a mouth. It was a salesman's, a consumer's society, wasn't it? The mouth was its paradigm. Thus he had never looked for any benefit to anyone or anything beyond his own satisfactions, appetites and requirements on his way to the top. So far, so good. He had heard that some who actually got [illegible] the top expressed disappointment with the limitation of [illegible] view, but he would worry about that when he arrived. [illegible] only trouble was, he hadn't arrived. He was deep in [illegible]mus.

[illegible]d up with nothing, in a pit, with earwigs . . . it [illegible] failure of approach. If they killed him they [illegible]en have to dig a grave.

Perhaps, after all, generosity and integrity might repay investigation. He had heard that honesty was a viable policy but he had always suspected that it only really suited the unimaginative. For the essentially fast-thinking guy it was a sucker's game. Still, if he ever got out of here, maybe he'd give it a try. He would tell Chloe that he was broke and in trouble. Maybe she would love him better for it. Maybe she didn't like the successful businessman image but she hadn't liked to tell him, maybe that was why she had been acting so strange, he had got it wrong. She would admire his candour, embrace his fortune (or lack of it), and make love to him without insisting that he dress up in her underwear.

Tony's self-righting mechanisms, his inbuilt buoyancy tanks, were his fatal flaw. They meant that he was incapable of learning from his mistakes.

He now found himself actually smiling at the thought of what the future might hold. Straight sex and new horizons. Surveillance was an overcrowded medium for his talents, but the tourist market in Britain was seriously in need of rationalization, in fact, come to think of it, the whole goddam country was.

It was then that he had an idea. It was so big, so bold, that he almost leapt, just like that, oblivious of danger, clotted with leaf-mould, straight from his dug-out, but at this moment a giant voice seemed to speak from the old-man's-beard right over his head.

'THIS IS THE POLICE. YOU ARE IN A PROTECTED WOOD. THERE IS A BERKS BUCKS AND OXON NATURALISTS' TRUST BIRDSONC PROJECT BEING CONDUCTED HERE. YC HAVE BEEN RECORDED. UNLOAD YC WEAPONS. PLACE THEM IN A PILE AT EDGE OF THE WOOD, AND COME OUT YOUR HANDS UP. IF YOU ARE NC WITHIN OH FIFE MINUTES, I REPEAT

MINUTES, WE WILL SEND THE DOGS IN. THIS IS THE POLICE . . .'

It might not perhaps have had quite the inspirational impetus of his brain-wave, but it still seemed a perfectly good opportunity to get off the ground, and so reasoning that his pursuers would not have the gall to do a kneecapping in the presence of the law, he extracted himself stiffly from his clammy bed and trudged back down the hill towards the cottage, further comforting himself with the thought that he, at least, had a cast-iron excuse for taking a walk in the woods.

A burly figure in blue stepped up as he emerged from the outskirts of a beech.

'You are under arrest.'

'No uh say, hold on there, will you? I live here.'

'Those are your premises?' The constable pointed at the flint-walled cottage.

'They are indeedy.'

'You have proof?'

'I have a key. See. The key.'

He dangled it like a talisman. There was a bit of faded label attached to the end that read 'Masthill Cottage.'

'You were shooting?'

'No, no . . . There were some guys up there fooling around. From London, I think. But I . . . I was bird-watching. I saw a . . . a woodpecker. They scared it. I'm really sore about that.' Tony brushed an earwig from his hair. 'May I go in now?'

The policeman relented.

'Very well, sir. Sorry you've been disturbed. We'll [illegible]e round later to take a statement.'

[illegible]hing the man good hunting, Tony walked briskly [illegible]o the little gate in the hedge that skirted the [illegible], and let himself in by the kitchen door.

[illegible]oney,' he called.

'Come in here, Mr Richmonde,' said a voice he recognized but was by no means expecting.

It seemed to stem from the living room. He walked into the hall and called up the stairs.

'Chloe? Where are you, honey?'

'In here, Mr Richmonde, if you please.'

He pushed open the door and stopped short at the threshold, momentarily overcome with surprise.

Chloe was sitting on the sofa, elegantly dressed. Her body under her summer frock had never looked more heartbreakingly, more unattainably desirable. In front of her stood the man Selvan, and beside her, looking like he was in a major disorientation situation, was the previously competent guy in the jungle hat.

His erstwhile guest advanced upon him, smiling.

'Sit down, Mr Richmonde. Have a drink. I think you are going to need it.' He handed him a glass of scotch, neat, and helped himself to Tony's eighteen-year-old Macallan. 'You no doubt are asking yourself what I am doing in your house?' he enquired.

'You're darn right I am,' said Tony.

'Well, you see, it isn't your house any more. It never was, to be accurate. It belonged to Mrs Richmonde, and now it belongs to me. Similarly, your apartment in Cadogan Square.'

'You . . .'

'Hear me out, Mr Richmonde. I also believe that you entertained a desire to marry this young lady here.'

'I did. I do.'

'She is coming with me. She understands that yo have not a dollar to your name, and she has a dislike poverty bordering on aversion.'

'She does?'

Tony's buoyancy tanks were taking a terrible ing.

At this point Chloe spoke.

'I'm sorry, Ant. It'd be like going back to the past. I ran away from all that years ago.'

'She will probably run away again,' continued Selvan. 'She is a runner. I will keep her for as long as she wishes or until she wants to get married, for of course that I cannot do. I have been explaining to our friend here,' he gestured at Jungle Hat, 'that he cannot take her back either. He was married to her once.'

'I am still married to her,' said Jungle Hat.

'It means nothing,' replied Selvan. 'A rapprochement would be out of the question. My lawyers will get to work on it immediately.'

'I . . .' Jungle Hat was suddenly galvanized out of his inertia, and made as if to reach for a weapon beneath his tunic, but Selvan forestalled him.

'Resistance is useless, versed though you are in the arts of war, my friend. You are covered from three points by my own personal security team. Your gun, if you will investigate, has only blanks in it, as has your Wingmaster. Any move by you would be imprudent if not terminal. My men may not be good in the trees but they are more than adequate in buildings.'

Bidwell sneered from a cupboard door. So it was he who had put the fatal 'soften-up' memo in the New Business file, the jerk.

Jungle Hat looked crumpled. He seemed surprised to see Bidwell, but then so was Tony. A confused trumpeting outside heralded the arrival of a particularly muddy wine-merchant and various Irishmen.

'Why are you doing this to me?' demanded Tony.

'You tried to deceive me. You tried to threaten me. wounded, or caused to have wounded, the cat Attis. the most unforgivable thing of all. The animal had no harm.'

lice . . . they will be here.'

l, indeed I have dealt, with the police. Now, if

you have finished your drink, my friends, you can both leave. Keep out of my way. Lie extraordinarily low. A great number of people will come looking for you if I give the word. You will rue the day you cross my path again.'

At last the never-failing buoyancy, the watertight doors, the double-hull of Tony's titanic ego all failed at once and sank without trace.

'Chloe,' he implored, 'stay with me, please, honey, I need you, don't do this to me, I can't live without you.'

And for once in his life he really meant it.

'You couldn't make me smile,' she said.

'Don't snivel, man,' said the Lebanese. 'Once you're on the bottom, you will find that there is only one way to go. Sideways.'

32

They are mad with their dreams and trust in technology.

I remember once in the Ulu, behind Port Swettenham, our Special Patrols cadre was visited by an American general. We were cooking up curry when he arrived. We all carried our pouches of garlic and curry powder in those days to give a fillip to whatever we found on the day's march; bat was good, deer a feast, snake less satisfactory but filling, wild pig succulence itself, monkey as I have mentioned sinewy and rich. But the meat was not as important as the actual fact of the cook-up; it was the best moment of the day, when you put down your pack, eased your limbs, and all gathered round to savour the preparations.

But this American general declined our offer of a mess tin full: it was bat on the menu that day. They hid in the bamboo stems to shelter from the sun, and you cut off the stem and roasted them just like that before putting them in the curry. Instead he undid his tunic, delved into the recess within, and finally produced two floppy polythene bags. Like nursing brassières, Corporal Armytage said – he had experience of such matters – full of rice and water as it turned out.

The idea, the general explained, was that they cooked in your own body heat. We all recoiled with disgust at the notion; it was somehow against nature. But when we had time to think about it, we realized it s a military disaster as well. Team spirit, so vital in Ulu, would be thrown out with the mess-pot; and e would talk to anyone and we would all wander round with our bags breast-feeding ourselves. We did not tell the general, he would not have understood. Indeed Corporal Armytage even volunteered to try a spoonful of the stuff, which was one of the bravest things I ever saw in all my days on the troubled peninsula.

I took the American home to the World's End in the Traveller.

Once again, as I crossed the Fulham Road and entered the network of neat little nineteenth-century streets behind St Stephen's Hospital (the only Casualty Ward still functional in inner South-West London, so much for the Welfare State), I marvelled at the aptly-named locality in which I had taken up residence, stemming from derisive references to its distance from the haut monde of Mayfair or a corruption of Earl's End, being due south of Earl's Court and next to the river. I even pointed out its relevance to my passenger's position, but he seemed too sunk in gloom to appreciate matters of topographical interest, absorbing though such details are – the past is all around us.

I was not feeling buoyant myself.

I had nursed the wild dream that my dear one could be brought back, but she had been snatched from me at the crucial moment just when it had seemed that my long and arduous journey, with all its dangers and privations as in days long past up the Ulu, would pay dividends. Instead of Eurydice, I had brought back one of the damned.

Damned or no, however, he did seem to be in such a state that I was obliged to put him to bed in the suite at the top of the house in Driffield Street that I had fondly reserved for the dear departed, with its special doors and windows – I had hoped it might one day serve nursery. Thereupon, I retreated to my little kitchen, where I sat in the luminous twilight of late summer cradling my Bovril and turning over my thoughts.

There was not a peep out of him until I knocked on his door next morning with a cup of Country House Breakfast Blend into which I had slipped a mild sedative, the soldier's friend.

'Who is it?'

'It is Croucher with your morning tea.'

'Why is my door locked?'

'For your protection. I do not altogether trust that Lebanese. Who knows but there may not be a hit-squad even now nosing at the gates.' I glanced, as I spoke, into the little street without, and could have sworn I saw a rough-looking gypsy gazing up at me from a basement across the way. 'We are under observation,' I confirmed, 'but you are not a prisoner. Pray take your leave. It is liberty hall here.'

But he did not wish to avail himself of my offer. He was a man with a brilliant future behind him, it is hard to follow.

And so it continued for many days. Richmond (I persuaded him to drop the e) and I had many discussions concerning the state of the world – America, Europe, Malaya, marketing, and the afterlife. He had started to read voraciously from my considerable library, and I was able to suggest passages that might be of special interest to him.

One of our favourite topics was the future of Britain. From his point of view I was able to concede that it must appear at times like a spent force.

'The body is cold,' he said in a vivid metaphor, drawn no doubt from his experiences on Mast Hill. 'The only real action's in the decomposition.'

But I countered strongly with a litany of our past greatness, and our legacy of living monuments to our forefathers' vigour, balancing our present picture of decay.

'Right,' he said, 'don't let it decay any more. We cannot bring the body back to life but we can mummify it.'

'It is not showing much faith in our traditional powers of resource and invention,' I objected. 'We have always been resilient.'

'Hear me out,' he said. 'This could be the most inventive step of all. At the moment all the Westernized nations are simply duplicating each other's activities, making automobiles, pig iron, steel bearings, sanitary fittings, kitchenware, surgical appliances, bicycles, coal, soap, disposable nappies, you name it, we all make it. In marketing terms, this is a no-no. The Age of Specialization is here. Each nation should make what it is best at, cutting out waste and increasing cost-efficiency.'

'All well and good,' I replied, 'but what *are* we best at? We seem to be overhauled on every side.'

'Exactly,' he replied, 'this is the glory of the idea. Britain's greatest resource is her history. Let us capitalize on it. Disney is doing it already. He is building a mini-Britain in Florida where you can experience something of the place on a one-day tour. How much better to do it on a grand scale with the real thing. Maxi-Britain. My vision,' he waved his arms expansively, 'is to turn over the whole country to tourism – except for a small industrial belt providing power centred on Glasgow. I see plexi-glass domes rising temperately over all your major centres of historical energy, to counter your only major drawback – weather. Here history can live. You are already high on the tourist ratings. This way you will lead the world. Visitors will be able to choose from whichever moments of your glorious past take their fancy. Like play bowls with Francis Drake, eat cake with King Alfred, spit pips with uh Nellie Gwynn, jostle in the Globe with Will Shakespeare, live it up in the greenwood with Maid Marian and Rob Hood, experience the communal spirit of the Blitz – we can have the East End burning nightly – sign Magna Carta with King John, and see a genuine hanging on Tyburn Hill. Most of the populace can play extras in the production – the element of capital punishment will do wonders to keep the crime rate down – and those who don't like it can man the services behind a security fence encompassing Clydeside, Paisley, East Kilbride and Rutherglen. Maxi-Britain Limited, a worker-management participating company. It is time the nations realized they are commercial enterprises. Japan of course has already, and adopted the disciplines of the same.'

I must say the effrontery of the scheme took my breath away. So this is what he had been hatching when I thought he had been reading *The Mill on the Floss*. I must admit I could see a deranged sort of logic in his reasoning.

'I anticipate obstacles,' I said cautiously, for I did not wish him to become over-excited, and I made a note to stiffen the bromide administered with his beverages.

'Obstacles,' he cried derisorily, 'there will always be obstacles in the path of concept. Did not Galileo have obstacles? Did not Newton have obstacles? Incidentally, that will be a particularly scenic module. Nothing worthwhile can be achieved without difficulty. Rome was not built in a day.'

'Not even by Disney,' I murmured.

He ignored me.

'I tell you,' he said, and there was the light of ·dness in his eyes, 'your future lies in your past.

That is the theme of my plan for Britain. Think about it. Live with it. Repeat it daily. Our Future lies in our Past.'

I have been for some weeks.

He is at present drawing up a master report (I am humouring him with some help on the military and natural history side) in order to put forward a proposal to the people of Maxi-Britain which would enable them to cast a vote on the issue. It has taken quite a hold of him. We sit together in the evenings in his room, and spread the day's work out on the floor in front of us. You could paper the walls with it.

33

The specialist was direct. She had asked him to be.

'I'm afraid the results are positive,' he said. 'The tests show malignant proliferation of the embryonal cells. The technical name for it is long and, one might say, unsuitably mellifluous. Chorionepithelioma.' He repeated the word as if its bell-like tones stirred a melancholy echo within him. 'Chorionepithelioma. Because of its location in the generative tissue, it grows rapidly. You left it very late, after your abortion, before coming to see me.'

She couldn't possibly have had Tony's child, nor drawn Henri's attention to the fact that she'd got rid of it, by being ill. She'd thought the trouble would clear up. Anyway, she didn't want to go into all that with the specialist.

'Is there anything you can do?' she asked.

'There is evidence already of secondary activity. I would recommend a course of chemotherapy at this stage, possibly followed by irradiation.'

'The sort that makes your hair fall out and your skin go yellow.'

'There are certain side-effects, regrettably.'

'The ugly face of sin.'

'I beg your pardon.'

'I mean, what'll happen if we do nothing?'

The specialist hesitated. He had grown used to the litany but it was still depressing.

'Go on,' she joked, using a Cheryl-ism, 'soonest said, least mended.'

'You will probably be dead in three months.'

'And if I have treatment?'

He wanted to tell her the truth, that she would probably be dead in three months either way. He was shuffling the palliative cliches around when she cut in on his thoughts. She was a very perceptive young woman.

'What would you do if you were me?'

He was tempted to say that he would go out and get drunk, but it seemed unethical.

'It is a very advanced carcinoma. The decision must be yours.'

'I'll keep my hair on,' she said.

The specialist looked at her sleekly shining head, now bent rather low.

'I would like you to come in for a few more tests anyway.'

Selvan visited her in the clinic, carrying pink champagne and orange roses. They chatted of this and that. Then she raised a matter that she had been saving for some time.

'It was funny you should turn up again like that,' she said, 'after our first meeting. I always remember how you talked so about women's role.'

She had never referred to the rape until now, but it seemed a good moment.

'I could not rest until I had seen you again.'

'You moved to London, bought a company . . . just for me?'

'I have never known such pleasure in pain, such pain in pleasure. You saved my life. Did you know that? You are a rare creature.'

'Rape isn't very fashionable, you know. What's a man like you doing going in for that sort of thing? You could buy anything you wanted.'

'That's just the trouble. When you have everything, you realize that you have nothing. It is a terrible thing n[illegible] to have to worry about money. All those restless li[illegible] winds of survival, paying the mortgage, saving fo[illegible] holiday, they protect the ordinary man from the terrible silence at the heart of things. The eye of the storm. It can drive you mad. Howard Hughes used to think he could hear microbes. I raped people.'

'You need a doctor more than I do.'

When he had gone, promising he would find her the best treatment in the world, she lay in bed for a while, watching the late afternoon sun wasting its strength on the ever-cheerful curtains.

'What was that poem you always used to spout, the one about the nightclub lady?' she said to Cheryl, who had come in with fruit and a gaily-ribboned box of joints specially flown in by Willis.

'I don't think you want to be thinking about that, dear,' said Cheryl. 'That's just for old war-horses like me.'

'No, go on.'

'Very well, dear. But I don't think it's very suitable.'

And Cheryl launched into her party piece, a poem she'd been taught long ago by a literary gentleman.

> '"I walked into the nightclub in the morning,
> There was kummel on the handle of the door . . ."'

She did it very well, rolled her rrr's in fine style over 'When Borrris used to call in his Sedanca', until she came to the last verse, which affected her so much she could hardly speak as the tears started, washing the powder down her cheeks like china-clay dust in a commercial estuary.

> '"There was sun enough for lazing upon beaches,
> There was fun enough for far into the night.
> But I'm dying now and done for,
> What on earth was all the fun for?
> For I'm old and ill and terrified and tight."'

'Cheer up, old horse,' said Chloe, 'have some pink champagne. You're not nearly tight enough yet.'

So they opened the bottle; and when they had got a little drunk, and had a little smoke, and each had a little cry, they both felt ever so much better.

34

I do not go out much. I get the feeling that I am being followed. It is an inconvenience for a man in my position.

Richmond keeps to his room.

You understand why I cannot encourage him to find other quarters: he would be locked up as soon as looked at.

Or worse, someone might take him seriously.

It is better this way.

Do you notice how the leaves on the plane trees at the end of the summer seem to wave like the hands of nigger minstrels in circular gestures of farewell?

I have prepared all that is necessary. My watch is synchronized. I have filled my pouches.

I am ready to leave at a moment's notice.

I am fit and in a state of readiness.